Dedicated to my readers. Thank you for inspiring me to continue this crazy career.

-DM-

Everything about me is a contradiction and so is
everything about everyone else. We are made out of
opposites; we live between two poles. There is a
philistine and an aesthete in all of us, and a murderer
and a saint. You don't reconcile the poles.

Orson Welles

-1-

"Hurry up. You're going to make your father late again."

Sun filtered through the window, bathing the kitchen in a warm yellow glow as Anna finished placing a plastic-wrapped sandwich into the padded lunch bag. She nestled it between a banana, a custard-flavored yogurt cup, and a can of organic soda. A smile flickered across her lips as she heard footsteps entering behind.

"Oh," came a voice from behind. "*He's* gonna make me late, huh?"

Anna turned, the smile pulling further across her lips as her husband, Dean, strolled into the room.

He crossed the space between them, set his laptop bag on the kitchen counter, and moved closer to wrap his arms tightly around his wife's waist. With a soft smile and a wink, he added, "I think you're going to have to take the blame for that one this morning..." He moved his hands down the small of her back, squeezing her hips tightly as he bit his lower lip.

"I didn't hear you complaining," his wife replied, a playful twinkle dancing in her eye as she reached up to fix an out-of-place curl that had fallen loose across his forehead. She reached down with her other hand, cupping the growing bulge beneath his slacks.

They stood, staring deeply into each other's eyes for a long moment.

"I think I could be a little later today."

She gave his crotch another soft squeeze, and then lifted his hand and pushed him away. "Later." Then she shifted her gaze to the doorway leading into the dining room. "Gabe," she called out. "Let's go."

Dean took a deep breath, letting it go in a shuddering release as he reached down, adjusting himself. "Coffee?"

"Where it always is," Anna replied, turning and making her way to one of the three bags lying on the counter.

"Late night?" Dean asked as she hefted his lunch, dinner, and likely late-night snack.

She turned, a grumbled sigh escaping past the smirk on her face. "Double rotation. Sam's *out sick* again this weekend..."

Sam was the charge nurse for her wing, and also her relief.

"Oh!" Dean replied, his eyebrows lifting. "Sick, huh? Crazy." His words dripped with sarcasm.

"I know, right!?" Anna replied. "Every time EDC weekend happens, he catches that same bug." She paused, a deep concern moving across her face. "I really feel bad for him. It's terrible." Her features tightened as she shook her head back and forth.

Dean chuckled.

"What about you?"

Dean was about to answer when their ten-year-old son, Gabe, strolled into the room, sleep still clinging tightly to his face.

Dean regarded him with a smirk and Anna shot him an incredulous look.

"Were you up all night playing your video games again? Didn't we *just* have this talk two weeks ago?"

Gabe exhaled in a sigh, ignoring them both and making his way to the fridge. Both Dean and Anna watched as he opened the door, pulled out the carton of orange juice, twisted the top off, and drank nearly a quarter of it before setting it back on the shelf and closing the door.

They exchanged a glance, Dean stifling a chuckle. "Normal day," he said, his gaze shifting back to continue observing his son's lackadaisical entrance in mild amusement. Then he turned his gaze back to Anna. "Jeannie's mom's in the hospital, so I told her to come in a couple hours late. I should be getting out of there by five."

"Oh. Is she okay?"

"Her mom?"

"No, dork. Her." She frowned at him. "Of course, her mom."

Dean smiled. "Yeah. Routine, I think. Heart stuff."

"Well. Tell her if she needs anything."

"I know," he replied, turning his attention back on his son. "You got everything? We're good to go?"

"Yeah," Gabe replied with a yawn, pulling a silver pack out of a Pop-Tart box and slipping it into his pocket.

"Alright," Anna said, hoisting her work bag over her shoulder. "I gotta go."

"Have I ever told you how sexy you look in scrubs?"

"Ew, gross," Gabe spat, his face wrinkling in disgust.

Anna looked down at herself. "Sometimes I think this is the only reason you asked me out."

"Didn't hurt," Dean said with a grin, shrugging.

The sounds of the city waking up had already begun to filter in through the window. A car horn bleated in the distance. A garbage truck trundled up the road, the grinding and squeaking echoing out. Sunlight fell through the window in beams.

Anna crossed the room, bending down and kissing Dean. She pulled back, her face hovering for just a moment. "You owe me..."

Dean smiled, his eyes working over her face. "Later."

She lifted her eyebrows expectantly. Then she turned and made her way to where Gabe was standing. "Give me a hug," she said, stepping in and pulling him close. "Love you."

"Love you too, Mom," Gabe replied.

Dean stood there, his coffee thermos in hand.

"Don't wait up," Anna said, making her way out.

Dean watched her leave, his gaze dropping to the back of her pink scrubs. A thin smile pulled at his lips. Then he turned his attention to his son. "All right, kiddo. Let's get a move on it. I'm already going to be late."

The sky overhead was clear, a perfectly warm spring day in L.A. Dean and his family—the Wilkinsons, as the carved wood plaque above their door said, lived in Lakewood, a small suburban community that was Long Beach adjacent. It was central to outdoor and indoor malls, with plenty of shopping and every type of restaurant one could crave. It had a great school system and was close to all the major freeways. These were just a few of the things the realtor had sold them on just three years prior.

Prior to their purchasing their small nine-hundred-square-foot dream home, they had been living in a two-bedroom apartment in the San Fernando Valley. But, with Anna working at County General, and Dean having accepted a transfer to a new restaurant in Long Beach, they had decided the commute wasn't worth it, and it was time to suck it up and put up a picket fence. Two months and six hundred thousand later, they had their little, two-bedroom Spanish-style home, complete with a turret entry and all. They'd had plans to convert the garage into a mother-in-law unit, to put in an above-ground pool, but then COVID happened and just like everything else in the world, those plans got put on hold. Dean was revisiting those very plans when Gabe broke the silence.

"Are we poor?"

Dean found himself stifling laughter, allowing just a little of it to come out in a snicker that Anna said reminded her of *Muttley* from the old Rocky and Bullwinkle cartoons. "Why would you ask that?"

"Billy told Romualdo that we were poor, because you drive an old car."

Dean looked shocked. For a moment he was stunned. "Our car's only four years old. It's still practically new." He tapped the dash beside the steering wheel. "She's only got fifty thousand miles on her."

"Yeah," Gabe replied. "Well, Danny's parents have a brand-new Mercedes and Billy says that's because they're rich."

Dean took a deep breath, slowing for the yellow light ahead. As the car slowed to a stop, he thought of the best way to respond, and the best metaphor to use. He sighed softly, turning to look at his son. "Look. Just because someone has a nice car, doesn't mean they're rich. I know lots of people who have a really nice car, but still live in a studio apartment and are up to their necks in credit card debt. And I know people who are incredibly successful and have more money than Billy, Romualdo and Danny's parents combined. And they drive twenty-year old cars with two hundred thousand miles on them. Having a fancy car doesn't mean you're rich." He studied the boy for a moment, his gaze flickering to the traffic light and back. "How about you tell Billy to mind his own business."

Gabe looked down for a moment, his gaze drifting out the window.

The light turned green and Dean started off again.

"But are we?" Gabe asked half a block later.

Dean scoffed. "No. We are not poor." He reached out, patting his son's leg. "You can't buy a house in L.A. if you're poor. Trust me."

Gabe nodded, settling back into his thoughts, when a flash of light caught his eye. He craned his neck, his body going rigid at the sight.

A sudden, blinding flash split the sky above them—a white-hot object tearing through the blue, so violent it seemed to slice the sky itself open. Dean's hands locked on the steering wheel, knuckles bloodless, as a roaring fireball screamed overhead. The heat was immediate, pressing through the glass and crawling across his skin like hot breath. The sky convulsed, vomiting a trail of black, viscous smoke that twisted and writhed, blotting out the sun. The sound came a heartbeat later—a thunderous, bone-shattering detonation that rattled the car's frame and set every nerve in Dean's body alight with terror. Birds exploded from the trees in a panicked, shrieking cloud, their cries lost beneath the relentless, unceasing roar.

Dean's breath caught in his throat. He couldn't move. Couldn't think. The world had shrunk to a single, impossible image: the raging inferno flashing past, the sky torn open by a second, then a third burning object, each one trailed by a cloud of oily darkness that tore through and blotted out the clouds. The air itself seemed to vibrate with a low, guttural rumble—the sound filling his chest.

All around them, cars screeched to a halt, doors swinging open as people spilled out and onto the street, All faces were turned upward, mouths gaped in silent horror. The world had become a tableau of fear, frozen in that terrifying moment. Then the ground shook—a deep, rolling convulsion that sent a sickening jolt through Dean's bones. Somewhere behind them, something massive struck the earth, the sound like the earth itself had erupted. The rearview mirror caught a glimpse of a wall of fire and debris erupting into the sky, swallowing houses, trees, and everything in between. The shockwave hit the car a second later, rocking it on its wheels. Glass shattered somewhere nearby, and someone screamed—a raw, animal sound that barely rose above the explosion.

Another impact lifted a plume of fiery debris into the air—closer this time. Dean's car lurched sideways as the street buckled. His heart hammered in his chest, a wild, frantic drumbeat. The dashboard lights flickered and died, the streetlights in the intersection doing the same. The world outside had fallen into frantic pandemonium, people running, stumbling, falling, their screams drowned by the relentless, inhuman rumble.

"Dad, what's happening?" Gabe sobbed, voice raw with terror.

Dean tried to answer, but the words stayed caught in his throat. He could only stare at his son, helpless, as the sky rained fire and the world fell into chaos around them.

They lived in California, and as such, were prepared for all manner of disasters, be it riots, earthquakes or fires. But giant objects falling from the sky... That wasn't on their bingo card. This wasn't something they could have prepared for, and he struggled to find the words. There was a tremble in his voice when he finally did. "I don't know."

Dean's left hand was locked to the steering wheel, sweat pooling beneath his palm. His right was clasped almost painfully tight around his son's. His breath came in ragged, shallow bursts. The world outside was absolute chaos—people screaming, running, some frozen in place, their faces twisted in disbelief. Dean wrenched his left hand from the steering wheel and fumbled for his phone, his hand shaking so badly he nearly dropped it. He pressed the power button again and again. Nothing. The screen was black, lifeless.

"Gabe, we need to—" he started, but the words were cut short as something massive slammed into the car. Metal shrieked, glass exploded, and the car spun, almost weightless, before crashing down with a bone-jarring impact. Dean's vision blurred, the world spinning in sickening loops. He was upside down, the seatbelt digging into his shoulder, blood trickling up his forehead. He realized in the hazy moment that gravity all wrong.

From somewhere to his right came a soft, broken whimper. "Dad?"

Dean twisted, pain lancing through his neck. His son was hanging from his seatbelt, eyes wide, mouth working soundlessly. Dean reached for him, fingers numb, fumbling with the buckle. The air was thick with the stench of gasoline and burning rubber. A thick bead of blood worked its way up the side of his son's face.

A breath later, a sound split the chaos, a screech so unnatural, so horrible that it froze Dean in place. The shrill warbling howl seemed to vibrate against the inside Dean's skull. Then there was the sound of metal being torn apart. Dean's gaze locked to his son's eyes. They were wide and pleading, his pupils blown so wide they seemed to swallow the color from his face.

Some *thing* came out of the smoke from behind— impossibly fast, a blur of glistening black and jagged limbs. The car rocked as the massive creature slammed into it, the impact so violent Dean's teeth clacked together. He tasted blood. Clawed hooks— long, jointed, slick with some viscous, stinking fluid, punched through the broken glass of the passenger window. Chitin scraped against metal, a sound like knives on bone. Dean screamed, but the thing was already inside, its limbs folding with sickening, insectile precision.

The creature's claws wrapped around the boy's torso, the tips digging in, drawing thick lines of blood. Gabe's mouth opened in a scream, but the sound was lost in the roar of the burning world outside. Dean lunged, fingers brushing his son's arm, but the alien creature yanked Gabe through the window in a single, fluid motion—so fast it seemed to tear the air itself. Gabe's seatbelt snapped with a sound like breaking bone, and the boy was pulled into the chaos outside.

For a heartbeat, Dean saw the creature in full: impossibly tall, its body armored in plates that shimmered with blood and soot, its eyes a cluster of black, soulless pits. Mandibles clicked, spraying droplets of saliva, and a nearly two-foot proboscis seemed to pulse with anticipation.

"GABE!" Dean howled, his voice raw and broken.

The creature turned, disappearing in a flash as massive wings unfolded from its back as it dragged his son away. Gabe's hands clawed at empty air, his mouth stretched in a silent, endless scream. Dean was helpless to watch, his vision beginning to swirl as the world spun away from him. A breath later, darkness closed in, thick and suffocating. The last thing Dean Wilkinson saw was his son's body vanishing into the smoke and fire.

FINAL DAYS

BY

DONALD MORRISON

Dean awoke to a darkness so complete it felt alive, pressing in from every side, thick and suffocating. The air was heavy, damp, and tasted of rust and old fear—a metallic tang that clung to his tongue and crawled down his throat. For a moment, he couldn't breathe. His chest heaved, heart pounding with a frantic, animal rhythm. He didn't know where he was, or why his skin prickled with cold sweat, only that something was wrong—terribly, irreversibly wrong.

Then the sounds came. Not the comforting noises of a world at peace, but the low, anxious murmur of voices, the shuffle of too many feet on concrete, the distant clang of metal on metal. Somewhere, a child whimpered—a thin, broken sound that echoed through the tunnels like a warning. Somewhere else, a man barked a command, his voice bouncing off the walls, sharp and desperate. Dean's eyes strained against the dark, searching for any sign of safety, but all he saw was the sickly yellow glow of bulbs strung overhead, bare wires, crisscrossing like spiderwebs, casting long, twitching shadows that seemed to move on their own.

He lay still, every muscle locked, listening for the sound that haunted his dreams: the clicking, the screeching, the inhuman chorus that meant death was coming. The memory of those sounds—wet, sharp, hungry—sent a shiver through his bones. He could almost feel the creatures moving above, their claws scraping against the world, searching for a way in.

The darkness pressed closer, thick with the stink of sweat, fear, and too many bodies packed together for too long. Dean's breath came in shallow bursts, each one tasting of panic. He tried to remember how he'd gotten here, but the memories were a blur of fire and blood, of Gabe's scream vanishing into the smoke, of claws and mandibles and the world ending in a storm of wings.

Somewhere in the black, a bulb flickered, casting the tunnel in a stuttering, jaundiced light. For a heartbeat, Dean thought he saw movement—something skittering just beyond the reach of the glow. He blinked, heart hammering, but it was gone. Only shadows remained, shifting and stretching, never quite still.

A voice whispered nearby, trembling with terror: "Did you hear that?" Another voice, rough and broken, replied: "Shut up. Just shut up." The silence that followed was worse than any scream.

Dean closed his eyes, but the darkness behind his lids was no safer. He saw Gabe's face, pale and twisted in fear, saw the thing that had taken him—its eyes like pits, its limbs folding and unfolding with impossible speed. He heard the clicking, the screeching, the promise of pain and death.

He opened his eyes again, desperate for any sign of hope. But the underground offered none. Only the endless dark, and the stink of fear.

He lay there for another moment, listening to what had once been the Los Angeles City Metro System thrumming. It had been over a year since he and the last remaining survivors had made their way down into the subway tunnels beneath the city. They had fortified the entrances, creating a working barricade system that allowed them to stay in relative safety during the day. Night was safe. It was when the sun was out that the creatures who had arrived thirteen months prior, emerged. Daytime was when people died, when the greater portion of the world had died.

The world had fallen into chaos in the first days. One by one, the creatures had emerged. At first, only a handful—massive, insectile shapes, their carapaces slick with the blood and soot. Then, as the sun's first rays pierced the gloom, the earth itself seemed to rupture. Hundreds—no, thousands—of the monsters erupted from their burrows, their wings unfurling with a wet, leathery snap.

The creatures rose as one, a living storm, their bodies writhing and shifting in perfect, unnatural synchrony. The sky darkened beneath their numbers, the sun blotted out by a churning cloud of chitin and hunger. Their wings beat in time, a thunderous, relentless pulse that drowned out all other sound.

It was mesmerizing, in the way a nightmare is mesmerizing—a ballet of death, beautiful only because it was so utterly inhuman. The creatures twisted and spiraled, their movements impossibly fast. For a moment, those original survivors could only watch, transfixed by the horror of it.

Then the hunt had begun.

In those first days, the survivors had huddled in the darkness, as the sky above became a canvas of slaughter. The world was no longer theirs. It belonged to the things that now hunted in the daylight, to the swarm that rose with the sun.

When as the last echoes of the feeding faded, replaced by the wet, satisfied clicks of the monsters returning to their nests, the survivors had come to understand there was no safety, not even in the shadows. The day now belonged to the creatures, and all they could do was pray for night.

The majority of the world's population had been eradicated by the end of that first week. And those who had survived had been forced to either quickly adapt, or die. It was a rapid and forced evolution that had set humanity back thousands of years.

Dean reached up, rubbing the last remaining sleep from his eyes. As he leaned up he saw a man with a small boy pushing a cart, make their way past. The subway tunnels had become home, the only refuge to the few thousand survivors within. The spanning network of tunnels had been divided into districts. The now-static subway cars had been repurposed to facilitate the most basic necessities. The blue line had been renovated into a medical clinic and pharmacy. The red line was a security station and the purple line contained a handful of trade shops. These shops operated on a barter system, offering items that one may not find in their nighttime runs on the surface, or things that had been scavenged in the beginning. The tunnels had become a sprawling city beneath the dead world above.

He sniffled lightly, clearing his throat as he stood. He lifted his arm, checking his watch. 4 p.m. Still light out.

He pushed himself upright, every joint aching, and looked around. The subway car was crowded with bodies—some sleeping, some staring into the dark, all gaunt and hollow-eyed. The air was thick with the stink of sweat, fear, and too many people packed together for too long. Beyond the car, the tunnels stretched away into blackness, broken only by the flicker of makeshift lanterns and the glint of desperate eyes.

"Dean."

Dean turned his face to see another man in his late forties approaching. "Hector," he said as the other arrived.

"Ronaldo wants us to check the traps up on Western."

Dean brought his hands out, interlocking his fingers and turning his palms out as he stretched. He looked at his watch again for effect. "Well. I suppose we'd better get moving then."

The other nodded. "Gather your stuff. Let's get going."

Dean was part of the security team, the large group who struggled to keep civility in the underground. In the beginning there had been fights over supplies and living spaces as hundreds had flooded into the tunnels every day. When one of the creatures had managed to claw their way in and nearly sixty people had died, some impregnated, the underground security force had been created. The creatures which had arrived didn't just hunt in the daytime. They also captured and used those surviving as hosts for their young. Humanity had become, in essence, not just food, but living incubators. If one of them didn't feed, which they did in the same manner as an orbweaver; by injecting their hosts with a venomous cocktail, causing near instantaneous paralysis. This was followed by a breakdown of the internal organs, which they would return to later to drink. That same proboscis was also used to inject its larvae. Those larvae, some twenty to thirty at a time, incubated over a period of about two days, before emerging. You were eaten from within before they burrowed their way out. The worst part. The host was alive and feeling every moment of it.

The security team had been trying for months to capture one of the creatures they referred to as bugs, or clickers; the name coming from the sounds they made while hunting their prey. Some had thought they were using some form of echolocation, but most just thought it to be no more than a sound one would imagine a spider making as it clicks its mandibles together in anticipation. Others believed it was a method to flush out their prey. This was also just as likely since these creatures hunt in large packs, or murmurs. As deadly as these creatures are, the sight of them rising into the sky in the dawn's light was mesmerizingly beautiful. Like an orchestrated ballet filling the sky, hundreds of thousands of them would rise up as one, shifting and swimming in unison like a cloud of six-foot, flesh-hungry starlings. They would ebb and flow, swimming through the air in shoals, before dropping to the earth in their hunt. Few that had seen this still lived to tell of it, but when they did, there was always a lamented awe in their tone.

The traps in question, the ones Dean and Hector were en route to, had yet to bear fruit. Many of the old-world style traps, those used for bears and large prey, only resulted in a captured limb. Any leg or *tarsus* caught was almost always torn free and left for the hunter to find. They had yet to obtain one live specimen. Dead, yes, but that was an incredible rarity, and had only been in the beginning when there had been more people and more guns. And even guns were iffy. The creatures were covered in a thick chitinous carapace, like armored plating that kept anything but the highest-caliber weapons from piercing. Grenades had seemed to work well in the beginning, but those were only kept for extreme circumstances now. Hunting rifles, pitfall traps and running were the most prevalent means of survival.

"Did you hear back from Carrie?" Dean asked as he hoisted his daypack onto his shoulders. His daypack consisted of a canteen filled with Pedialyte, a handful of Clif bars, and a diary he kept for nothing more than nostalgic purposes. Anna had forced him to start keeping one as part of a couple's therapy thing they had done prior to... Everything. He had decided to keep it going if only to keep that dedication.

"Not yet," Hector replied.

"They were due back yesterday."

Carrie, another survivor that had made her way into the tunnels at the same time Dean and Hector had, and a small group had decided to make their way south, to San Diego. They were going to check for other surviving communities before making their way back with their report. They had left six days prior and had been due back the day before.

"Yeah," Hector replied, eyeing a small group huddled around an old street vendor grill. "Well. You know how that goes."

Dean did. Many people had gone out and not come back, especially those who had left with the plan to travel long distances. With radio communications down, they were back to the Pony Express days.

"They probably just got held up," Hector added, trying to stay optimistic. It was a trait that Dean both admired and despised at the same time. "Or maybe they found another community down there and decided to stay." That was less likely than them having found their slow deaths at the spiked feeding prong of a bug, but minutely possible nonetheless.

"Yeah," Dean replied, his nose dragging his face toward the smell of cooking meat. "It's possible."

The pair continued on, making their way from the Seventh Street station where they resided, through the spanning tunnel, up through L.A. and into Hollywood. Over the past year, the rails had been covered with wooden slats, nearly all the lumber in the city's yards being utilized to make a twenty-foot-wide path the entire way. The large exchange areas and maintenance bays became smaller communities. Some of these housed the renovated subway cars.

The entire subway system was illuminated. Even though electronics had been fried upon the creatures arriving, traditional wire relay systems still worked. This was another thing those few remaining scientists still struggled to understand. With an endless supply of generators and enough gasoline and solar panels to power them for the next five-hundred years in supply above, they were able to keep the lights on. Power was regulated; the use of portable speakers or personal devices limited to one hour a day in order to conserve. But that was something that was only lightly enforced. The security detail had bigger things to worry about than little Timmy playing his video games for a few hours, *much* bigger things. They passed the MacArthur Park community, the Beverly community and Santa Monica. By the time they reached the Sunset station the sun had already begun to lower beneath the horizon above. It was a little after six.

As the pair made their way up the small staircase that led from the tunnel to the platform, they could see the small security detail near the shutters.

Each of the subway stations had massive security shutters installed in those first few weeks. It had been an incredible undertaking and had cost them many lives. From ceiling to floor, thick steel panels were welded into place, gun ports dotting the base. There was a large steel door that operated on a large rack and pinion system that was manned by no less than four security personnel. Some of the larger stations, like Union, had a full security detail monitoring it at all times. These teams were responsible for keeping track of those coming and going, checking in new arrivals and escorting them to one of the station's mayors. The mayor was the person who oversaw all the day-to-day activities in their respective community. As the Western station was among the smaller of them, the mayor presided over that and the North Hollywood community. Western was more of a transition point.

"Reggie!" Hector called out as he approached the two guards near the door. "What's going on, man?"

The security guard, a rather large African-American man in military fatigues, smiled. "Oh. You know. Another day keeping her puckered up for you."

Dean listened to the exchange, his gaze wandering across the multicolored tiles that surrounded them.

"That's what we do," Hector replied.

"How are things over at Metro?"

Reggie was referring to the Seventh and Metro station, the one that Hector and Dean called home. Beyond that was Union Station, the largest hub and central settlement.

"Good," Hector replied. "Still secure."

"You still getting new arrivals?"

Hector stepped up, shaking Reggie's hand. "Not like we used to. The occasional straggler here and there. It kind of tapered off a couple months ago."

"Yeah," Reggie replied. "Same here. Some of the folks up in the hills come down to check on us every now and again. To trade supplies and see how we're doing."

"Brave or stupid."

"You know most of those big ass houses have panic rooms and underground compounds. They're just as safe up there as we are down here."

"I suppose so," Hector replied.

"So," Reggie added, glancing at Dean and nodding. "Headed up?"

Dean nodded. "Ronaldo wants us to check the traps."

Reggie smiled. "Better you than me."

"Eh," Hector replied, giving a passive waive of his hand. "It's nighttime."

"Still. Gives me the creeps going up there."

Dean drew in a breath, held it for a moment and then exhaled. It still did him as well. He didn't think he'd ever get used to the quiet, the death. He supposed that was one good thing about the way the bugs fed. Once they drank you up, there wasn't much left to rot. All the organs and fluids that would create the stink, is drunk away, so there isn't much left to create the smell. The hosts on the other hand... Those were entirely different altogether.

"Well," Reggie said, nodding to the other guard who engaged the large door mechanism. "Be safe out there."

"Always," Hector replied.

"Dean."

"Reggie," Dean replied, giving him a quick but firm handshake.

The steel door groaned to the side and the last of the day's light could be seen warming the stairwell leading down. A scattering of detritus covered the stairs and non-functioning escalator, and even though they had a cleaning detail clear it out once a week, leaves and old papers carried by the wind always managed to build up at the base.

"Lock her up," Hector said as he started up the stairs.

Not a moment later, the door creaked closed behind them.

The city above was a graveyard. Dean and Hector emerged from the subway's mouth as if surfacing from a tomb, the moonlight painting the ruins in a sickly, blue-white glow. The air was sharp with the scent of dust and weathered rot. The silence was unnatural— no distant traffic, no voices, not even the hum of electricity. Only the faint, ever-present stench of decay, and the soft crunch of broken glass beneath their boots.

The moon overhead bathed the sidewalk ahead in its gentle glow. The last of the day's light played out across the sky in thin ribbons of fuchsia caught in the clouds. There was a gentle touch of coolness to the air, and a soft breath of summer whispering past. All of the city's past reminders of the coming season were gone, the layered haze of smog and wafting odors of jet fuel drifting up from LAX. All the familiar smells of the city were gone, replaced with decaying reminders of what had passed. The soft summer breeze carried a foul odor, just hinted at behind the not-so-distant smell of salt water, dirt and pine.

As the pair exited the stairwell, Dean glanced up, his gaze working over the nearly stagnant clouds above. "Fresh air," he said, his words nearly conceding a faint tremor of lament.

"Come on," Hector said, slapping him lightly on the back of his shoulder. "Let's go see what we caught."

"A whole lot of nothing," Dean responded, stealing one last glance at the fading color above. "Just like the last hundred times."

The pair started making their way toward the intersection. Just three blocks away was the first of the traps. The underground had been trying to trap one of the creatures for months. If they could just catch one, they could study it, or at least they thought they could. Really, they had no idea what they would have done if they'd managed to snare one of the things. With the goddamned feeding tubes and six-foot reach ending in a spiked tarsus, even getting close proved to be an obstacle in and of itself—a deadly one. But, they'd decided to go with the plan, constructing a handful of crudely built traps near the entrances to the subway stations. The one that they were currently making their way toward was an old North Hollywood Ice truck that had been converted into a MacGyvered, catch-and-release type trap that old exterminators had used prior to the creature's arrival. It worked in the same fashion, with a small animal, in this case, a stray dog tethered to a leash, and a trigger pad that would cause the back of the truck to seal up the moment pressure was put on the plate. The dog was placed at the back of the truck, the pressure plate trigger set, and a generator rigged up to kick on the moment the trap would spring. The idea was to lure one of the bugs in and turn the truck into an icebox. They had no idea what effect the cold would have on one of the things, but there were educated assumptions. First, they only came out in the daytime. They nested underground, which meant that they used the warmth captured by the earth to help regulate their temperature, and the fact that they shared very similar physiology with Earth's insects led the surviving members of society to believe they were also poikilotherms, or cold-blooded in layman's terms. This meant they couldn't self-regulate their temperature. Those left alive assumed that was why they only came out during the daytime and stayed underground at night. Though all of this was still purely theoretical speculation. No one had really had a chance to study one.

As they made their way down Hollywood Boulevard, Dean glanced at the fading orange letters on the front of the plaza. "Man, I miss that spot."

Hector looked over, reading the sign. "Norms?"

He nodded, looking into the grimy window. "I'd give my left arm for a Lumberjack right now..."

"They did have some good hotcakes, didn't they?"

"They had good everything," Dean replied, the saliva beginning to build in his mouth.

"Don't let Carol hear you say that. She might think you're speaking ill of her cooking."

"Oh," Dean replied mockingly. "We wouldn't want that now, would we?"

Hector chuckled. "She does make a mean goulash."

"Kind of hard to mess up a goulash..."

Hector shot him a sidelong glance. "Remember Clayton...?"

"Jesus," Dean replied, thinking about the younger, head-smart kid who'd claimed to have been a Michelin-rated chef before the invasion, and the insufferable slop he'd put together that their district would have to choke down, using an unhealthy amount of salt, pepper, and sauces to make it palatable. "Don't remind me."

Clayton had died just a few months prior, deciding to tempt fate while out on a supply run. He'd stayed just a little too long after dawn and had found a quick end at the pointed end of a bug snout. That had ended his kitchen tirades rather quickly. Carol, a slightly older woman from the Midwest had stepped in to fill his shoes, and while her offerings weren't as fancy and decorated as the kids, they tasted light years better. They actually looked forward to mealtime now, and the salt and pepper had gone back to being on reserve.

The two of them continued down the boulevard, weaving through the stalled vehicles. Some of them still contained the original owners, preserved for all time behind the seatbelts that held them in place, the ones that had secured them during the initial attack. Countless had died in those first few days, immeasurable numbers in those that followed.

"I was thinking," Hector said, looking past the windows of a Thai restaurant. "Maybe we could take a trip. Head up into the mountains. Find a nice lake to sit around for a few days. Be nice to get out for a time."

"Oh," Dean replied flatly. "Why don't we just pack up the car. We could grab a couple girls, a twelve-pack. Hell. We could probably even rent us a nice cabin for the weekend."

"I'm being serious," Hector replied with mild irritation threading his words. "I think we could make a go of it."

"I think we should just stick to the task at hand," Dean replied. "Having thoughts like those will only get you killed. You know as well as I do that being anywhere outside during the day is suicide. Doesn't matter where you are. We're safe underground. That's how we stay alive. That's how we survive."

Hector clenched his jaw. He grunted, "Yeah. You're right..."

They passed the next block, cutting through a small parking lot. The tiny plaza was empty, the liquor store barren, looted to empty shelves months prior, and the sign above the old strip club had been broken. All that remained said *O's OM*. There was an old clip-art-style image of a woman bathing in a large cocktail glass above the word cocktails. The faded red entrance stood out in stark contrast to the gray that surrounded it.

"You ever go there?" Hector asked as they made their way around to the side street.

"Once or twice," Dean replied. "Before Anna and I were a thing."

They turned the corner and stopped.

Just up the street was the old refrigeration truck. The back door was closed and the generator atop it was thrumming.

"Oh, shit," Hector said.

Neither of them moved. They stood there, staring at the truck, listening as the generator rumbled above.

"No way," Hector whispered after a moment. "You think we actually caught something?"

"I don't know," Dean said, his voice low. As he spoke, he pulled the thin leather strap off the hammer of his revolver. He pulled it, giving an instinctual check to the cylinder. Then he nudged Hector with his elbow and started forward. "Let's find out."

Hector pulled his pistol, a nine-millimeter Smith and Wesson M&P that he'd had long before the bugs had arrived. He drew in a sharp breath, shoving it out in a gust and started after.

As they approached the truck, Dean could feel the sweat beginning to build between his palm and the pistol grip. He edged forward, reaching out and placing his hand against the door. He felt the chill press into his palm. He nodded to Hector and stepped back. One hand lifted, a closed fist held out. Hector mirrored the motion.

"One," Dean mouthed, lifting his hand and dropping it back to level. "Two. Three."

On three, they both dropped their hands. Dean's stayed a fist, but Hector's dropped open, the first two fingers extended. "Shit," he growled, clenching his fist.

Dean stepped back, taking two steps before stopping. He leveled the pistol and pulled the hammer back.

Hector reached out, grasping the canvas strap attached next to the locked latch. He nudged the latch to the side and took three steady breaths before jerking his hand up, sliding the door open and stepping back.

A blast of cold air rolled out, thick with the stench of rot and something chemical, alien. Inside, sprawled on the metal floor, was one of the creatures.

It was huge, its limbs twisted and frozen mid-reach, carapace cracked with cold. Its eyes clusters of black, soulless pits, were wide and empty, staring at nothing. The dog's body lay nearby, torn and slick with viscous fluid. The creature's feeding tube was still embedded in its side, frozen in place.

Dean's stomach lurched. The thing was dead, but the horror of it was undiminished. Its claws were as long as his forearm, hooked and stained. Its mandibles were parted, frozen in a final, silent scream.

For a long moment, neither man moved. The city seemed to hold its breath.

"Oh, shit!" Hector said, his knuckles whitening around the grip of his pistol.

For the next thirty seconds, the two men stood there, weapons trained on the creature. They didn't move. Each of them kept their gaze locked on the bug, scrutinizing it for any movement.

Dean was the one that finally reached down, hefted up a small rock, and tossed it underhand into the back of the truck.

The stone landed against the insect's back and rolled to the metal floor with a clatter. There was no movement.

"Is it dead?" Hector asked, still not moving, or lowering his gun.

"Why don't you give it a poke and find out?" Dean replied, equally locked in place.

The moon overhead shone down on them, bathing the street in light. It was a clear night and the nearly full moon offered them a good view of their surroundings. The dim glow that fell out of the back of the refrigeration truck caught the cool steam pouring out in ribbons. Frozen fog swirled under the single interior light, twisting and churning with the air pouring in.

It was Hector who finally stepped forward, climbing into the back of the truck and stopping. He could see the rope tied to the back of the truck and the large shepherd lying on its side beneath. He edged forward, the barrel of his pistol trained on the bug's head. Slowly, he brought his foot out and tapped the creature with his toe. He jumped back, nearly firing off a round. Relieved that it hadn't reacted, he repeated the process—one more tap, this time without the frightened reaction. "I think we got it," he called back, his gaze moving to the dog.

The brown-and-black shepherd lay on its side. There was a thick, viscous coating around it, and Hector could see a large puncture wound in its side. Then, he saw a ripple of movement just beneath the fur. "Ah, shit," he growled, turning to watch Dean hoist himself up into the truck.

Dean made his way over, his gaze working from the bug to the dog. "I hate these fucking things," he growled, bringing his pistol up and sending a round into the dog's head.

The truck echoed with the gunshot, filling their ears with a high-pitched ringing. The movement beneath the dog's fur slowly stilled.

"Cold," Hector said, a moment later, his words just below a shout.

"What?" Dean asked, the tinnitus still ringing.

"Cold kills them."

Dean looked down at the bug. "Cover your ears," he said, allowing Hector a moment to do so before painting the floor with the inner contents of the insect's head.

"Let's go tell the others," Dean continued. "I'm sure Jim will want to send his guys out here to collect this. Maybe we can get a few extra rations out of this."

"I wouldn't get your hopes up," Hector replied. "It's Jim we're talking about."

The Jim in question was the mayor of the Seventh and Metro district, and the man responsible for overseeing the distribution of supplies and rations.

"One can hope." He reached out and tapped Hector on the arm. "Come on. Let's get back."

The pair dropped out of the truck, making their way back to the boulevard. They made their way back to the train station and settled in for the long trek back to downtown. A little over two hours later, they were back.

That night, the tunnels pulsed with a feverish, electric dread. Survivors gathered on the Seventh Street platform, their faces gaunt and hollow-eyed in the jaundiced glow of bare bulbs. The air was thick with sweat and fear, every voice pitched too high, every movement edged with panic. The news had spread like a virus: one of the monsters was dead. Killed by cold.

For twenty minutes, the crowd seethed, hope and terror clashing in every word. Some clung to the idea that the creatures couldn't survive the cold, their voices trembling with desperate optimism. Others argued back, voices raw, insisting that a single, frozen bug in a truck was no proof at all. The bug's death could have been caused by anything. Maybe it was sick. Maybe it was dying already. Maybe it was a trap.

Jim had sent a small group with a handcart to retrieve the bug, and those men, along with two folks who had been in the science department at USC, were doing their best to analyze the creature and determine the cause of death. Until they had concluded the autopsy, there would be no way to know *what* had killed the thing. At this moment, it could have been indigestion for all they knew. Though, it *had* chosen the dog as a host, not food. But still.

"Just because it was in the refrigeration truck, doesn't mean it was killed by the cold. It could have been anything."

"We've captured them before," Hector barked back. "And they were still alive. This one was dead."

"You said it had laid its eggs in the bait dog," another member of the large group replied loudly. "Why would it do that if it knew it was going to die from the cold?"

Hector shot the man a puzzled look. He glanced at Dean.

"Maybe it laid its eggs *knowing* it was going to die," Dean said. "*Maybe* it knew that the cold was going to kill it, that it couldn't escape, and did that so that its *offspring* could have a chance to survive. The larvae would survive off the body heat of their host. At least for as long as the host survived the cold."

"But that's also suggesting that these things are capable of complex thoughts. That implies reasoning and higher cognitive functions," another person blurted out. "They've already proven to be incapable of that. They operate in a hive mentality."

"Exactly my point," Hector remarked. "One sacrifice to continue the hive." He paused. "I remember hearing something about bees or ants doing something like that."

Another person was about to blurt out when Jim lifted his hands into the air. "Okay!" he said loudly, grabbing everyone's attention. "Okay."

At that moment, one of the scientists stepped in from the tunnel, her face pale, eyes wide. Jim's words died in his throat as she approached. "What do you have for us, Amelia?" he asked, voice barely steady.

The woman walked up to where Jim stood. She looked at him for a moment before nodding. "It was the cold," she said, her voice carrying over the silence.

Jim stared at her.

The woman turned to the crowd. Again, she nodded, a tired look of relief on her face. "Exposure," she said, her voice lifting. "It died because of the cold."

A murmur rippled through the crowd—relief, disbelief, fear, all tangled together. Dean felt it in his gut: a flicker of hope, instantly smothered by the memory of the surface, the certainty that the monsters were still out there, learning, adapting.

"Its carapace showed structural cracks, consistent with extreme cold," the woman continued. "Cold fractures."

Dean watched as a mixture of fear, relief and skepticism worked its way through the crowd. He wondered how, if they knew so little about the monsters, they could have determined that conclusion. But they were the scientists, not him, so he dropped the thought and pulled his attention back to the moment.

"Then we need to seek higher elevation," an older man, who had been standing next to him, shouted. "We should go north."

A low rumble rose up, most of the group grumbling about the time it would take to get there. They complained about not being able to travel during the daytime, and said it would be nothing but suicide. Most of them were content with their current situation. All in all, they were surviving rather comfortably. Sure, they lacked modern amenities, but they had the basics: food, shelter, working toilets, and a lifetime supply of toilet paper. It was enough, spread out across the city. For all intents and purposes, they had calculated that they would be able to comfortably survive in the tunnels for the next two hundred years if they continued to ration their supplies. Maybe even longer if they came up with a farming system—which they had already begun working on. But there were those who weren't happy with spending the rest of their days living underground and sneaking out at night to scavenge. There were those who just wanted to find a place where the bugs didn't exist, to be able to go out under the sun, to not have to hide during the day. But those voices were few and far between. At that moment, only the man standing next to Dean seemed to hold that desire.

"And what are you going to do when you get there?" another barked in response. "How do you plan on surviving in the winter with no working power grid? And how far north do you think we'd need to go? Canada? Further?"

"It's not realistic," a woman chimed in. "They can't survive in the cold, but neither can we."

"Eskimos have been doing it for thousands of years," the man replied flatly. "No electricity. No cellphones. No heaters. And they've managed just fine."

"So, you want us to become Eskimos?"

The man's mouth opened to respond, but quickly snapped shut when he realized the futility of trying to argue his point.

"Not a bad idea," Dean said, craning his neck toward the man who had just spoken. "You aren't wrong. But I think the term would be Inuit."

The older man turned his dark brown gaze on him, nodding softly. He extended his hand. "George."

Dean took the man's hand and gave a firm shake. "Dean." He noticed the streams of grey running through the man's black, ear-length hair.

Another in the crowd said that he had family in North Dakota. He said it was cold nearly year-round, and all they had to do was make it there. Sure, it got warm in the summer, but they'd be far enough out that the bugs wouldn't likely be out looking for them. He thought it would be safe. This drew a better response than George's Canada plan, and more than a handful of people co-signed it almost immediately. There was something about being in the frozen tundra that deterred most of them away from that plan.

"What about heat?" another shouted. "What if we go somewhere hot?"

There was a scattering of scoffs and stifled laughs.

"Military tried that," an older man replied. "Remember that? Oakland?"

The military had firebombed the city in the first weeks of the attack. They had carpet-bombed the city nearly to rubble in an attempt to take out a large swath of them. But the bugs had only burrowed further. The earth had kept them safe from the napalm. The buildings that thousands of survivors were holed up in were not so much.

"We have *proof* that the cold kills them," another person added. "How is this even still a debate? We should leave tomorrow. That guy says he has a place in North Dakota. Right?"

The man who had made that announcement chimed back in, reiterating that fact, adding that there was plenty of acres to start rebuilding. This created a large stir, drawing a divide between the people.

"I'm with you," Dean said to the man beside him.

George nodded in reply, holding Dean's gaze for a moment.

The crowd around them continued with their animated conversation that bordered at points on all-out argument. When it was over, Dean found George and asked him if he was serious about heading north. George looked at him for a moment. He could tell he was sizing him up. Then, with a single nod, he replied. "Hearing that today—that's all I needed to hear. I'm tired of hiding underground."

Dean nodded. "Yeah. Me too."

"Are you all planning on heading north?"

Dean and George both turned their gazes to the man who had just interjected himself into their conversation. He stood there, flanked by another man around the same age, and a young boy who couldn't have been a day over ten. His gaze worked between them. He licked his lips, waiting for their response.

Dean and George exchanged a quick glance. "That's what we were just discussing," George replied.

"Well," the man replied. "If you are, my family and I would like to tag along, if that's alright."

Dean and George exchanged another quick glance.

"That's fine by me," George said, glancing at the man and the kid behind. "But I don't assume it's going to be an easy journey. I'm guessing most of the roads are gridlocked, and we're limited to traveling at night. Are you sure your family is up to it?"

"We've survived this long," the other man replied, peering down at him.

George felt a smile creep across his face. That little spit of fire told him everything he needed to know. "Well, alright then. You should probably be a part of this conversation."

The man's face didn't soften. He simply reached out, patting his boy on the back and gesturing for him to take a seat at the table. The man introduced himself as Bill, and the other man, Gary, was his husband. The quiet boy was Simon, their son, and George had been nearly spot-on. He had just turned ten the week prior.

"Well," George replied. "I'm George, and this is…" He looked at the other man, seated across from him. "Sorry. Terrible with names."

"Dean," Dean replied, offering a hand.

Bill grasped the outstretched hand and shook it. His husband offered a polite nod.

"So, where were you thinking?" Bill asked.

George told him they had been discussing Alaska. Either Anchorage or Fairbanks. It was far enough north that he doubted the bugs would be able to survive, being cold-blooded. Alaska still had permafrost, which meant burrowing wouldn't be feasible for them and some parts of Alaska were dark up to two months a year. As long as they could figure out some type of farming situation, they would be fine. But again, this was all speculation. Nobody really knew what it was like up north. Hell. The bugs could have adapted for all they knew. But the one thing they could all agree on was that it was better to take a chance and find out they were right in their assumptions, rather than to stay hiding underground. Everyone knew it was just a matter of time before the bugs figured out a way to get in. If that happened, they'd have nowhere to hide, and that would put a pretty quick end to their happy underground society. None of them wanted to be there if and when that happened. So, they spent the next few hours working out their plan.

"I think, if we stick to the 1 the entire way up, it will avoid the nightmare which is bound to be the 5. I can guarantee it's gridlocked the entire way."

"I don't know about that," George replied, watching as the lantern light flickered across Bill's face. "Up through the Grapevine, probably, but once you get past that, gotta be open highway. Plus. Taking the 1 has a lot less options for places to take cover in, should we find ourselves in a tricky predicament."

Simon had sat quietly, listening to the adults talk. He wasn't interested in what they were talking about. It was all about traveling and surviving. What had captivated his interests was the large, black German Shepherd that belonged to George. He'd introduced him as Coal, and at that moment, Coal was lying contentedly on the floor, getting a lifetime's worth of neck scratches. He'd been almost hesitant at first, but now his eyes were closed and his neck arched up. His foot twitched slightly, as if he were running in a dream.

"I think both options are good," Dean said, glancing at the boy who was lost in the abyssal fur. "But, I think George has a point. The 1 is wide open. Lots of space between towns. We don't know what's out there. Bugs could be the least of our problems. We all went through the COVID lockdown. Apocalypse scenarios don't exactly bring out the best in people."

"That's what I was trying to avoid saying," George added. He'd been thinking it, but with the boy there, was trying to tactfully dance around saying that there was a possibility there could be militias, or gangs, or roving packs of rapist cannibals for all they knew. He was ex-Army, and he'd been on the front lines. He knew what people were capable of. He'd seen it firsthand. That was partly the reason he was still there, hunkered up underground.

"How far of a walk are we talking?" Gary asked, glancing at his son.

George pulled a map from beside him and laid it out on the table. "We're here," he said, stabbing his finger down in the center of downtown. "I can say from experience, that at a mild pace, it takes about five hours, give or take, to walk to the North Hollywood district. For that part, we can use the underground. The tunnels are a straight shot and will allow us to avoid any of the unnecessary detours taking the surface streets would. From there." He moved his fingers to where the 5 freeway cut up and through the mountains toward Santa Clarita, the next city outside of the San Fernando Valley. "That's about the same distance, give or take. I'm guessing it'll take about the same amount of time to get there." He pulled his finger back, glancing at Gary. "If we leave North Hollywood, just as the sun is going down, that puts us out of the valley and onto open roads by, and I'm throwing a guess here, eleven or twelve. That gives us a good five or six hours of walking before we have to find a good place to hide for the day. We might even find us a car by then. Then we could really put some miles on us before we have to stop."

"How many miles is that?" Gary asked, a worry in his tone. "On foot?"

George looked down at the map.

"A lot," Dean answered for him. "But it's the only way out." He glanced at the boy. "If we have to get a wagon, or a cart or something, we'll figure that out."

"I don't need a wagon," Simon said, glancing up at the adults. "I like walking. My dads took us on a hike that was almost fifteen miles. I could have done it twice."

Bill smiled, feeling a gentle rush of warmth in his chest. "Yeah, we did," he replied, the smile growing. Then he looked at George. "He'll be fine."

"This is a lot more than fifteen miles we're talking about."

"I could do fifty," Simon added, just for good measure.

"Okay," George replied, hands lifted. "Alright. I get it. You can walk." He glanced at the others. "Look. I think it's pretty straight forward. Go pack up whatever it is you're going to bring and meet us at the North Hollywood station at six. We'll leave the moment you arrive."

"So, we're taking the 5 then?" Dean asked, just to confirm.

They all shared a quick glance, and when nobody spoke up to challenge the plan, George nodded. "Looks like that's the plan."

The group disbanded, Simon taking slightly longer than the others in order to give Coal a proper goodnight hug. George liked that the boy had taken such a shining to him. Coal was a good boy, and he knew having someone younger around would probably breathe a new life into the young dog. He was still a pup, so George liked to say. He was just over five. He had a lot of life in him and more energy than he at his age was able to disperse. Sure. He'd play fetch with him, or send him tracking, but in the attention department. Coal had become more of a partner than a friend. They relied upon each other, and George had tapered off the training a year or so back. Bugs invading earth and killing ninety percent of the population could have that effect on a man. He missed their outings, the hikes, the camping, hunting. Coal had gotten pretty good at tracking and retrieving small game. He'd also fallen into a slump when they'd gone underground as well. It hadn't gone unnoticed. So, as he was packing his belongings up for the trip, he smiled knowing that Coal had no idea the adventure he was in for, and the fact that he'd have plenty of high energy company along for the trek.

Dean was seated next to George when Bill and his family emerged from the southbound tunnel and up the stairs to the platform. The air in the underground was thick with anticipation, every movement edged with nervous energy. The knowledge that the cold could kill the monsters had spread like wildfire, igniting both hope and fear in equal measure. For every person eager to act, there was another paralyzed by the risk of leaving the only safety they'd known.

George didn't waste any time. He hoisted his bag onto his shoulders, cinching the straps tightly. "Ready to go?" His voice was low, but there was a new urgency in it—a sense that the world above was shifting, and they had to move before it shifted again.

Bill nodded, and Dean could see the sleep still clinging tightly to the faces of his husband and son. A tiny smile tugged at the boy's face as he saw Coal sitting alert next to George. A yawn wrenched his mouth open. They had slept in the Hollywood Highland district the night prior, shaving nearly three hours off their commute. They had woken up at four to make the two-hour trek to the North Hollywood station. The cup of coffee he'd shared with Gary that morning had already run its course.

"We're really doing it then?" Dean asked, his voice barely above a whisper, as if afraid the tunnels themselves might overhear.

George nodded and Dean found himself mirroring the motion. "Better than waiting around to..." He cut his words short, glancing at Simon. "Well. You know."

Bill nodded. "That's why we're here."

"Then what do you say we get this show on the road?"

George turned and made his way to the large steel-grated blockade. The guards opened the door, and the last clinging remnants of daylight filtered dustily through the rectangular space. Particles danced in the waning coral light. There was a thin bustle of activity as they reached the top of the stairs. Scavenging groups had already begun to gather, preparing for their nightly runs. Another group, dressed in tactical gear, military-style helmets, flak jackets and high-powered rifles, eyed them with a mixture of camaraderie and suspicion.

Dean recognized one of the men, who turned and made his way over. "Heading out?" the man asked as he approached.

Dean saw Gary tense. Bill maneuvered himself slightly between them.

"Heading north," Dean replied, reaching out to shake the man's hand.

"North?" the other replied, glancing between them. "Like, North, north?"

Dean nodded. "That's the plan," he said, adjusting the hunting rifle slung over his shoulder.

"Oh," the man in soldier attire replied. "Well, I wish you the best. You be safe out there."

"That is also the plan," Dean replied, forcing a thin smile.

The man's gaze lingered a moment longer, as if weighing whether to say more, then he simply nodded and turned away.

The group made their way away from the station, turning onto the miles-long parking lot which had once been Lankershim Boulevard. Once out of earshot, a familiar silence drifted between them. The quiet of the city nestled thickly around them, and after a short time, they had all settled into their paces, the sounds of their shoes scuffing the dirty concrete rising into the air.

Every step away from the underground felt like a gamble, the city above a vast, unpredictable board. But beneath the fear, hope flickered—a stubborn, defiant thing. They had a plan. They had each other. And for the first time in months, the monsters weren't the only ones adapting.

═7═

Dean had lived in Los Angeles for most of his adult life. Prior to moving to sunny SoCal, he'd lived in a tiny town in Southern Utah. Like death and taxes, the only things assured in Utah were snow and Mormons. Oh, and dry Sundays. But those were things he had put behind him decades ago. Now they were just conversational talking points, like, 'You see how the Packers did last week?' After living in L.A. for so many years—as with any place—you get to know the different neighborhoods and the unique aesthetics each part of the city offers. The section of the city they were currently walking through, North Hollywood, he and his wife, prior to their marriage, had lived in for a short handful of years. The city they were currently walking through looked nothing like that city. The city that surrounded them was a vague, skeletal mockery of a once-bustling corridor. They made their way up the wide boulevard, their quiet procession of footsteps keeping rhythm to their strides. Someone had cleared the gridlocked traffic to the sides of the road with a bulldozer some months prior, allowing a single lane for getting from the NoHo district to the foothills some miles away. Whoever had overseen that undertaking had also cleared traffic a good portion of the way down Ventura Boulevard as well. Likely for scavenging and supply run purposes. But at the moment, it was affording them a straight, no-hassle shot to the 5 freeway near the mountains. From there, it was another straight shot up and over the pass.

The last of the day's sunlight dimmed below the distant horizon, a gentle, blue-grey padding overhead, ribbons of peach dancing just at the edge. There was a faint flicker of a chill on the air, a tickle of frosty breath in the breeze, just enough to raise the hairs on your arms.

"I thought summer was just around the corner," Bill said, his gaze working across the last of the sunlight clinging to the bottom edge of the sky. "Oof." Bill and his family were from Arizona. They weren't acclimated to the strange ping-pong effect that happened in Southern California as the seasons went back and forth, unable to make up their mind which one was going to show up for the day. It would go days at a time, hovering in the low sixties, and then, bam, ninety-eight the next day, and into the triple digits for the next three, followed by cloudy skies and rain for another two. Spring to summer in Southern California was like being in the middle of a debate between two people with dissociative identity disorder. This was one of the good days.

"This is tank-top weather," George replied. His gaze shifted toward Bill. "Wait till we get further north…"

Bill smiled. "We're from Flagstaff. We know cold."

George smirked.

"So," Bill asked, glancing between the two men. "What did you all do before this?"

George glanced at Dean.

Dean took the visual cue and was first to respond. "Suppose I'll go first." He took the next two steps, gazing at the quickly fading dusk. "I was a restaurant manager. Little spot in Long Beach, called Harlan's." He drew in a breath, memories of the restaurant and staff filtering past.

"Restaurant manager, huh?" Gary replied. "Okay."

"What about you?" Bill asked, looking at George.

"Retired," the older man replied, offering no more than the one-word response.

"What about you?" Dean asked, looking at the burned-out husk of an abandoned pickup truck off to the side.

Bill pondered the question for a moment, drawing in a deep breath and responding in a tone that was almost lamenting. "I was a market analyst."

George caught the questioning tone in his reply. "Is that regret, or longing I'm catching there?"

Bill scoffed, letting a single chuckle escape. "Just didn't do much to prepare me for all of this, you know."

Dean looked at him. "And being a restaurant manager did?" He shook his head. "Find me one job that could have prepared you for this..." He opened his arms, swinging them wide to accentuate the desolate landscape surrounding them.

Bill nodded.

"Seems like you're doing a pretty good job to me," George replied. "There's a lot of folks alone now, who had family before all this."

The words stabbed into Dean like a serrated knife, the memories twisting it deeper. "Yeah, I guess so."

George stole a glance back to where Gary and his son were walking. "How's the boy adjusting to all this?"

Bill shot a quick glance back. "Simon?" He scoffed. "I wish I had half his resilience. Other than missing his friends, this has been one big adventure for him." He let out an exasperated gust. "Part of me thinks he prefers it this way." The next two steps went by in a gravel-crunching silence. "No school. No chores. No homework. That boy's living the childhood dream."

Dean thought back to his own son, Gabe. A smiling memory was quickly replaced with him being dragged backwards on his stomach, a scream erupting from his terrified face. He shoved the thought back.

"Gary's the one that's having the hardest time adjusting," Bill continued. "He's been through a lot. This was just the cherry on top."

Neither of the men questioned further, and Bill left it at that as they fell into a cadence down the street.

The group had traveled another ten blocks in silence, when Dean spoke up, shattering the still monotony of footsteps. "I used to work there," he said, pointing at a black wall with Jeremy's written in sparkling orange letters across the front.

"Jeremy's?" George asked with a smirk.

"Bar?" Dean smirked.

"Something like that," he replied. "It masqueraded as a nightclub," he added, reminiscing about the blur of drunken nights. "Place almost cost me my marriage," he added, thinking about that tumultuous time in his and Anna's relationship.

"Bars'll do that," George replied matter-of-factly.

Overhead, a small group of pigeons cooed, the last of the fading light lulling them to sleep on the overhanging traffic light pole.

Dean sighed. "Yeah. They will..." His thoughts drifted back to the low amber lighting, polished bar-top and brass railings beneath. He thought about the DJs that had taken up residencies there, the good, the bad. He thought about the staff and realized this was the first time since everything had happened that he'd even thought about them. He wondered, in that moment, if any of them had made it. He doubted it. Most hadn't.

"Did your wife...?" Bill started, ending the incomplete sentence when he realized he didn't know how to ask the insensitive question.

"Yeah," Dean replied, looking at the small plaza of shops next to the bar.

"I'm sorry," Bill added. "I didn't mean to..."

"It's fine," Dean replied, his brow furrowing.

"Look!"

The three men spun their heads, Dean turning to walk backward, hand darting to the pistol at his waist.

Thirty feet back, Simon was waving a stick in the air. Coal was dancing around, lifting up onto two feet and making a series of short hops to grasp at the dangling piece of wood. His tongue was hanging out to the side and his eyes were pulled back and wide. The three men watched, smiles growing on their faces as the interruption pushed bitter memories back to the dark.

George let out a chuckle. "Crazy dog," he said, a thick country accent filling the words.

Dean watched a moment longer before spinning back around. "Seems like a good kid," he said.

Bill gave another backward glance. "That he is. We hit the lottery with that one."

The group fell back into silence as night enveloped them. There was a warm breeze drifting past that smelled of ocean and kapok flowers.

For the next four hours they walked in silence, taking in the neighborhoods that folded past. By the time they reached the end of the valley, it was just after midnight.

"How you doing back there?" George asked, looking back to where Gary and Simon were walking.

Gary looked down to Simon. "We should probably take a rest," he said, looking back to them, his gaze settling on Bill. "Forrest here might have embellished a bit in his endurance."

George glanced at Bill who offered a smirk. "Alright, yeah," he replied, glancing around. Just off the freeway was a small restaurant. "Why don't we stop for a bit," he suggested. "We could take a load off in that restaurant right there. I could use a bite myself."

They all agreed, making their way off the freeway and over to the tiny Mexican spot.

"So, I said, if you don't either change those socks or stop taking those damn boots off, we're gonna have a problem…"

The others laughed, Gary and Bill sharing a loving glance.

George had just finished telling a story from his time in boot camp, about the guy in the bunk next to him who had an affinity for wearing the same socks for days in a row.

"Man," Dean said, sipping the room temp instant coffee in his cup. "I could only imagine…"

Gary looked over to where Simon had fallen asleep in one of the booths opposite theirs. "You remember that time we caught the bus to Riverside?" he asked, looking back to Bill, whose eyebrows rose up nearly to his hairline.

"Riverside," he replied as if the one-word response said it all. He let out a scoffing chuckle. The smile faded as his eyes traced a deep set of claw marks that gouged the opposite wall. The reminders of what hunted them were everywhere, even here, in the places that should have been safe.

"So," Gary began. "Bill here, decided one day that Simon hadn't experienced public transportation. So, he found this fun little nature exhibit in Riverside, and decided we should take the bus there and back. An *experience*…" He shot Bill a smirk. "It was an experience all right, because he didn't bother to check the bus schedule."

"Oh, man," George said.

"Yeah," he replied with a snap. "So, by the time we got out of the exhibit and back to the bus stop, Riverside Transit had stopped running."

This got a chuckle out of Dean. "And mind you, Simon was four at the time, and this was before rideshares had gotten big—and my paranoid husband here didn't bring his credit cards—because he was worried about someone stealing his wallet..."

A smile spread across George's lips.

"So, needless to say, we had about twelve dollars to our name, a four-year-old child and no way to get home until morning." At this last part, he leaned in, staring at Bill. "So," he continued. "We went to a Denny's nearby and had coffee. Three hours later, the waitress asked if everything was alright. I told her what my stupid husband had done and said we were just waiting as long as we could before we were kicked out." He shook his head, smiling at the memory. "The waitress spoke to the graveyard manager, and they actually offered us a booth at the back of the restaurant. I'm pretty sure they felt sorry for us because Simon was already asleep in the booth. So, we spent the night like homeless people in a booth at the back of a Denny's."

George laughed. "Bet you didn't do that one again."

Bill shook his head. "No. I didn't."

Gary sighed, a gentle smile on his lips. "We've had some adventures, haven't we?"

Bill reached out, placing his hand atop Gary's and squeezed lightly. "Yeah, we have."

"Well," George added, glancing over to where Coal slept beneath the table where Simon was sleeping. "Let's see how they stack up against the one we just started."

Bill squeezed tighter and Gary brought his other hand atop his, reciprocating the gesture, the warmth of the moment fleeting. Around them, the darkness pressed against the windows, every gust of wind, every distant sound sending tendrils of adrenaline through them.

"We should probably get moving though," George said, glancing out the window. "I'd like to get out of the valley before sunrise."

Gary looked over to where his son was sleeping.

"Can he ride a bike?" Dean asked. the flicker of paternal worry flash through Gary's eyes, a look he'd seen in his own wife more than once.

Gary nodded in response.

"We taught him right before all this," Bill said, nodding as he realized what the older man was suggesting. "Not a bad idea."

"Might make it a little easier on him," Dean added.

"We'll keep our eyes open," George said, lifting his cup and draining the last of its contents.

"How far do you think we'll make it tonight?" Gary asked.

"As far as we can," George replied, pushing his cup a few inches forward. "If we get up and over the hill, it's a clear shot to the other side. I figure we can find a house with a basement, or a place with shutters we can draw." His mind was already racing with possibilities.

"Okay," Bill said, nudging Gary with his hip. "Let's get the boy up."

The group had walked the rest of the night. It had only been a short time after leaving the restaurant that they had found a small bicycle for Simon. He'd taken to it immediately and had spent the next five hours weaving through the stalled vehicles on the freeway as they wove their way past. Coal had chased after him for a bit at first, racing and trying to keep up, but eventually he'd settled into a mellow pace alongside George, who welcomed the furry company. By the time they reached the city of Valencia, a soft glow was beginning to hint at the horizon. George looked over to where massive monuments to the past rose up, twisting, looping, and turning. The abandoned amusement park's rollercoasters stood tall, giant steel megaliths from a quickly fading society. "There's a hotel over there," he said, glancing at the distant horizon behind him. "Let's call it a night." The others agreed. They were tired, their feet hurt, and their shoulders were sore from the straps pulling them downward for the last nine hours. The group made their way to the hotel.

The front door was unlocked. Like most of the stores and homes, it had been quickly left during the initial attack. So, they made their way through, finding stairs that led down to a laundry room a short time later. They dragged four mattresses from the rooms above and laid them out on the floor. Then they went upstairs, locked the front doors, and made their way back down, settling in for the day. Less than an hour had passed before the first screeches rose up outside, heralding that the alien creatures had awoken and were rising up for the day's hunt. For the next three hours, they lay there, listening to the echoing screeches and clicks as the winged insects flew across the landscape in search of prey.

Every sound outside was a threat. The walls felt paper-thin, the windows like fragile barriers against the chaos beyond. The group huddled together in the dim, musty laundry room, every muscle tense, every breath shallow. The screeches outside grew louder, closer, sometimes so near it seemed the monsters might burst through the walls at any moment. Simon clung to Coal, burying his face in the dog's fur, while Bill and Gary exchanged anxious glances, both trying to hide their fear for the boy's sake. Dean sat with his back to the door, rifle across his knees, eyes fixed on the thin line of light beneath the frame, as if expecting claws to appear at any second.

Time crawled. The screeches ebbed and flowed, sometimes fading, sometimes swelling into a frenzy that made their hearts race. The group barely spoke, afraid that even a whisper might draw attention. The world outside was a nightmare, and all they could do was wait, hoping the walls would hold, hoping the monsters would pass them by. In that darkness, hope was a fragile thing, but it was all they had. They clung to it, each in their own way, praying for the sun to set, for the monsters to retreat, for another chance to move, to survive, to keep going north—toward the cold, toward the only future that might still be possible.

—10—

Gary awoke with a start, his heart pounding in his chest, the darkness of the room pressing in on him like a physical weight. For a moment, he couldn't remember where he was, or why the air felt so heavy, so thick with dread. Then the memories returned— the frantic escape, the endless hours of walking, the desperate search for shelter. He blinked, trying to orient himself, and saw Simon curled up nearby, one arm draped protectively over Coal, who slept with his head nestled against the boy's chest. The others were scattered around the cramped basement, each lost in their own uneasy sleep, haunted by dreams of what waited above.

A faint glow seeped in from the narrow window near the ceiling, signaling the approach of dusk. Gary listened, straining to hear any sound from outside— any hint that the monsters had moved on, or that something worse was coming. The silence was absolute, broken only by the slow, rhythmic breathing of his family. He let out a shaky breath, trying to convince himself that they were safe, that the walls would hold, that the horrors of the day would not find them here.

But the fear never truly faded. It lingered in every shadow, every creak of the floorboards above, every distant echo that might be the first warning of another attack. He remembered the way the creatures had swarmed the hotel, their screeches rattling the windows, their claws scraping against the walls as they searched for a way in. He remembered the way Simon had clung to Coal, his small body trembling with terror, and the way Bill had tried to hide his own fear, offering comfort he barely believed himself.

Now, as the last light faded from the sky, Gary felt the tension ratchet tighter. They would have to move again soon—back out into the open, back onto the road, back into the nightmare that waited for them beyond the thin safety of these walls. He glanced at Bill, who was barely beginning to wake, his eyes hollow and red-rimmed.

"Is it morning already?" Bill groaned, sighing and wincing as he rolled over and extended his legs.

"Yeah," Gary replied. "Get Simon up; I need another two."

Bill lay there for another moment before Gary reached out and shoved him gently. "Go. I need two more minutes."

Bill grumbled, grunting with a snort as he pushed himself up. He let his eyes adjust to the dim light and then forced himself to his feet.

George was already gathering his belongings. "I'm gonna head up," he said, already sounding like he'd been awake for hours. "Take a look."

Dean grunted something that could have been construed as an *okay*.

A moment later, light filtered dimly in from the open stairwell as George made his way up.

Daylight had already faded to dusk, the blanket of indigo pushing the remaining coral hues beneath the horizon. The night air whispered across George's skin with a soft breath as he stepped out into the waning light. He drew in a deep breath through his nose, exhaling as his gaze scanned the distant horizon. A moment later he felt the familiar comfort of fur pressing against his leg. Without looking, he lowered his hand, his fingers drifting through the soft fur between Coal's ears and stroking them gently. "Hey, buddy," he said, his gaze drifting up to the large moon already hovering above. "Full moon," he said, still rubbing his companion's head. "Good night to travel. At least we'll have plenty of light."

Coal snorted, moving away and finding a sprouting of weeds sticking through the concrete in the parking lot a short distance away. He half squatted, half lifted his leg and offered a quick watering.

"That's not a bad idea," George said, and in turn made his way to the edge of the building to relieve himself.

A few moments later, Dean emerged from the hotel lobby. "Full moon," he said as he approached where George was standing. "That'll make it easier to see where we're going."

George smirked. "That's what I was thinking." He was about to ask about the family, when the door to the hotel opened and Gary stepped out, followed by a very sleepy-looking Simon. "How'd you sleep?" he asked as they approached.

"I could get used to sleeping in a bed again," Gary said, his gaze moving to the fading palette on the horizon.

The door to the hotel opened again and Dean stepped out, adjusting the straps on his pack and starting toward them.

"Well," George replied. "We manage to get to where we're going, I'm sure we'll each be able to have our own bed." He pondered the thought. "Me. I'm just looking forward to getting back into a circadian rhythm."

"What's a sycadian rhythm?" Simon asked.

"*Circadian*," George corrected politely. "It's our natural sleep cycle. You know. Going to sleep when it's dark and waking up when the sun comes up. How our bodies are meant to function."

"I miss the sun," Simon said, his voice tinged with sadness.

"Yeah," George sighed. "I know. Me too." He gestured toward Coal with a nod. "Even Coal here misses the sun." He smiled. "He used to run around and roll in the grass and chomp his sticks. He'd lay out in the sun and cook himself until I had to drag him back inside, panting and sweating." He looked at Coal. "You know. They used to say dogs can't sweat. Something about only being able to release sweat through their paws or some B.S. like that. I can't tell you the amount of times I'd put my fingers through his fur and they'd come back wet." He looked at Simon and made a face. "And stinky. Coal's got funk. Don't let that handsome face fool you."

Simon smiled, letting out a soft chuckle.

"Whelp," Dean said, looking between Bill and Gary. "Y'all ready to put in some miles?"

They both nodded, telling Simon to go get his bike.

For the next six hours, they made their way along the gridlocked freeway. Up and over the pass and into the Santa Clarita Valley. They stopped for an hour and rested, getting their strength back with some coffee and a light meal. Then they were back on the road. As they pressed on, the tension never truly faded. It clung to them like a second skin, a constant reminder that safety was an illusion, that hope was a fragile thing, easily shattered. And yet, as the sky brightened and the road stretched out before them, Gary felt a flicker of something else—a stubborn, defiant spark that refused to die. They were still alive. They were still together. And as long as they kept moving, there was still a chance. By the time the sun was beginning to whisper across the horizon, they were already coming up on Castaic Lake.

The area they stopped didn't have a lot of options for safe places to stay, so they opted for a side-of-the-road truck stop. The storage area was located in a small basement, and by the time the sun was just cresting the horizon, they were locking the door and making their way down.

Moments later, the faint sound of insectile screeching sounded out in the distance as flocks of alien creatures rose into the air, murmuring in shifting clouds before fanning out in search of their next meal.

"I found the underground right after it started," Dean said, looking across the small candle at Gary, who'd asked the question. "After losing my wife and son..." He drew a deep breath and exhaled with a sigh. "I'd lost a big portion of self-preservation. I wasn't suicidal or anything, running around in the daylight, but I wasn't exactly careful either. One of those careless days I'd decided to leave my place and just wander. See where the night took me. It took me downtown, and before I knew it, light was peeking up on the horizon. I knew I had to get somewhere safe or—well, you know. So, I figured the subway tunnels would be the best way to go. That's when I met Jim Bayless, and he introduced me to the Underground. I ended up sticking around, and it kind of became my home."

"Did you ever go back?" Gary asked.

"Where?" Dean asked in response. "My old house?" He shook his head, smirking. "No. I don't think I could have handled revisiting those old memories." He paused, remembering the photos on the walls, the pictures and smells. He remembered the last set of sheets he and his wife had put on the bed, and the way the sun danced under his son's door in the mornings, and how he could tell if he had gotten out of bed yet by the shadows cast. He remembered the strange, little things, like the smell of the linen closet and feel of the hardwood underfoot and the places it squeaked when stepped on. "No. Maybe one day. But not anytime soon." He lingered in that moment, oddly comforted by the thought a moment longer.

"What about y'all?" George asked. "How'd you end up underground?"

Gary looked across at Bill. "We were visiting Bill's sister, in Pasadena. She'd wanted to take us shopping, so, we ended up downtown in the jewelry district. That's where we were when the things first arrived."

"Visiting?" Dean asked. "Where from?"

"Flagstaff," Bill replied.

"Arizona," George said. "I've been there a few times. Used to have friends that lived in Fredonia."

"Fredonia," Bill smiled. "That's a few hours north. Small town. Gary used to work with a woman that lived there." He looked at Gary. "What was here name? The little old lady that shot off half her thumb with that shotgun?"

Gary pondered it for a moment. "Juanita."

"Shot off half her thumb?" George interjected. "With a shotgun?"

"Yeah," Gary said. "She was in one of those old west gunfighting groups. The ones that would put on shows and act out old west gunfights."

"Oh, man," George said. "I used to love those as a kid."

Gary smiled. "So did she. But it turns out, even with blanks, if you put your thumb over the end of a shotgun barrel and thump it cocked against the ground, it can still go off. And it'll take your thumb with it."

Bill smiled. "You remember. Everybody was running around looking for the top half of her thumb so she could try and get it sewed back on?"

"Yeah," Gary replied. "All the kids were running around like it was an Easter egg hunt."

"Man," Bill smiled, turning to Dean. "What about you? Where were you from?"

"Whoo," Dean replied. "Feels like a lifetime ago." He paused, thinking about it, letting the time catch up. Then he sighed heavily. "I was living in Long Beach." He smirked, pausing. "Lived in a little town called Escalante, in Southern Utah for a few years in my early teens though."

"Utah?" Bill asked.

"Yeah. My dad got a contract there. Since he was the worker and my mom was a stay at home, we packed up and moved. Six years were in that tiny little town."

"How was that?"

"I had long hair, wore baggy pants and had both ears pierced. Take a guess."

George scoffed.

"Let's just say, I didn't make a lot of friends quickly. Not to mention, my mom's first generation Guatemalan."

"Mmmm," Gary replied, completely understanding.

"De donde?"

Dean looked over at George, shooting him a puzzled glance. "Antigua."

George smiled. "Mis padres son de Huehue."

"No shit," Dean replied with a smile.

"So, you speak Spanish then?" George asked.

"Mas o menos," Dean replied with a grin. "Suficiente para meterme en problemas."

George grinned. "Any amount of Spanish can get you into trouble. That's what's beautiful about the language."

"Well," Dean said, looking at George. "Since we're on the topic. What about you?" He pondered the thought a moment. "I just realized, in all the time we've spent together, I've never thought to ask."

"Long Island, New York," George replied.

"Long Island," Dean replied. "You don't sound like a New Yorker."

"Not every New Yorker sounds like Tony Soprano," George replied. "That's a stereotype."

Dean smirked. "Well. How did you end up in L.A.?"

"I went online about a year ago and bought a ticket for one of these things they used to have, call aeroplanes. Believe it or not, you actually get inside one and it can fly you across the sky to wherever in the world you want to go." George smiled, offering a quick wink. Then he let out a small laugh, amused by his own wit. "Same as these two," he added, gesturing toward Bill and Gary with a nod. "I was visiting family. My tíos live in Lawndale. I had come out for a week to help them do a kitchen remodel. Everything went to hell a few days after I arrived, and like the rest of you, I ended up in the Underground."

The others stayed quiet for a moment, a distant screech drawing their attention toward the basement door.

"Where were you when you first saw them?" Gary asked, looking at George.

He shook his head. "Getting hardware supplies from a wholesaler in downtown." He sat with the memory a moment, allowing it to play out in his mind's eye. The screaming, the chaos, the panic.

"Where do you think they came from?" Bill asked.

Dean and George both shook their heads.

"I remember NASA had said something about an asteroid coming within close proximity of earth right before they appeared. Maybe that. Maybe they hitched a ride, and when they got close enough to Earth, they," he skipped his hands together, making a soft clap. "Skipped off and flew the rest of the way here."

"It doesn't matter," Dean said. "They're here now, and in less than a week, they nearly wiped all of us out."

"Have you seen one?" Gary asked. "Up close?"

Dean and George exchanged a glance.

"Yeah," Dean replied. "Actually. Right before we left. That's how we figured out that the cold can kill them. We'd been setting up traps in Western district," he continued. "One of them was a freezer truck. A buddy of mine and I had baited it, and when one of them took it, it got itself locked inside. By the time we got there, it was dead. Frozen stiff. Medical examiner said the cause was exposure, and that was when we realized it might be a good thing to make our way north, where it's colder."

"So, wait," Bill said. "You two were the reason for that whole townhall gary'g?"

George shook his head. "'Not me" he replied. "That was all him," he added, glancing at Dean.

"Are they as scary as they sound?" Simon asked from a short distance away, where he was seated with Coal beside him, enjoying a healthy dose of pets. Simon had heard of the monsters, but had never seen one. In the chaos of them making their way into the Underground, he had been too busy running to look around.

George looked at Bill and Gary, who nodded acceptingly.

"They are," George replied. "Do you know what a wheel bug looks like?"

Simon shook his head.

"Well. It's a smaller insect, with six legs and a large abdomen. There's a small, spiked ridge along it's middle section and it has wings that fold out from along its body. These creatures look something similar to that. But these have what's called a *proboscis*. It's like a long, straw that sticks out from its mouth. But like, this big." He held his hands out as wide as he could. "And it's this big around." He brought his thumb and forefinger together in a circle. "And that's what it uses to eat."

"Gross," Simon replied, his face scrunching in disgust.

"Yeah," George added. "Do you want to know how it feeds?"

"I think he's okay not knowing the finer details," Gary said, interjecting before George could share.

What George didn't say, was that the creatures fed by piercing their victims with the venom tipped proboscis. The venom at its tip would act as a paralytic, allowing it to inject them with a powerful toxin. That toxin would rapidly liquefy their insides, allowing the creatures to return and drink them to a husk. Those who weren't chosen for food, were turned into hosts, where the insects would inject them with larvae from the same tube. Those larvae would gestate inside them while, all the while leaving them paralyzed while consuming them from within. Once the larvae were done gestating, they would bite and claw their way through muscle, flesh and skin, to the surface, allowing the host to finally die once the transformation was complete. Then they would rise up into the sky and start the entire cycle all over again. It was these finer details that Gary felt his boy could live another few years without knowing. It was these finer details he wished he had gone another few years without knowing. What was even worse was that the creatures didn't limit their diet to humans alone. Horses, cattle, deer, dogs, cats. Anything large enough to survive the piercing stab of the creature's proboscis was on the menu. Most life on the planet had been eradicated within the first few weeks. Those that still lived, had quickly learned to adapt.

"What are we going to do once we get to Alaska," Gary asked, quickly changing the subject. "How are we going to survive?"

"Like I said in the townhall, Eskimos have been doing it for thousands of years. We'll just have to adapt. That's how. We learn to hunt, build shelters, live off the land. We can use greenhouses for gardening and get a solar grid up and running." He paused, having thought it out repeatedly in the past days. "That should keep us going most of the year."

"It's summer that I'm worried about," Bill said. "Twenty hours of daylight for three months... And it isn't exactly freezing during that either. It can get up into the seventies."

"That's true," George added. "But if those things can't make the trip, or survive the night, we won't have to worry about it. Remember. They're cold blooded and need shelter just as bad as us. Why do you think they burrow. The underground temperature stays pretty well regulated. That's why their nests are underground. And even in the summer, Alaska is still covered in permafrost." He paused, brow furrowing at his next thought. "And as shitty as it is to say. I think it's safe to say that the bugs took care of our climate problem. I think they were pretty effective in lowering carbon emissions."

"I guess that's one way to look at it," Dean said, his brow furrowing as well at the thought.

"That's what always scared me about the underground," Gary added. "What was stopping those things from burrowing into the tunnels?"

George looked at Gary. "They can burrow through dirt with those claws, but not concrete."

Bill yawned, reaching up and rubbing his face. "As lighthearted and engaging as this conversation is, I think I'm gonna turn in."

"Probably a good idea," George added. It was getting lighter outside and they all needed to allow their bodies as much rest as they could get. Especially their feet.

"My feet are hurting a lot more than I thought they would," Gary said as if on cue.

"If we pass a shoe store, or an outlet along the way, we could stop and swap out," George added, nodding toward his walking shoes. "Might want to get something a little more durable too, like a good pair of hiking shoes."

"There's an outlet further up the 5," Dean said. "It's along the route. And we should have transportation by then. The freeway's already starting to thin out a bit."

"Good," Bill said. "My feet aren't doing much better. I'm looking forward to sitting down for the rest of the journey."

"Don't get too comfortable with that thought," George replied. "Probably going to get pretty congested in the bigger cities. We're gonna likely finding ourselves having to make our way through on foot and switch out vehicles on the opposite sides."

Gary looked over to where Simon was not laying, his chest moving up and down rhythmically. He'd fallen asleep, and Coal was lying right there, next to him. Eyes trying desperately not to close, but falling repeatedly shut. "Yeah," he said, pulling his gaze away. "I'm going to sleep."

The group turned in, each sprawling out and falling asleep no sooner than the light went out.

A short time into the day, the group was awoken by a loud screeching sound, followed by a series of distant gunshots. They all sat there, awake, listening. Then, the world outside fell silent and they eventually fell back asleep.

"Alright. Time to get a move on."

Gary opened his eyes to see George, Bill and Dean standing a short distance away. Even Simon was on his feet. "Ugh," he grunted, shoving the blanket atop him down forcefully. "I just fell asleep."

"Well," George said. "Then you'll be happy to know that I've procured us a ride, and once we get topside, you can go back to sleep. But we should probably get a move on. We're burning moonlight."

He stared at him for a moment. "You think the freeway's clear enough?"

"Should be," he replied. "It was already lightening up as we arrived here. And I chose a good, all-wheel drive SUV. We'll be able to maneuver around most things we come across. And if we can't, we'll figure that out then." He paused, looking down at him as the others started their way up. "Now. Up and at 'em."

Gary dragged himself to his feet, rolling the blanket up with numb fingers and following after a moment later. When he emerged at the top of the stairs, the sun had already dropped below the horizon, leaving the world outside bathed in a cold, uncertain twilight. A sprawling blanket of stars hovered overhead, thin traces of lacy clouds sitting stagnant between. He could feel a light chill dancing on the soft breeze, a reminder that the world was not as it once was. There were days back in Flagstaff that had felt just like this, and for a flicker of a breath, he felt a ping of homesickness tug at his heart.

Sitting a short distance away, engine idling, was a large, dark blue SUV. The headlights illuminated a tractor trailer parked directly across from it at the opposite end of the parking lot. He looked at the fast food spread painted across the side and his stomach grumbled.

"Here," Bill said, walking up beside him.

He looked down to see his husband holding out a nature bar.

"Figured you'd be hungry. They had a few boxes of these next door."

"Thanks, Babe," he said, reaching out and taking it.

He leaned in, giving him a kiss and then turned, making his way to the vehicle, backpack held in one hand. "You ready?" he asked, looking to where Simon was standing with Coal.

"Yeah," Simon replied, starting toward the SUV.

Dean made his way over to where Gary was standing, leaning in as he passed. "Let's get off our feet."

"Thank God," Gary said, slinging his pack over one shoulder and starting forward.

One by one they climbed in, securing their seatbelts in place and settling in for the ride. It was a few minutes later that they were making their way down the freeway, wind blowing in through the open windows, tossing their hair as it did. The world outside was a blur of shadows and ruined shapes, the silence broken only by the hum of the engine and the distant, ever-present threat of what might be waiting in the dark.

Gary looked out the window, watching as moonlight illuminated the rolling hills going past. There was a stillness to it all, a quiet abandon that the world now whispered. Many of the cities' automated grids were still powered, the valley glow not allowing the full effect of the stars above to emerge, and he found himself pondering what that would look like once the last of the power grids went down. He imagined it would look like the Instagram pictures he'd seen in his feed prior to everything, the ones where photographers would play with light setting and exposure to show clear images of the Milky Way galaxy and the billions of stars that surrounded it. It was that same thought that scared him, because once the power grids went down, they would truly be back to the stone age. Except for the people still alive, now, didn't have the wherewithal or knowledge possessed by their ancient ancestors to allow them to comfortably survive in the desolate, creature-filled wastes that for the last year had been slowly edging in around them. Once the power went down, and the gas stopped flowing. Once they had to go back to creating fire by hand and learning to filter water. Once they were truly dependent upon hunting and growing their own food, because everything on every shelf was well beyond its expiration. That was what terrified him the most. It wasn't surviving the creatures. That, they had done easily enough. It was what waited for them further in time that brought his true fear. It was the future that awaited his son that he could never truly get from festering in the back of his mind. That single thread of thought scared him the most.

The group made their way up and over the grapevine. As they were beginning their descent, traffic once again began to fill the lanes. They were able to circumvent the first few miles, but near the base they saw where a tractor trailer that appeared to have jackknifed and sat overturned, trailer spreading from one edge of the freeway to the other. A pile of cars sat impacted against it.

George slowed the SUV to a stop. "Well, shit," he grumbled. "That was short lived..."

"What is it?" Bill asked, leaning between the front seats to get a better look.

"Pile up," George replied. "There's no getting around it." He sighed heavily. "Looks like we're back on foot." He paused. "Unless there's another vehicle on the other side, which I highly doubt." He glanced back at Bill through the rearview mirror. "I'm guessing we're hoofing it to the next town." He lifted his hand, checking his watch. "We got time, so..."

"Ohhh, God," Gary grumbled, his feet already beginning to throb at the suggestion.

"Sitting here groaning ain't gonna move that semi," George replied, his gaze shifting to his. "Let's just get this over with." He reached out, opening the driver's door and stepped out.

Getting past the overturned truck was easy enough. And it was just as George had guessed. The freeway was clear all the way to the small town they could see a handful of miles in the distance. "On the bright side," he said as they started down the vacant asphalt. "We can at least see the town we're headed to. It could be worse. We could have ended up stranded in the middle of nowhere."

"Always a silver lining," Gary grumbled.

George smiled, glancing back at him. "Think of it as an adventure."

Gary scrunched his face. *"Think of it as an adventure,"* he repeated in a mocking tone.

George chuckled, taking a tiny bit of pleasure from the exchange. But as they pressed on, the tension never truly faded. Every step away from the underground felt like a gamble, the city above a vast, unpredictable hellscape. But beneath the fear, hope flickered—a stubborn, defiant thing. They had a plan. They had each other. And for the first time in months, the monsters weren't the only ones adapting.

=12=

A little over two hours later, the group made it to the small city of Gorman, spending the better part of another hour going car to car, trying to find a set of keys. The search was frantic, every minute spent in the open a risk, every shadow between the abandoned vehicles a possible hiding place for something hungry. The air was cold and thin, the silence broken only by the distant echo of wind and the nervous shuffling of feet. Eventually, after what was beginning to feel like far too long looking through vehicles for keys, they decided to continue on to the next town a short distance away. The roadside sign had indicated that Wheeler Ridge was only a few miles further down the road. They decided they may as well keep moving, since they'd had no luck procuring another vehicle.

By the time they reached the small town, it was already nearly five o'clock in the morning. The walk down the bottom of the grapevine and time spent trying to find a working vehicle had cost them hours. Now, with dawn kissing the horizon behind them, they decided it was best to simply find shelter and begin their search for a vehicle the next evening. The tension was palpable—every step felt like a countdown, every glance over the shoulder a silent prayer that nothing was following.

"There's a truck stop a little further," Dean said, nodding down the freeway.

"I don't want to risk getting there and we're stuck wide open or spending the night trying not to freeze in a walk-in," Bill said.

"What about that?" Simon asked, pointing to a large distribution warehouse a short distance away.

"That's not a bad idea," George said. "It's big, flat. Heavy roll down doors." He looked at Simon. "Good eyes."

"Alright," Dean added, starting forward with a glance at the growing light behind them. "We should probably get a move on. We're already pushing it."

By the time they reached the warehouse parking lot, the group was nearly at a jog. The sun had begun to rise behind the mountains, though its light was still hidden from view. Every footfall felt like a countdown, the growing brightness at their backs urging them forward. Their breaths came in ragged bursts, boots slapping against the asphalt as they scanned for any sign of movement.

"We gotta get a move on," George shouted, moving nearly to a slow run.

Behind them, a sound brought a chill to their blood—a sharp, inhuman screech echoing across the fields. The first of the creatures had awoken, and a small flock was already rising from a distant burrow, swirling together in a dark, fetid cloud. The mass of leathery wings twisted in the air, then turned, arrowing straight toward the warehouse.

George was the first to reach the pull-down gates. He skidded to a stop, dropping down and grasping the handle. He yanked, but it didn't budge. "Shit!" he barked, rushing to the next. The same. "They're locked!" he said, looking back to the others, and the swirling cloud of creatures just a few short miles away.

"Try one of the trucks," Dean suggested, turning and running to one of the parked tractor trailers a short distance away. A few moments later, he spun around the end of one of the trailers, skidding to a stop. He reached out and saw a lock attached to the latch. He cursed under his breath, moving to the next. When he stepped up to the next trailer, he saw there was no lock hanging from the latch. It was likely empty, so they hadn't bothered. He reached out, unlatching the handle and lifted.

The sliding door opened with a protest, screeching as the metal lifted up the tracks. "In here," he shouted, directing the others to the trailer.

In the distance, the sound must have caught the ears of the first murmuring mass, because the screeching sounds rose to a frenzy, and the shifting cloud turned, starting in their direction.

"Hurry your asses!" Dean barked, waving the others forward.

George was the first to climb up, tossing his pack inside and rolling his body over the lip. Bill helped Gary and Simon scramble in, then Dean hefted Coal up and dove in himself, slamming the door shut behind them. The five of them pressed to the back of the trailer, Coal right beside Simon, all of them straining to hear the chaos outside.

They stood there in the pitch dark, time rotting past as they listened silently to the sound of the creatures drawing closer. They could hear the flapping of wings as the creatures approached and the chorus of staccato clicks sounding out.

Early on, people had realized that the creatures not only hunted by sight and sound, but by smell. Much in the way a mosquito can find its meal from dozens of feet, and sharks from miles, these insect-like creatures could detect the slightest odor of sweat and blood. And right then, at that moment, the five sweat-drenched survivors had all but left a bread crumb trail right to where they were hiding.

It was only moments later before they heard the first heavy *thud* as one of the insects landed atop the trailer. Less than a breath later, it was followed by another, and then another. The creatures skittered about overhead, their feet landing in a flurry of movement as they studied the container below them, searching and prodding for a way in. Loud, shrill screeching sounded out as the frustrated monsters outside prodded and stabbed at the container with their long cartilage proboscis'.

For nearly an hour, the assault continued. The group huddled at the rear, hearts pounding, every muscle tensed for the moment the monsters might break through. More than once, the latch outside jiggled, and each time, their breath caught, certain this was the end. But after a time—perhaps from frustration, or the lack of an easy entrance—the sounds faded. The creatures moved on, their screeches receding as they searched elsewhere for prey and hosts for their young.

Dean had lost track of time, completely unsure of how long they had been there, standing in silence, weapon cradled in hand. He pulled his thin jacket off, setting it quietly beside him. The inside of the trailer was already beginning to warm up, and the sun hadn't even crested fully overhead yet. He, like the others, knew they were in for a long, very hot day, and by the end of that afternoon, they had stripped down to just their pants, save for Gary who wore a sweat-drenched t-shirt.

"I have to pee," Simon whispered in the dark.

Only the sound of breathing answered back.

"Dad," he began again.

"Okay," Bill said in a whisper. "Go to the front," he said. "Try to get it in the crack so that it doesn't come back this way, okay."

He couldn't see it, because other than a tiny sliver of light where the trailer rolldown sat latched, the interior was pitch black. Neither of them had dared to turn on any lights. A candle would have only served to heat up the interior even faster, and the smoke it would have put off could have served to attract even more of the creatures. So, they had simply resigned to sitting in the dark for the prior six hours, sweating and waiting.

Simon felt his way along the trailer wall toward the sliver of light. When he reached the end, he unclasped his belt and unbuttoned his pants. He lowered the zipper and pushed them down, pushing the front of his underwear down at the same time. He stood there for a moment, hearing the soft breathing behind and trying not to focus on it. He had always had trouble peeing in front of other people. He didn't even like using public bathrooms. It gave him anxiety. And forget about pooping. Unless it was an emergency, he was the type of person that would hold it until he got home. He was grateful that wasn't the current case. But now, standing there in the dark, his gaze locked on the tiny sliver of light showing the crack in the door, he focused on willing his bladder to release.

Bill swallowed, wiping the line of sweat from his brow. "I'm cooking," he grumbled.

"It's not even noon yet," Dean replied.

"Yeah. Thanks for reminding me…"

"It's gonna be a long afternoon."

At the other end of the trailer, they heard the first trickle of urine as Simon was finally able to let his flow begin.

"But," George added in a whisper, just above the sound of the stream. "We're alive."

"Until we cook to death in here," Gary said.

"Oh, it ain't that bad," George rebutted. "I've holed up in worse. Spent an entire day in a meat locker once. Almost suffocated that time."

The sound of Simon peeing stopped, and they could see by the thin shadow that he had turned and was edging his way back along the wall.

"Think we're gonna find another car?" Gary asked as Simon approached and sat back down.

"Of course," Dean replied. "We just ran out of time. There's gotta be something out there. And this time we have all the time we need to look."

"Should we have gone with the others?" Gary asked after a few moments of silence.

"We already went over this," Bill answered. "North Dakota is only cold in the winter. What are they going to do with the other nine months out of the year?"

"I don't know," he replied. "Just. Strength in numbers and all that. I mean. I just keep thinking. What kind of life are we going to have? What kind of life is Simon going to have?"

"No worse than he was going to have growing up in the underground," Bill replied.

"But at least there were other kids his age," Gary added.

"And I'm sure there will be other kids in Anchorage as well. If it's like George and Dean say, and those things can't survive the cold. Then, Alaska may not have even been affected in the first place. They may have been going on like nothing ever happened this entire time."

"We would have heard something, on the radio," he responded flatly.

"How?" he asked. "Communications went down the first week. Internet, phones. All that was dead when people were still trying to escape."

"We didn't hear anything," George said, interjecting himself into their conversation. "Because we only had short range communications. But there were folks in San Diego and parts of Mexico still surviving, just like we were. So, we have to assume that folks up north are still surviving too."

"Dad?"

"Yeah, Bud," Bill replied.

"Can I play my game?"

"Sure," Bill said. "But no volume."

"K."

A moment later, a soft glow illuminated Simon's face, spreading out to give a soft light to the trailer.

"How much battery you got left on that?" Bill asked, watching as Simon stared at the screen.

"Forty percent," Simon replied.

Bill nodded. "I suppose we're going to have to figure out a solar charging situation for you sometime soon."

"It's fine," Simon replied. "I have my charger."

"Yeah," he replied. "But that's not going to work when the power goes out."

Simon looked up at him for a moment. "When is that going to happen?"

"There's no way to know." He replied, not enjoying the thought. "Hopefully not for a while."

"As long as the gas stays on and I can keep taking warm showers," Gary replied. "That's the thought I'm lamenting. When there is no more hot water…" He let the thought linger for a moment before shoving it back. It was one more thing that had kept him company since the beginning, constantly nipping at his mind's heel. Once the gas went out and the heaters stopped working…

A distant screech pulled him from the thought and he reached out, placing his hand over the lighted screen in his son's hand.

They sat there for the next few minutes, listening.

"I think maybe you should turn that off," He suggested a moment later. "Try to get some sleep."

"But it's hot…," Simon complained.

"I know, but you need to try. We all do."

"Think of it this way," George offered. "If you're asleep, you won't feel the heat. And when you open your eyes, it'll be night again and we can get out of this stupid trailer."

Eventually, the light from the console faded, plunging them back into darkness.

The sun had dropped below the horizon, taking all the horrors of the day with it. The creatures had returned to their nests, or burrows, or whatever hellish hole they slank to during the night. A light drizzle fell from the blanket of quickly darkening gray above and a sheen of moisture glistened across the vacant, dull gray parking lot.

A low, metallic groan sounded out, sending a nearby murder of crows into the air, their wings flapping loudly as they rose. A series of angry caws accompanied their startled escape.

George stepped out, his revolver moving from one direction to the next. The parking lot was vacant, the surrounding valley as well. At least the view standing in the trailer afforded looked that way.

The ground squished as George's weight dropped from the truck, his boots impacting against the wet cement. "Looks like we're clear," he said, still scanning the sky around them. "Yeah. We're clear."

A moment later the sound of boots landing sounded behind him and Dean stepped up, his rifle cradled across his chest. "Wasn't expecting this," he remarked, referencing the light drizzle falling around them.

George glanced at him. "They get the forecast wrong?"

Dean smiled, shaking his head.

"Dad," came Simon's voice from behind them. "It's raining."

"Raining?" Gary said as she stuck his head out from inside the truck. "You better put on your jacket."

Simon unslung his backpack and fished out a light hiking jacket from within. He put it on and returned his pack back in place.

"There was that travel center a little ways up the road," George said, pulling his gaze from the blanket of gray above. "We should probably check there first."

"And what if we end up in the same situation?" Bill asked. "A bunch of cars and no keys?"

George shrugged. "I suppose I could try and hotwire one."

Bill looked at him, his brow furrowing at the thought that they had spent almost an hour the prior evening rummaging through vehicles only to end up walking miles because they hadn't found a set of keys. "This whole time you could have just hotwired a car and saved us all the walking?"

George looked at him. "Never said I knew how. I said I could try." He reiterated, shrugging as he did so. "Can't be too hard. People used to do it all the time. Looks easy enough in the movies, right?"

Dean chuckled, patting him on the shoulder as he walked past, starting back toward the freeway. "Come on, old man."

The group started off, crossing the massive parking lot and making their way back out onto the freeway. A little over an hour later they were making their way off and into the small community of Wheeler Ridge. Though, using the term *community* was being generous. It was more of a roadside stop, with a handful of fast-food restaurants, a big-rig travel center and a couple cheap motels and gas and gulp stations. The biggest attraction that brought people there was the large outlet mall. The rest of the community seemed to be built around it.

"I used to stop here at least twice a year," Dean said as they were making their way down the small road leading to the outlet. "Anna, my wife. Her boss had a cabin up at Lake Isabella. They used to let us borrow it twice a year." He smiled at the memory. "Every time we'd go up, we had to stop here." He scoffed, sadness working its way in. "This was one of the rituals."

They walked the next few yards in silence.

"Mugs," George said a few minutes later.

"Come again?" Dean asked, glancing over at him.

"Mugs," George repeated, as if saying it again offered all the explanation needed. "Coffee mugs."

Dean looked at him, eyebrows raised questioningly.

George drew in a lungful of moist air and exhaled with a heavy sigh. "My ex-wife, Carmela. She collected coffee mugs. That was her thing, her ritual." He took the next few steps in silent remembrance. "She used to drag us out on these long, aimless road trips. Thirty, forty hours of driving. And every little roadside dive we stopped at, she'd have to get one of their mugs as a souvenir." He scoffed. "By the time we split, she must have had at least a hundred of the damned things. She had so many coffee mugs that three-quarters of them were packed up in boxes in the attic. I used to tell her, you got six dozen of those things boxed up in the attic. Why the hell are you buying another? *Because it's my thing,*" he finished in a mocking, heavily accented tone. "Never understood it."

"Do you miss her?"

George thought about it for a moment, putting genuine thought behind his answer. "No. She was crazy."

Dean shook his head, a smile creeping across his lips.

"But," George continued. "I would never have wished this on her. I hope." A soft gust of breath escaped. "I hope she is alive somewhere. Making someone else's life miserable."

This brought a laugh out of Dean, who shook his head, smiling.

"That bad, huh?"

George looked at him. "She was a demon."

"Oh, shit," Dean said, his gaze working to the outlet a few blocks away.

Behind them, Simon and Coal were making their way along the edge of the road. Coal was sniffing and Simon was whacking at the tall grass with a stick he had picked up a short distance back. Behind them, Bill and Gary were engaged in their own private conversation, one that unbeknownst to the others, had been revolving back around every few months over the past twelve.

"I just don't see the point," Bill said, looking up to where Simon was hitting the tops off a cluster of sunflowers. "There's a lot more important things he should be learning other than math and science. Eventually you're going to have to face the reality that things aren't going to go back to the way they were. This is how it is now."

"You think I don't know that?" Gary barked quietly. "You think I haven't come to terms with that? I know this is the way things are. I'm not an idiot, Bill. But just because the world stopped being like it was, doesn't mean our son needs to grow up ignorant. You want him to stop studying and focus on things like survival and hunting. And yeah, I think those things are important. A lot more now than before, obviously. But that doesn't mean we need to stop teaching him the basics. He still needs to learn mathematics, science." He glared at him. "Look me in the eye and tell me that biology won't help him." He walked the next few paces, waiting for his husband's response. "You used to tell me that a good education was more important than anything else in the world. When did that change?"

Bill snapped his gaze to him. "When the fucking world ended, Gary."

Gary stopped, his eyebrows lifting.

Bill slowed to a stop, exhaling in a gust. Slowly his eyes closed and then opened. "I'm sorry." He swallowed. "That was. Out of line."

"You fucking think?" Gary snapped, folding his arms across his chest.

Bill stepped forward, reaching out to place his hands on his shoulders.

Gary twisted, avoiding his grasp and stepping back. "No. I don't need your touch."

"I'm sorry."

He stared at him, anger churning in his chest. "That was an *asshole* thing to say."

"I know—"

"No," he interrupted. "I'm not done." He stared at him. "That was an asshole thing to say, and I don't deserve to be spoken to like that. Especially when all I'm trying to do is look out for what's best for *our* son's future. Now, you can teach him all the survival stuff he needs to know. But he *is* going to continue to study, and we *are* going to continue to offer him the basic fundamentals of an education. And I don't want to hear any of this, *things aren't like they were before,* bullshit." He stared his husband down. "And this is the last time we have this discussion."

Bill stared at him, the low churning of embarrassment working in his gut. Slowly he nodded.

"Good," he said, unfolding his arms and walking past him.

Bill pulled in a deep breath and held it for a moment, before releasing it through puffed cheeks.

"Goddamnit," he breathed, bringing his hands up and wiping them down his face. Then he turned and followed after, allowing the dozen feet of space to stay between them.

It was only a few minutes later that the group were making their way through the massive parking lot surrounding the outlet mall. There were a handful of scattered vehicles left parked throughout. George and Dean had settled on a smaller, hybrid SUV, having a conversation about gas milage and comfort.

Dean had stayed a short distance back, watching as they used a hunting knife to break open the steering column, and after a handful of tries, finally managed to get the engine to turn over. During this process of trial and error, George had explained that a few years back, someone had broken the steering column on his Four Runner, and for the three months following, while the insurance company tried weaseling their way out of paying for the repair, he'd had to use the exposed wires to start it. In telling the story, he found another thing he didn't lament being lost to the world prior; insurance companies.

Once they got the vehicle running, they made their way into the outlet. They spent the better part of three hours changing and stockpiling weather appropriate clothing and gear for up north, and when they were successfully outfitted, they had made their way back out to the vehicle. A short time later they were back on the freeway, the wind blowing through their hair.

"I really thought it was going to start coming down hard," Dean said, looking over to where Bill sat, driving.

Bill had offered to take the first shift. Things had been awkward after his and Gary's argument, and he didn't want to sit quietly in the back with the fog that all arguments like that left between couples, the kind that hung thick and persistent. It hadn't been their first argument over how to parent their son, far from it. It had been one of the better ones, however. Both Bill and Gary were strong in their parenting beliefs, and those differences had reared their heads on more than one occasion. Gary was more conservative and down to earth, believing in fostering a childhood filled with preparation for adulthood and how to navigate the trials and tribulations the world had to offer, especially a boy being raised in an untraditional household consisting of two fathers. Bill on the other hand believed in teaching him to face those adversities head on, not backing down and always being open and receptive to whatever life might throw at him. This was one of the things that had led to the argument they had earlier that afternoon. Gary wanted to keep teaching Simon the way they had been prior to the world being ripped apart, and Bill felt it was more pertinent for him to learn to adapt to how things were and would be. They were both right in that sense, and they both only wanted what was best for their son, but it was the method in which they guided him that could often be disparate. Bill had said once, during a small dinner party they had hosted, that nothing in the world could truly test a relationship between two people like raising a child. And that it had, and still was. Patience, humility, sacrifice and compromise. These were all things that had been tested and still were, even after the alien bug apocalypse.

George sat in the back with Gary; Simon tucked between them. The boy had his console in his hand and was playing some game, completely oblivious to the world around them. Coal was in the back, sitting up, looking out the back window.

"Yeah," George said from behind. "So did I." He glanced down at the game console in Simon's hand. "What are you playing?"

"A game," Simon replied, sounding as if he was on auto response.

"Well, I figured that much out on my own," George remarked. "I may be old, but I'm not *that* old. I meant, what game are you playing?"

"Mario," Simon replied flatly, offering no more information.

George smirked. "Okay."

"Don't take it personal," Gary offered. "You should be honored he even took the time to respond." He looked down at him. "Half the time he acts like he doesn't even hear you."

George looked past the boy at him, smiling. "Technology…"

In the distance, a thin line of blue rippled across the horizon, illuminating the sky in a glow that hung suspended for a moment as the haze of bluish white flickered away.

"Speaking of which," George said, reaching up and tapping Dean on the shoulder. "How about you give that radio a try."

Dean reached out, flipping the radio on. He scanned a full rotation on the FM band and then flipped it to AM. Another rotation later, they realized that all the stations were dark. He turned it off, letting silence fill the interior.

George nudged Simon in the side with his elbow. "How much charge you got on that thing?"

Simon took a moment to check. "Full."

"You mind if I borrow that cable for a bit?"

"Okay," Simon replied, pulling the cable from his console without taking his eyes off the screen.

George reached out, pulling it from the rear charging port and plugged it into his phone. "You mind plugging this in for me?" he asked, handing the other end to Dean, who took it and plugged it into the accessory port at the bottom of the center console. "You wanna flip that to auxiliary?" he asked.

Dean reached out, flipping the input setting on the radio, and a moment later, an older, Spanish guitar fell out of the speakers.

"Allow me to introduce you to Buena Vista Social Club," George said with a smile. "You can turn it up."

Dean reached out, turning the volume up, and for

the next hour and a half, the tropical Cuban music
filled the inside of the car.

Bill had driven just over thirty minutes before the freeway once again backed up. Coming into Bakersfield, another large accident had gridlocked the freeway. They had decided to make their own road, cutting through a swath of agricultural fields, and making their way across smaller roads in order to circumvent the city. A little over an hour later, they had made their way back onto the freeway. Another three after that and they were pulling to a stop just outside of Stockton.

"That's not good," Dean said as the SUVs lights illuminated a large pile of burned-out vehicles scattered from one end of the freeway to the other.

Bill slowed the vehicle to a stop, and they sat there, staring at the pileup.

"I supposed we could backtrack," Dean suggested. "Make our way around using the smaller highways."

George shook his head. "Give me a minute," he said, pulling up the map on his phone. He traced the highways, looking for a good alternate route. "If we cut back a ways, we can catch the 4 East. We can take that around and up to the 160. There are some other smaller roads we can take to circle around Sacramento." He paused. "But I'm gonna be honest. It looks like nothing but farmland out there, so if we get stuck, or stranded. We're gonna be hard-pressed to find a place to shelter down for the day." He pondered the thought for a moment. "It's a risk."

Dean leaned his head around, glancing back at George. "This whole trip is a risk. But I think we should probably avoid going through any major cities, so if your route avoids that, I think that's the one we should probably take." He glanced between Bill and Gary. "What do you guys think?"

Bill nodded, glancing in the rearview mirror at Gary, who looked back blankly at him. "Yeah," Bill said after a moment. "I think we should avoid major cities. Safer that way."

Gary nodded. "Yeah. I agree."

"Alright then," George said. "Let's flip around."

Bill turned the vehicle around and started back to the highway they had passed a short time before. As they made their way back, he couldn't help but feel the nervous pang of driving the wrong way down the freeway. He was about to say something when Dean spoke up.

"Doesn't feel right, does it. Driving the wrong way down the freeway."

Bill scoffed. "Yeah."

"You remember Ireland?" Gary said, finally shattering the frozen sheet of ice that had been hovering between them.

Bill chuckled. "Yes. I remember Ireland..."

A moment passed before George bit. "Go on. This was going somewhere."

Gary smiled at the memory. "Bill and I had just gotten married. Simon wasn't part of the picture yet and we decided to take a little European vacation before settling down. The whole trip we'd been in the main part of Europe and had taken taxis and public transportation to get around. But the last place on our list was Ireland. And to get around Ireland, you need to rent a car. So, we booked a car rental. The part we hadn't thought about, was that in the UK and Ireland, traffic is on the opposite side. When we landed in Dublin International and got our rental car, I told Bill he had to drive."

Bill huffed, clicking his tongue.

Gary smiled. "Right when you leave the airport, there's this big roundabout that connects you to three different highways." He chuckled. "We entered the roundabout, and Bill, just starts going around and around, in circles. After about the third time, I asked him. What are you doing?" He shook his head in amusement at the memory. Then, in his best impersonation of his husband, added. "*I'm just getting my bearings, okay?*" He shot Bill a playful glance. "We went around what had to be another three or four times before he finally exited and we started our way down the highway." He sighed in a huff. "For the next three hours he kept saying he felt like he was going to get into an accident because it felt like he was driving on the wrong side of the road."

"In my defense," Bill remarked. "Have any of you ever driven in Europe?"

Dean shook his head.

"Nope," George smirked. "Can't say that I have."

"It feels exactly like this," Bill said, glancing into the rearview and smiling.

Gary looked at him flatly, shaking his head. The gesture was all he needed to see to know that he had been forgiven for his prior idiocy, and that his husband was allowing the night to move past it.

"Let's just hope we don't come across any roundabouts along the way," Bill said, glancing back again. "I might have to take a few spins just for old times."

Gary smiled, a renewing sense of warmth moving through him as he looked into his husband's eyes.

They reached the smaller highway a few minutes later and cut right, following the two-lane road a good thirty miles before it curved and started north. Another hour later they were making their way around the outskirts of Sacramento. It was another hour before they were edging their way back onto the freeway.

Ten minutes later the SUV pulled to a stop and the engine fell into park.

"Whelp," George said from behind. "Looks like we've gotta backtrack..."

Bill and Dean stared out the front window at the power pole splayed across the freeway and the three vehicles that sat crushed beneath. On the opposite side of the freeway was another large pileup, likely caused when the electrical wires flipped over the center divider into oncoming traffic.

"Ain't nothing back there," Dean replied. "Just a few farmhouses and some old barns. Not sure we want to risk getting caught out in the open."

"Then what do you suggest?" George replied.

Dean leaned over, looking at the eighth of a tank left on the gas gauge. "I was banking on us being able to reach a gas station. I don't think we have enough to get us back to the one we passed an hour back." He paused. "Unfortunately, it looks like we're back on foot until we can get past all this."

"Well," George added. "At least we're not in the middle of nowhere. Shouldn't take us long to find another ride." He glanced at Gary. "You up for another hike?"

He looked at Simon, who was asleep, his video game console still held in his lap. "I can't wait till we're past all this."

George nodded, reaching out to open his door.

The night air was crisp, a cool breeze working past as he made his way to the back of the vehicle. He opened the rear hatch and Coal dropped down to the pavement. He reached in, fishing out his bag, and slung it over his shoulders. A moment later, Dean reached past, grabbing his backpack and rifle. He slung the pack over his shoulder, sticking his arm through the other strap and then slung the rifle strap over his shoulder. A sleepy Simon walked up a moment later, reaching in to grab his bag. A few moments later they were making their way past the wreckage, careful not to get too close to the downed wires.

The group continued, making their way down the wide-open freeway. After the large pileup, traffic had disappeared. The two-lane freeway was empty, and the silence that surrounded them only served to fuel the desolation. Above, a blanket of stars flickered through the hanging clouds.

The sky had cleared slightly, the rainy drizzle being left behind and making way for a patched, star-dotted cloudy sky. The waning moon hung silver above, its glow illuminating the dotted pavement stretching into darkness beyond.

The stretch of highway they were on was lined with farmhouses, spaced out with a few miles between them. Beyond them lay endless miles of agricultural fields. Silos stood tall, illuminated by the night sky, clouded shadows rolling past.

George pulled his gaze from the sky above, lifting his wrist and looking at the time on his watch. "It's getting late," he said, glancing to a large house about a mile in the distance. "We should probably start thinking about where we're going to stop for the night. We can figure out what we're going to do for transportation in the morning."

"I still find it funny that we refer to dusk as *morning*," Dean remarked.

"Old habits are hard to change," George replied.

"Do you think this is what our ancestors saw when they looked up?" Gary asked from behind.

"I think they saw a lot more than this," George said. "You have to think. There are still a lot of power grids up and running. Most of the streetlights and storefronts are still automated. There's still a good amount of light pollution keeping us from seeing what's really up there. San Francisco is only a few hours that way," he said, nodding to the east. "And most of Sacramento's still lit up. All of that adds up." He took a moment to admire the sky overhead. "What our ancestors saw was pure. Undisturbed." He smiled. "It must have been magical. It had to have been. Entire civilizations revolved around the sky and constellations. I come from the Mayans. Their entire society was based on astrology. The Aztecs, the Toltecs, Egypt and Greece. They were mapping the sky thousands of years ago. Tens of thousands. Some of the earliest megaliths ever found were aligned to the constellations." He walked in silence, admiring the twinkling stars above. "This is just a fraction of what they saw. Just give it a few years. Once the grids go down and the world is plunged back into darkness. It'll be beautiful..."

"Didn't realize you knew so much about history," Dean said with a smirk. "Were you a teacher before all this?"

George smiled, looking over at him. "Netflix."

Dean let out a loud laugh, the sound rolling off the edge of the highway. Even Gary joined in.

"That's hilarious," Gary said, shaking his head. He chuckled twice more, the sound fading. "Do you think they knew?" He asked a moment later. "That there was life out there?"

George pondered the thought for a moment. "I'd find it hard to believe otherwise," he said. "Have you ever been out in the ocean?"

He nodded. "I went on a cruise once. Does that count?"

George smiled. "In this context. When you were out there, did you get a chance to look up at night?"

He smiled, nodding. "I did."

"Do you remember it?"

He did. It was a vast, unimaginable amount of stars, like a sea of crushed diamonds. "I do."

"After seeing that, could you say without question, that we are the only life in the universe?"

Gary shook his head, looking up. "I didn't think so before, but I get what you're saying."

"Now. Did they think there would be giant alien insects that would eradicate all life on the planet? That I highly doubt. But. There's that famous Mayan carving of the man who appears to be seated in some type of spaceship, and one that looks like he's wearing an astronaut helmet. I think we'd have to look at those examples for a better answer to your question."

"It's different now," Gary replied. "Before, I'd look up at the stars and feel nothing but wonder and amazement. Now. I can't look up and not feel fear." He took the next few steps, letting the sound of feet pressing into pavement accompany his thoughts. "I used to love going camping. My parents would take my sisters and I every summer. I couldn't wait for the sun to go down. Marshmallows and campfire. But mostly, the stars. I would lay on my back and just stare up. Now, every time I look up, I can't help but wonder. How many of those bright, twinkling stars are full of terrifying creatures that would love nothing more than to come here and..." He let the sentence fall off, looking over to where Simon was quietly walking.

"Call me a kook," George said, taking the opportunity to lighten the tone. "But I don't think this is the first time we've been visited. I think it's a little difficult to pass off everything we've been shown and seen over the decades as hoaxes. Area Fifty-One, sure. Maybe. But the thousands of videos and documented evidence. Some of that even being video footage taken by military pilots." He shook his head. "I have to believe that at least some of it is true. Some of it. It would be statistically impossible for it not to be."

"So," Dean asked with a slight grin. "You're saying you believe in Bigfoot and the Loch Ness Monster?"

George regarded him with a lack of amusement. "There's no scientific evidence proving they're *not* real."

Dean chuckled, nodding in reluctant agreement. "Touché."

"Before this, three quarters of the world believed in God. A significant number more than that, in Allah. There was even less proof that they existed than aliens, but people fought and died for thousands of years over their belief in either of the two. Yet. You mention you believe in aliens, and everybody looks at you like that guy with the hair." He brought his fingers up, mimicking a wild mess on his head. "I think people were just desperate to find a way to validate their own existence. Accepting that we came from tiny organisms in the cosmic ocean of life just didn't have enough magic to it, I suppose." He took the next few steps with his gaze lifted to the stars. "I think we came from out there. Just like the bugs. I think maybe a spaceship, or some type of interstellar ship crash landed here millions of years ago, and we just happened to survive. Maybe we'd already destroyed whatever world it was that we were originally from, just like we were about to do to this one before the bugs showed up and hit the reset button. That's what I think. It wouldn't surprise me if we were the bugs, just on a different world." He scoffed, shaking his head. "We've done the same thing to our own. Native Americans, Mayans, the Jews. We're no different. Conquer and spread. The only difference is that we do it for greed." He paused. "Do you know how much of the world has Genghis Khan's DNA in them...?"

"I'd like to believe that there's a higher power," Gary replied after a moment. "Something that makes this all make sense. I'd like to think that once we... *pass*, that it's not just the end. I'd like to think that there's more."

"Well," George said, looking up at the stars again. "It may be a messed-up way of thinking about it, but I suppose the bugs could serve as ammunition for your hope. It's proof that there is other life out there. It all had to come from somewhere." He paused, pondering that thought. "So much for the Fermi Paradox..."

Gary scoffed, shaking his head. "Great. Thanks. With that thought, God could be some planet killing insect alien?"

George shrugged. "He did it once right? That's what the bible says."

"Did what once?"

"Destroyed the world."

Gary looked at him, his gaze narrowing. "I don't think the flood, and giant, flesh-eating insects are the same..."

He smirked with a shrug. "End results..."

He exhaled in a quick snort, shaking his head as he fell back to a silent cadence. But, for the next twenty minutes he found himself pondering the similarities in the analogy.

"We should probably check that house," George said a short time later, gesturing toward a large, two-story farmhouse that sat a half mile off the highway. He checked his watch once more. "It's getting to be about that time."

The others looked back at the eastern horizon. It was still dark, but it wouldn't be long before dawn was whispering behind the hills, and they all shared one sentiment. None of them wanted to spend another night in the back of a dark tractor trailer.

A short, single-lane asphalt strip led to the large farmhouse a quarter mile back. It stood tall and proud, all white with a columned foyer entrance at the front, and a large, curved driveway around a central rock formation.

As George passed, he looked at the piled boulders and the large hole that had been dug at the base. A collection of pipes and black vinyl tarp lay illuminated in the dim moonlight nearby. He hadn't realized he'd slowed down when Simon made his way past, climbing atop one of the large stones.

"Be careful," Bill called out, eyeing his son.

"Yeah," George added, watching as Coal was beginning to entertain the thought of trying to join the boy. "Might wanna come down. The last thing you want to do is slip and twist an ankle. Especially with all the walking we have to do."

Simon entertained the thought for a moment, eyeing the next stone up, and then took the advice, carefully jumping back to the ground and making his way toward the house after his dad.

"We might want to announce ourselves," George suggested as they made their way across the driveway. "Just in case." He took the moment to scan the multiple windows. "Rather not catch a bullet for trespassing."

"Good point," Bill said, glancing back at where Simon was.

"Hello?" Dean called out, eyeing each window carefully.

The house was dark, most of the curtains drawn closed. Moonlight bathed the house in a soft, bluish-white glow. A cloud had just begun to drift past, the shadow creeping slowly across the ground, edging toward the sprawling home.

"Anybody home?" Dean added, waiting a moment.

George came to a stop beside him. He too was searching the residence for any signs of presence.

"Look," Dean called. "We ain't bad people. We're just looking for a place to wait out the day. We're gonna approach now, nice and slow. There's no need to shoot. We'll gladly find somewhere else to spend the day."

George gave it another few moments before reaching out and nudging Dean with his elbow. "Let's check it out."

Dean smirked, unslinging his rifle and drawing it to his chest. "You take left? I go right?"

"Meet you 'round back," George agreed.

The two started forward.

"Hang back," George said, removing his pistol from its holster and glancing at Bill. "We'll go check it out."

Bill nodded, letting his gaze drift to the house.

The cloud overhead continued to drift slowly, the shadow now nearly encompassing the house. The field behind was completely dark, the obscured moonlight rendering whatever lay beyond nearly invisible.

As George made his way closer, he jutted his lower jaw out, popping his ears in order to better hear his surroundings. Old instincts smiled from his inner shadows as he approached. He moved heel to toe, rolling the sides of his feet first, the knife edge of his foot cutting silently across the pavement. As he drew closer, he pulled the pistol to his chest, reaching down and removing the flashlight from his belt. He brought it up in his left hand, moving it beneath his right and clicking it on. Then he brought both hands up, still close to his chest and continued forward.

There was a light creak as he made his way up the three steps to the front entrance. His gaze flickered between the two front windows, scanning the curtain drawn across the front door. It was large. It had to be nearly eight feet tall, a towering testament to the flaunted wealth expended in the home's construction.

He made his way past the window, flashlight pointed at the floor. He saw no sign of occupancy from within. The interior was dark, not so much as a shadow moving. Satisfied, he continued his way to the side of the home.

A few minutes later, George was edging his way around the side of the house. As he reached the back corner, he brought his lips together and gave a light whistle. A breath later it was answered by another from behind the house. He brought the end of the flashlight from against his jacket, releasing the light to the ground and made his way around. "Anything?" he asked as he started toward Dean.

Dean shook his head with a smirk. "Looks empty."

"Famous last words," George said, shining his light on the back door. "Should we give it a try?"

"Might as well," Dean replied, bringing his wrist up to look at his watch. "Doesn't look like we have much of a choice. Sun's going to be coming up in less than an hour. Sky's already getting light."

"Guess we better get to it then," George said, walking to the door and putting his hand on the knob. "Get my back," he said, waiting for Dean to bring his rifle to bear before twisting the knob. It moved about an eighth of an inch before stopping. He gave it another jiggle and then looked back at Dean. He shook his head.

"Well," Dean said, eying the windows. "I doubt the front's going to be unlocked."

"What do you suggest?"

George looked back at the door, eying it for a moment. Then he looked around the base of the small steps. Sitting near the bottom one was a small stone frog holding an American flag. He bent down, picking it up and glancing at Dean. "Hoo-rah," he said, turning and bringing his arm up to shield his eyes. Then he swung out, bringing the frog against the glass near the corner of the door's window.

The glass shattered, dropping broken pieces to the cement stairs.

George dropped the frog to the dirt and reached carefully in, feeling for the lock. A moment later there was a soft *click* and he twisted the knob, pulling the door open.

"Guess it's a good thing they didn't have an alarm set," Dean said.

"I'd thought about that," George replied. "Let's make sure it's clear."

George stepped in, calling out once more. The small mud room they were standing in led to the kitchen. Beyond that, they could see the large living room. An equally large dining room was off to the side.

They made their way through the house, Dean turning and making his way to check the left side, and George the right. Outside, the others watched their lights snaking through the interior.

"What are they doing?" Simon asked, watching as a flashlight beam illuminated a white curtain.

"They're just making sure it's safe," Bill replied.

"They have to make sure no bad people have already claimed the house," Gary added.

"Are there bad people?" Simon asked, a hint of worry in his tone.

"Of course," Bill replied. "But I don't think there are any here."

"Are there bad people where we are going? In the north?"

Bill exchanged a glance with Gary. "Well. Maybe," Bill replied, not wanting to lie, but also not wanting to scare his boy. "But from what your dad and I have seen, most people are like us, just trying to survive."

"I'm sure there are bad people out there," Gary added. "Somewhere. But most of those people were... Most of those people disappeared in the beginning."

"It's okay, Dad," Simon said. "You can say they died."

Gary glanced at Bill, a smile tugging at his cheeks. "Okay. Most of the bad people died in the beginning. The rest, like your dad said, are just trying to survive, like we are."

"Do you think there's more undergrounds? Like back home?"

Gary exchanged another silent glance. "I'm sure there are," he said. "Lots of big cities have subway stations and tunnels beneath them. I'm sure there's lots of people surviving just like we were, using the subways and tunnels to stay safe during the daytime."

"Why can the monsters only come out during the daytime?" Simon asked.

"Well," Bill said, glancing at the house as a flashlight moved through a second floor room. "Because the creatures are cold-blooded. Do you know what that means?"

Simon shook his head. Beside him, Coal whined, his tongue coming out in a pant as he eyed the house impatiently.

"It means they can't regulate their body temperature. So, if it gets really cold, they freeze."

"Don't we freeze when it gets cold?" Simon asked.

"Yes," Bill replied. "But it's different. See. Our bodies can regulate the temperature, which means we can get colder for longer periods before our bodies start to shut down."

The front door to the house opened, pulling their attention away from the conversation.

"We're clear," George called out. "You can come in."

"Well," Bill said, putting his hand on his son's shoulder. "You gonna sleep out here tonight?"

Simon looked at him, his face splitting in a large grin.

"Race you," Bill said, feigning as if starting to sprint.

That was all it took for Simon to charge away, shouting for Coal to follow, who immediately turned into a dash, sprinting past the boy and rushing full speed up the stairs and into the house.

"I think we should be good for the night," George said as Bill and Gary made their way in. "There's a basement, and Dean found a truck in the garage."

Bill's nose wrinkled as he sniffed the air.

"It'd be best if we stay off the second floor," George replied to the unasked question. "Be sure to keep Simon down here."

"How bad is it?" Gary asked.

"They took the quick way out," George replied.

George and Dean had made their way to the second floor when the smell had first wafted past. They'd followed it to the master bedroom, where they found who had presumably been the home's owners. A couple lay in bed, three empty bottles of wine and a bottle of pills lying empty beside it. Their dull, bloated corpses lay on the bed, melted together in eternal embrace. The open window had allowed for most of the smell to escape, and the following months had nearly removed all traces. But death has a way of leaving its mark, in the form of a pungent, sweetly sour smell that never truly dissipates.

"Oh," Gary replied.

"How's the basement?" Bill asked.

"Do you like wine?" George asked, a thin smile working across his lips.

Bill stared at him, a smile growing across his face.

"Well," George said, turning and making his way to the door leading to the basement stairs. "Come on."

He made his way to the stairs and opened the door. "Watch your step," George said, shining his light down the staircase. "Power's out. Dean's out back checking the breakers." He turned and started down the stairs. Behind him, a flashlight illuminated and he heard footsteps follow.

"Careful," Gary said as Simon started down, Coal just behind him.

They had just made their way to the bottom of the stairs when the lights came back on. Instantly the basement was illuminated in a soft glow.

"Oh, my God," Gary said as he stepped out to the bottom. "This basement's bigger than our entire house was."

"So," George said, holding his hand out. "Like I was saying about wine."

Bill made his way over to where he was standing and stopped. His mouth dropped open. "Holy shit."

From floor to ceiling, spanning one wall to the next, were hundreds of bottles of wine. They were separated into varietals, and those into vintage. Each one was marked with tabs, showing exactly what they were. Beyond that was a large, walk in cooler with racks on both sides and the back. An ornate sign hung over the glass entrance, reading *Whites, Rosés and Bubblies.*

Bill stood there, gobsmacked by the sheer volume of wine before them.

"I call the couch!" Simon shouted from behind, rushing over and leaping onto the large, curved couch. Coal climbed up, curling up and resting his chin on his paws, watching as Dean slowly started forward.

"Oh, great," Gary said, watching Bill make his way to the wall of reds. "Looks like we're going to be staying here for a few days."

"Holy shit," Bill repeated. He reached out, removing a bottle from the shelf and admiring it like a newborn child. "They have six bottles of Lafite Rothschild." He held it out for Gary to see. "Six."

"I take it that's a good one?" Dean asked as he entered the room from the bottom of the stairs.

"Good?" Bill remarked. "This is almost two thousand dollars a bottle," he said, looking down in awe. He turned, looking at the wall once more. "There has to be a quarter million dollars' worth of wine in this basement."

Gary looked between George and Dean. "Bill was a sommelier."

"*Am* a sommelier," Bill corrected, continuing to eye the wall. "Oh, my God. Romanee-Conti. Chateau Mouton Rothschild." He paused. "What...?" He reached out, pulling another bottle from the shelf. "They have freaking Screaming Eagle..." He turned, looking at Gary. "Yeah. We're going to have to stay here for a few days..."

Gary looked back at George. "Is there hot water?"

"I don't see any reason why there shouldn't be," Dean answered. "There's still power. It was just a flipped breaker."

George looked at his and then at Bill. "I think the safest option would be to spend the day and head out at dawn. This house isn't exactly fortified."

Gary looked at where Simon was seated on the couch, face already stuck to his video game console. "I think we could really use the break," he said. "We've come a long ways, and Simon's walked more in the past three days than he has in his entire life. And I think my blisters have blisters."

George glanced at Dean, drawing in a deep breath and exhaling quietly. He nodded, looking to where Bill was pulling another bottle from the wall. Then he looked at Simon and Coal. "I suppose we could set up some type of perimeter alarm. Something to alert us if anyone comes snooping around."

Gary looked at him, his gaze softening. "Thank you."

George nodded, turning his gaze to Bill. "So. Which one of those is the best?"

"So," Bill says, looking across at Gary with a smile. "We get to the restaurant, and it's our first date, so, you know. I decided to go big. I pulled out all the stops. I made reservations to this five-star steakhouse, had a nice corner booth reserved. The whole nine yards."

Bill looked at Gary again, scoffing with a smile.

Gary lifted his glass, watching his husband over the rim as he took a sip of what was about to be his third glass. Three empty bottles sat on the table between them and a nice, rosy glow was worn across the group's faces.

"So," Bill continued, stealing a quick sip from his glass. "They send over the sommelier, who starts recommending different wines. Now. I didn't know anything about wine at this point. Wine for me was Boone's Farm and Mad Dog."

"Whooo," Dean said with a laugh. "MD-2020."

Bill's brow lifted.

"Boy," Dean added. "I've spent *way* too many mornings feeling pain and regret because of a night out with 2020..." He let out an exaggerated shudder.

"Tell me about it," Bill added. "But, anyways. The sommelier is rattling off this list, a bunch of names I've never heard. And I pick a random one, trying to pretend like I know exactly what it is. And I say, *we'll take a bottle of that*. The part I didn't realize, was how expensive wines can get." He lifted his glass, taking a sip. "Ugh. That is amazing," he said, looking down into the glass.

"Then the server brought the check," Gary continued, smiling.

"Then the server brough the check...," Bill repeated. "I put my card in the presenter and the server took it to the front and ran it. Three minutes later he was back. *I do apologize sir, but there seems to be an issue with your card.*" He smirked. "That's when I looked at the check and realized that the bottle of Opus One that the sommelier had suggested was four hundred and fifty dollars..."

"Yeah," Gary said, giving him an accusatory look, before glancing between the others. "And can any of you guess who wound up getting stuck paying?"

George let out a laugh, the sound filling the basement. "Oh. That's rich," he said, lifting his glass and draining the last of it.

"Yeah," Gary said, shaking his head and smiling at Bill.

"Oh," Bill sighed. "Man." He drained the last of his glass and reached out to open a fresh bottle.

"I think I'm gonna go on and cut myself off for the night," George said, gesturing with a wave of his hand.

Dean yawned, nodding. "I think this is putting me to sleep."

Bill paused, his hand hovering just at the edge of the bottle. He glanced at Gary who gave an almost imperceptible shake of his head. He sighed heavily.

"Eh. You're probably right. We can continue this tomorrow."

George patted his knees and stood. "If you all will excuse me. I'm gonna go visit the little boy's room."

"That's not a bad idea," Bill said, reaching out and setting his glass down before rising and following behind.

Filtered sunlight filled the first floor of the house as George stepped out. It was well into morning, and he took a moment to listen before making his way into the dining room.

Dean stepped up behind him, bringing his hand up to block his eyes. A small grunt fell from his lips. "Gonna feel this one tomorrow," he said, following behind George, who was making his way to one of the two bathrooms on the first floor.

"Yep," George said quietly. "But it felt good. Almost *normal*, you know."

"I think we all needed that," Dean replied, watching as George made his way into one of the rooms.

He continued past, working his way through the living room and into a smaller room off to the side. This one appeared to be a study. There were books from floor to ceiling across one wall, and a large, ornate wooden desk and leather chair against the other. Large, curved windows ran the length of the back wall. Dark burgundy curtains blocked out most of the light beyond.

He crossed the room to the small half-bath and stopped in his tracks, fingers just inches from the knob.

Outside, a series of clicking screeches sounded out. From where he stood, it sounded as if they were just outside the window. He stood frozen, half his buzz dissipating nearly instantly. Again, the screeching sounded. This time it was followed by a *thump* coming from above. He stood there, his breath held in his throat as he waited for what was going to come next. He swallowed, the dry taste of cabernet edging down his throat. Then another thump sounded, and he heard the familiar sound of rapidly flapping wings.

Dean stood there for the next few minutes, finally releasing the breath he held before reaching out and opening the bathroom door. He slipped inside and quickly relieved himself, sitting down in order to reduce the sound of his urine hitting the water. When he was finished, he shut the lid and crept back to the basement door.

As he was passing the second bathroom, George stepped out, turning his gaze to them. They held a silent conversation with their eyes and a couple of nods and then made their way back downstairs.

By the time they reached the bottom, they could hear the sound of light snoring. Apparently, the sounds above had gone unnoticed by the family below.

George looked over at the curved couch, where the boy slept, Coal curled up at his feet. Gary had taken a plush chaise lounge near the wine wall and Bill was asleep in a foldout chair by the table. He exchanged a quick glance with Dean and then made his way to the nearby loveseat.

By the time George finally fell asleep, the midday sun was almost directly overhead. The creatures that had landed above had scraped a small portion of roofing tiles from above and they lay in a scattered pile near the back door. In the distance, a large murmur of creatures rose, spiraling up and twisting in a flourished display before turning west and flying away.

It was a little after seven when George pulled himself awake. He looked across the dim room to where Bill still slept in the recliner. Simon was still asleep on the couch, though Coal had shifted and was now facing the other direction. He shifted his gaze to see Dean in the loveseat, a book held in his grasp, reading glasses resting at the edge of his nose. He cleared his throat lightly and Dean peered at him from across the cream-colored pages. He nodded politely and George responded in kind. He slowly pulled himself to a seated position, resting there for a moment before bringing his watch up to check the time. A moment later he stood, making his way to the small bathroom near the back corner.

George stood there, feeling the gentle tug of a hangover on the back of his eyes as he relieved himself. He zipped up, moved to the sink and washed his hands. As he did so, he caught the streaks of dirt that hid beneath the ends of his sleeves. He sighed, turning the water off and flushing the toilet before making his way back out.

As he stepped out of the small bathroom, Gary was already pulling himself to a seated position. He cleared his throat and smiled. "Morning."

George nodded politely. "Morning. How you feeling?"

"As could be expected," Gary replied. "Better than him when he wakes up," he smiled, gesturing toward Bill with a nod.

George smiled. "I'm gonna go ahead and take advantage of the nice shower upstairs. I think I'm a little overdue."

Gary nodded in reply. "That's a good idea. I've been waiting for that before putting on the new clothes we picked up."

George made his way to his pack and slung it over his shoulder, moving to the stairs.

As he made his way through the house, he took the time to admire the décor. There was a large taxidermied elk head over the main entrance, and a chandelier in a tall domed space. He looked at a large nature painting and a vintage wine advertisement as he made his way toward the bathroom.

A short time later, steam had blanketed the large, round mirror, fogging everything into obscurity. Hot water flowed down over George's head and shoulders, draining into the sedimentary pool that swirled muddily at his feet. He stood there, head bent forward as the water flowed down his naked form.

George had been a clean man prior to the invasion. A military man of nearly twenty years, he'd lived a tightly regimented life, his clothing clean and pressed, not a hair out of place. He'd spent weeks and months at a time in combat situations, much of that spent in Afghanistan, with a three week stint in Falluja, so he wasn't a stranger to going days and sometimes weeks at a time between showers. But he'd retired nearly fifteen years prior, and after that, he was a shower a day type of man, who still kept all of his clothing clean and pressed, folded and organized. This was one of the things that he had battled with the most after the bugs had arrived. Adapting to a life at night. He likened it to pulling third watch. That was easy. Going months at a time without seeing the sun. That he was able to deal with as well. But showering only when safety and time would allow, and never wearing clothes that were truly clean. That still drove him crazy.

As he stood there, enshrouded in fog, his thoughts wandered back to the day the bugs had first appeared. George had been at a store recommended to him by his elderly uncle, who he had come out to help remodel his and his aunt's kitchen. He'd just come out of the hardware store, paper bag in hand, when he saw the first fireball drop out of the sky. He had stopped where he was and followed the object as it burst past, impacting against the side of a high rise building a block away. Then he heard another and looked up to see six more of the objects burning their way across the sky. By the time he'd pulled his gaze back to the burning hole in the high rise, he could already hear car horns blaring and the panicked screaming. When he looked up, staring, unable to believe what he was seeing. A large, clawed foot had emerged from the hole, followed by another. A breath later, a massive, chitinous insect emerged, climbing out and across the side of the building. It hovered there for a moment and then dropped. The creature landed on the ground, six stories below and darted forward, impaling an incredibly confused homeless man through the torso. That was when George had dropped the bag and turned to run.

The water pooling around his feet was now clear, spiraling down the drain. He shook the memories away and lifted his head, bringing his hands up and brushing the water from his hair. As he did, he realized he was in dire need of a haircut. His gray hair was well below his ears, and he was beginning to feel like the hippies he and his military buddies had made fun of in the seventies. He reached out, twisting the shower knob and killing the stream. He stood there a moment longer, the screams in his memory fading away. Then he pushed the glass door aside and stepped out, grabbing a towel.

By the time George arrived back down in the basement, the others were already up and about. He was surprised to see that Bill had already opened a new bottle of wine, and was going on about it being one of the best, and most expensive bottles of wine in the world. As he walked up, Bill brought a glass to his lips and drank.

"Ugh!" Bill barked, pulling the glass away, a look of disgust on his lips. "That is terrible..."

Dean laughed and Gary watched him, a slight amusement on his face.

"Right back at it I see," George said, pushing his suggestion that they pack up and get moving down.

Bill made a bad face and hefted the bottle up.

"Corked?" Gary asked.

Bill shook his head. "No. Just bad..."

He smiled. "Well. The whites have had a day to chill. I'm going to go find myself a nice, New Zealand Sauv."

Bill nodded, still flabbergasted at how a six-thousand dollar bottle of wine could taste so bad.

"We should probably start thinking about what our next move is going to be," George said, dropping his pack next to the couch and taking a seat. "As much as I'm sure we'd all love to stay here and get hammered for the next six months, we should probably get moving."

"Especially after last night," Dean added.

This grabbed Gary's attention. "What happened last night?"

"Nothing," George said, pulling his attention to him. "We had some company."

Fear warped his face.

"Bugs," George added. "But none got in. We can't even be sure they knew we were here. But, they were crawling around on the roof."

"Bill," Gary said, the tone in his voice telling him everything he needed to hear.

Bill nodded. "Yeah. Okay. We'll leave at sundown, tomorrow."

"That's pretty much what I was thinking," George replied. "It's too late to get started tonight, and I'm thinking we should probably take the time to see if we can find anything useful here."

Bill thought about making a joke about the wine and its uses but kept it to himself.

"We should look for first aid kits, medication, things like that. If they have *this*," he said, looking around the room. Then they likely have a pantry. Wouldn't hurt to stock up on some canned goods or anything else we might find."

"There's a truck in the garage," Dean added. "We should probably look for the keys. Make sure it's gassed up."

"That's a good idea," George agreed. "We can load up the truck, and if we have to ditch it somewhere, we can take whatever we can carry and leave the rest for other folks that might come across it."

The group made their way upstairs, Gary making his way to the kitchen and rifling through the cabinets. Bill found a small pantry and began removing canned goods and setting them on the kitchen island. Dean found the keys to the truck hanging near the door to the garage, and a few minutes later had the engine fired up. It read a little over a half a tank of gas. George had gone upstairs, locating the master bathroom and a small stockpile of ibuprofen and aspirin and a small bottle of antibiotics. Alongside that, he discovered a nearly six-month supply of insulin and clean syringes.

These he all piled into his pack before returning back downstairs. A little over an hour later, the group was once again congregated downstairs.

Bill had found his way inside another bottle of wine, though verbally limiting himself to three glasses, max. George was seated at a small table, playing gin rummy with Dean. Simon sat on the couch playing his game and Gary was lost in the pages of a book he had found. Coal had made his way upstairs and was snooping around the house.

"I really think Coal's taken a liking to your boy," George said, pulling Gary from his book. "Did you all have a dog before all this?"

Gary set the book down in his lap. "No. Our HOA didn't allow pets." his gaze drifted to his son, resting sadly on his son for a moment. "He always wanted one though."

"On that note," Bill added. "At least we don't have to deal with Cindy Lauper anymore..."

George offered a puzzled glance. "The singer?"

"No," Gary smiled. "Heather Tran. She was the head of our HOA committee and an absolute horrible human being." He shook his head. "She used to do her hair all up with Aqua Net like it was nineteen eighty-five. We started calling her Cindy Lauper because of that, and the ridiculous jogging apparel she'd wear when *patrolling* the neighborhood."

Bill groaned. "I wanted to beat that woman with that damned clipboard..."

"Well. Hopefully she got hers," Gary added.

"Knowing our luck, we'll get to Anchorage, and she'll be their self-appointed mayor..."

"Don't you even put that out there, Bill Tanner."

He reached out, rapping his knuckles three times on the table before him.

"My ex-wife tried to get me wrapped ip on one of those HOAs when we were shopping for our first house. One of those, new master-planned communities or whatever they're called. Almost had me to, but I'd happened to make a comment as we were talking with our realtor, about putting a big flagpole in the yard and hanging the stars and stripes. They were real quick to tell me that that was a big no-go, that the community had a strict, no flag policy." He paused, smirking as he remembered. "I'm pretty sure she never stopped hating me for that one..."

"Yeah," Bill said in a sigh. "We didn't really know what we were getting into until after we moved in and I went to put a couple flowerpots on my porch. Cindy Lauper showed up about ten minutes later, clipboard in hand, telling me I had until the end of the day to remove them, or I was going to be fined a hundred dollars, per the HOA agreement." He scoffed. "That was the beginning of a very long seven years..."

"Sounds like my marriage," George chuckled, moving his attention back to his game.

"Dad?"

Gary looked over to where Simon was sitting.

"Can I go upstairs with Coal?"

"Sure," he replied. "Just stay off the second floor, okay?"

"Okay," he said, setting his game console on the couch and making his way toward the stairs.

"And don't go outside," he added as the boy was starting his way up.

"Okay," Simon called back down, quickening his pace to two stairs at a time.

Gary lowered his gaze back to his book, hearing Simon call out for Coal a moment later.

"Damn." Dean grunted, slapping the cards in his hand down on the table. "You're cheating."

George laughed, setting his cards down. "Don't be a sore loser," he said, pushing his chair out and rising to his feet. He sighed in a gust. "I'm gonna hit the head."

Dean glared at him as he turned and started his way upstairs. As George disappeared at the top, he looked over at Bill, whose face was illuminated by his phone's screen. "I'm gonna take a walk," he said, standing up.

Bill pulled his gaze from his phone and Dean could see the thin lines of tears on his cheeks.

"You want some company?" Bill asked, turning his phone off. "I could use some fresh air."

"Sure," Dean said. "Why don't you bring that bottle." He gestured to the half a bottle of wine on the table with a nod.

Bill smirked, rising up and grabbing the bottle by the neck.

The air was crisp, the light smell of moisture hanging in it as Dean stepped down the back stairs. Bill followed right behind.

"Want to walk the perimeter?" Bill asked, looking up at the half-moon overhead.

"Sounds good to me," Dean replied.

It was nearly silent as the pair made their way around to the front of the house. There were no crickets, no frogs, just the soft, almost unnoticeable sound of a breeze working through the tall grass and weeds in the surrounding field.

"You think you'd get used to it," Dean said, glancing back to Bill and holding his hand out.

"To what?"

"The quiet," Dean answered, taking the bottle and holding it to his lips for a moment before taking a sip.

Bill chuckled.

Dean looked at him and gave a questioning nod.

"It's just funny," Bill replied. "We're standing outside of a farmhouse with the owners dead inside, and we're drinking a twenty-five thousand dollar bottle of wine straight from the bottle."

"Don't forget the part about the world having been invaded by alien insects."

"Oh, yeah. Of course. And the world's been invaded by alien insects that either want to drink us dry, or implant us with their young." He scoffed again, reaching out for the bottle.

Dean took another sip and passed it back. "Twenty-five thousand, huh?"

"Twenty-five," Bill replied.

"Hmph. Would never have guessed it. Tastes like a six-dollar bottle of Vons special to me."

Bill chuckled. "Not much difference to be honest. At the end of the day, you're really just paying for the name."

Dean looked up at the night sky. A blanket of twinkling stars hung suspended in the endless black. "Never in a million years would I have ever thought something like this could have happened." He shook his head, watching as a thin line of red streaked across the sky. "I really hope we're right," He added.

"About what?"

"Going north. The cold."

Bill scoffed, taking another sip and look up at the sky. "We all knew it was only a matter of time before they figured out how to get into the underground. I think all of us knew we were living on borrowed time. We had to do something eventually. At least this plan seems to make sense. It was better than going to North Dakota…"

"I wonder how that group's doing," Dean said, reaching out and taking the bottle.

"They've got a longer trip, and most of it's spread out and in the open. Not to mention. Like you said, it really only gets cold enough to keep those things away a few months out of the year. I'm happy to be taking my chances in Alaska. Sure, it stays light for a portion of the year, but for the rest. I think it's a good trade off."

"I suppose we'll see," Dean added. "But we gotta get there first."

Bill chuckled. "I just hope it involves less walking than we've been doing. My feet are still killing me."

"You and me both," Dean replied, taking another swig from the bottle and handing it back. "Twenty-five thousand..." he said, his gaze narrowing at the thought. "Who the hell has twenty-five thousand for a bottle of wine. Must be nice..."

"You don't drink a twenty-five thousand dollar bottle of wine," Bill replied, holding the bottle out and admiring the faded label. "You collect them."

"To each their own, I guess."

Bill smirked, taking another swig and then cocking his arm back and flinging the bottle as far out into the field as he could. A long, rooster-tail of wine flared out, spraying in a circle like water from a sprinkler head, before the bottle *clunked* into the dirt somewhere in the weeds.

Dean turned to him, his brow furrowing. "Dude. That was like six grand right there..."

Bill smiled, the grin spreading as Dean began to laugh. For the next few moments, they stood there, laughing at the ridiculousness of it all.

Dean sighed, the laughter falling away. "Come on," he said. "Let's get back in. They're probably worrying about us."

Bill nodded, looking up at the sky a moment longer before turning and following Dean back to the house.

The sun was still clinging desperately to the distant horizon when the garage attached to the house opened. A tracked chain pulled it back, a grating sound echoing out as the last of the fading sunlight illuminated the front of the large white pickup truck.

The group had awoken a few hours prior, loading the last of their things into the truck's bed. They had spent the prior night loading as much as they could, a stockpile of canned goods and packaged foods and three large, five-gallon jugs of water.

The truck's engine roared to life, and a moment later they pulled out onto the long, circular driveway.

"We ready?" Dean asked from the driver's seat.

A quiet agreement was shared, and he took his foot off the brake, allowing the truck to start forward. Moments later they were pulling back onto the main road and making their way back to the freeway.

"I'm really going to miss that house," Bill said as they pulled onto the two-lane highway leading north.

"You're going to miss that basement," Gary said with a playful smirk, scoffing lightly as he shook his head.

In the front, George shifted his gaze to a large field they were passing. In the fading daylight, he saw dozens of shapes scattered, small mounds dotting the open space. As they drove past, he saw one of the lumps lying close to the fence just beyond the dirt road paralleling the freeway. A gentle breeze ruffled a tuft of fur, and he instantly recognized the crumpled shape as what had once been a cow. His gaze moved past to the dozens of other corpses lying they were either fed upon or made host to more of the alien insects. He pulled his gaze away, shifting it to the glowing horizon.

They drove the next thirty minutes in silence, all but Simon watching the desolate world drift by. He had fallen back asleep after having stayed up far too late playing his video games.

It had been the second or third day of the invasion, when Bill had realized the scope of what was happening. In what he still considered possibly one of his greatest feats of fatherhood, he'd told his son to download as many games as he could fit onto the console. He'd given him extra SD cards and told him to fill those too. He wasn't sure if he'd ever seen Simon so happy in his life. Simon had worried about how much it was going to cost, but Bill had told him not to worry about it. He was sure that wasn't going to matter. So, nearly four thousand dollars later, Simon had pretty much every game released on the console packed onto a small package of SD cards. He had so many games, he wasn't sure he'd even get to them all. Simon was still doing his best to assure him he would.

Bill looked over at his son, bringing his hand up and patting him lightly on his leg. He was the greatest thing that had ever happened to them.

Prior to adopting Simon, Bill and Gary had spent most of their free time outside of their house. They'd go days at a time, camping and taking road trips. They'd figured out how to balance both their schedules in order to get the maximum amount of time possible together. Bill could still remember the moment Gary had pulled him in close and whispered into his ear, "I want to have a baby." They had been sitting atop a massive boulder formation in a campground just inside Joshua National Park. The sun had been setting, and a million colors had been painted across the horizon. He could still feel his heart melting when Gary had whispered those words. It had been three weeks later, after many long discussions, that they had put in their application. Three months later, a seven-month-old Simon had been placed into their lives. Not a single moment went by that either of them regretted it, even though their personal and together time had taken an incredibly large hit. And the long road trips... Simon had spent the first four years of his life getting over carsickness.

Bill looked past his son at the other love of his life and smiled, the gentle warmth moving through him. Gary must have felt him staring and looked back, a puzzled look working across his face.

"What?"

Bill smiled. "Nothing."

"Weirdo," Gary said, smiling at him for a moment before shifting his gaze back out the window.

The next forty-five minutes drifted by like this, the only sounds heard, those coming from the truck's engine and large tires rolling down the freeway. That's when the truck's headlights fell upon a long, stalled procession of vehicles across both lanes, and a handful of cars stuck on the shoulders and median.

Bill slowed the truck to a stop twenty yards before the jam. "Well," he groaned. "Shit…"

Simon woke up, yawning as he wiped the sleep from his eyes.

"Can we get around it?" Bill asked, leaning over for a better view ahead.

"We'll have to cut that fence," George said, gesturing to a barbed wire fence twenty feet away. "Don't wanna risk getting that barbed wire all tangled up in the tires. We do that and this thing should have no issues going around."

"There's bolt cutters in the toolbox," Dean said, putting the truck into park and killing the engine. "I put them there myself."

"Alright," George said. "Why don't we get out and stretch our legs for a bit."

Once outside, Dean looked at George.

"Come on, sleepyhead," Gary said, tapping Simon on the leg. "You heard the man. Time to stretch our legs."

"We've been stretching our legs," Simon groaned. "This whole time. I'm tired of stretching my legs."

Gary looked at him lovingly and smiled. "You know what. You're right. Why don't we stay here and let them figure it out."

Simon smiled, turning to pet Coal, who shifted only his eyes up in recognition.

Dean made his way to the toolbox and popped it open, shifting some of the contents around before coming out with a short pair of bolt cutters. He made his way over to the five-foot fence and started cutting. George offered a hand, grasping the wires as he cut in an effort to keep them from springing back and slicing through Dean's arm. When they were finished, Dean stepped back. "Think we can fit through?"

George and Bill eyed the space and then the truck. "It'll be tight," Bill said. "But I think I know a good paint guy if we scratch it."

This got a chuckle out of George.

The moon was just a crescent above, a thin sickle of silver casting a dim glow across the landscape. For as far as they could see were sprawling agricultural fields. Though, with the irrigation systems having been inoperable for the last thirteen months, it was beginning to look more like a vast swath of Southwest desert. Tall weeds and bushes grew out, sparsely dotting the nearly smooth surface. Somewhere far in the distance a lone owl hooted, the sound reminding them that nature was still out there, just as they were, fighting to survive.

The door to the truck opened and Bill climbed in. Gary gave him a quick questioning nod and he smiled, confirming they had completed the task. A moment later, George and Dean climbed in.

"Alright," George said, glancing out of the side window at the opened fence. "Let's see what this baby can do."

"Famous last words," Gary said from the back.

Dean dropped the truck into gear and turned off the freeway. It jumped a bit as they dropped down the shoulder, the front tires dropping into a small ravine. A moment later they were scraping their way through the fence. Metal grated on metal and there was a screeching sound as the truck bent the fenceposts out, and they drug across the sides.

"Better call that paint guy," George said from the front, chuckling at his humor.

Bill gave a small laugh, and a moment later they were making their way through the vast field.

They drove through the fields on the side of the road in four low for the next hour, before a central irrigation canal forced them back onto the road. By then, traffic had cleared a bit, and they were able to slowly weave their way through, utilizing the center median to traverse the endless parking lot.

Another hour further and traffic once again slowed them to a stop.

"Suggestions?" Dean asked, sighing as he looked at the two lanes of blocked traffic, and cars stalled out, blocking both the center median and shoulder.

George stared out, looking at the truck stop illuminated a few miles away. "Rinse, lather, repeat," he said, shaking his head.

Dean nodded, dropping the truck into park.

They stepped out, making their way to the toolbox and once again cutting the fencing away. Then they squeezed the truck through and followed the dirt path another two miles, cutting through another field around the back of the packed travel center.

"Looks like we found the cause of all the traffic," George said as they pulled around the side of the truck stop.

The travel center was filled with abandoned vehicles. Three, endless lines of traffic all flowed into the center island of pumps. Dozens of red gas canisters lay strewn about below the charred remains of the burned overhang. The pumps were blackened husks, and the dozens of vehicles that were piled up to them were burned down to nothing more than rusting frames.

"Looks like something big went down here," George said, noticing the dozens of shell casings littering the ground. Then his eyes caught the bullet holes pockmarking the abandoned vehicles. He eyed the carnage for a moment longer, when Simon's voice pulled him from the recreation his mind was in the process of doing.

"I have to use the bathroom."

"Yeah," Gary added. "Me too."

"Let's take a minute," George said, pulling his eyes away from charred wreckage. "How are we looking on gas?" he asked.

Dean looked at the gauge. "Little over a quarter of a tank."

"We'll probably have to do something about that soon," he said, glancing at his watch. "We better not spend too much time lingering about," he added. "We only got a few hours of dark left."

Bill nodded, glancing at Gary and gesturing for him to take Simon to the bathroom with a nod.

Gary nodded in reply, tapping Simon's leg. "Come on."

The group started toward the front doors.

The interior of the place was trashed. Shelves lay off kilter and knocked over and there wasn't much more than empty wrappers and air fresheners lying about. The entire place had been ransacked.

"It looks like a hurricane blew through here," Dean said as they made their way through.

Each of them played back their own memories of those first few days in vivid detail.

"Let's check the supply room," Dean said, making his way toward the back.

They crossed the empty facility, their feet crunching through plastic and broken glass. Only trinkets and useless knickknacks were left. Everything else was gone.

A familiar sound caught George's ear, and he looked down at the handful of spent shell casings his foot had sent clinking across the floor.

Gary and Simon had followed the overhead signs to the left and were making their way to the bathroom. Simon made a reference to some post-apocalyptic video game he had played, and how the truck stop looked just like it. Gary had seen some of the games he had played, and though a few of them he didn't agree with, his only being ten years old and the games being quite violent, he had never fallen into the whole, video games cause violence nonsense. He'd remembered the campaigns when he had been a boy, and even though he hadn't been a gamer himself, he still thought it ridiculous.

Simon pushed open the bathroom door and started in, when a soft squeak escaped his lips, and he nearly fell backward out of the doorway.

"Simon!?" Gary burst, pulling him back.

As the door closed, he caught the grisly sight of two bodies splayed out on the bathroom floor. Nothing more than cloth covered bone, the long-decayed corpses were sprawled beneath the handwashing sinks.

He pulled him in, hugging him as he took two steps backward.

"Sorry, Dad," he said.

Gary squeezed him tightly. "No," he replied, exhaling slowly. "I'm sorry. I'm sorry things are like this. I'm so sorry."

Simon pulled away, turning to face him. "It's okay. I'm fine."

Gary stared at him. He knew he wasn't. There was no way he could be. But he had to keep reminding himself that children were far more adaptable than adults. Covid and the resulting fallout had proven that. But it still didn't make it right. He should be growing up in a normal world, having a normal life. Not...

"What happened?"

Gary jerked to the side, startled by Bill's voice.

"Are you okay?"

He swallowed, nodding.

"Sorry, Dad," Simon said, looking at the bathroom door. "There were..."

"He saw two bodies. In there," Gary said, nodding toward the bathroom. "It just startled him. That's all."

"Are you sure you're okay?" Bill asked.

"Yeah," Simon replied. "I'm fine. I've seen dead people before."

Bill and Gary exchanged a glance. "Yeah. I know," Bill reassured. "But it doesn't make it any easier."

"Come on," Gary said, putting his hand on Simon's shoulder. "I'll check this one first."

He gave Bill a reassuring glance and turned, pressing the door to the women's open and peering in. "We're all clear," he said, holding the door open for Simon to enter.

"Hey," Bill said as he was about to step in. "Are you okay?"

He nodded. "Yeah. Thanks."

His husband nodded in reply, and he turned, making his way in.

It was twenty minutes later that the group had made their way back to the truck and were edging their way around the mile long line of abandoned vehicles.

"It must have been a nightmare," Bill said, his gaze drifting to an ambulance with its back doors standing open. "I mean. We all had it bad, in the city. But imagine being stuck out here, in the middle of nowhere, and people are shooting each other over gas..." He paused on that thought. "After surviving the bugs and the chaos, to die because of selfish ignorance..."

"It's human nature," George replied from the front. "Charles Darwin at his finest."

"I don't think that's Darwin," Gary replied. "I believe that would be Hobbes." He paused. "Thomas Hobbes was the one who stated that humans are naturally selfish and wicked, and therefore cannot be trusted. He believed our natural state, as a species, is violent and brutal. It's our innate behavior."

A moment of silence passed through the cab.

"Hobbes, huh?" George replied with a gentle smirk. "I think I might be inclined to agree with him. It isn't until the world is falling apart, and people need each other the most that they truly start to tear each other apart."

"People were just scared," Bill said, glancing out the window at a passing structure.

"I was scared," George replied. "Shitting myself terrified. But I didn't go and murder anyone for a package of toilet paper."

The truck fell silent again. In those first days, when the looting and riots had begun, tens of thousands of people had been killed in the ensuing chaos. It had felt like humans were killing themselves almost as much as the bugs. Panic had gripped the world, and the resulting nightmare had been hordes of people trampling and killing each other for the finite resources and supplies. The world had torn itself apart and only the smartest, strongest and most willing to do whatever was necessary to survive, did so. So, maybe they were both right. Maybe Darwin *and* Hobbes had equally good points.

"So," Dean said, his eyes glancing at the line of cars as they slowly passed. "How did you all wind up in the underground?" He shot a glance between them in the rearview.

"Well," Gary began. "We had flown out to visit Bill's sister, Claire, in Pasadena." He paused, remembering the day. "We'd gone to the Macy's in downtown, and she was planning on taking us to the jewelry district. That's when..." He remembered the fiery objects blasting across the sky, and the exploding glass and steel as they impacted into the tops of the skyrise buildings. "Everyone was running and screaming. That's when Bill saw the subway entrance. We ran down with a crowd of people and hid in the tunnels. We just stayed down there. Eventually people went back up. We realized that the *bugs* only hunt during the daytime." He paused. "We thought about trying to get back home. But after that first week. We knew we were never going back. Not with Simon. We couldn't risk it. We were too afraid to even go back to his sister's house."

"Did your sister...?"

"No," Bill replied. "She's still at the Union Station district. She. She wanted to stay." He scoffed. "She always was the stubborn one."

Gary smiled, glancing at him. "The apple didn't fall far, sweetheart."

Bill smiled, shaking his head.

"Those first few days...," Bill added, sighing heavily. "And then the quiet."

Dean exhaled in a sound that resembled a stifled sob. "That was it," he said, his gaze locked to the road ahead. "That was when I knew it was real. That first night I went up and there was no sound. It was so quiet. No dogs barking, no birds, even the wind seemed to be hiding. That's when I knew. The world we knew was gone. All of it."

Another moment of silence passed. "But you know what's funny?"

George glanced back at him. "Huh?"

Bill smiled. "I didn't even know my sister was still alive until almost a month later."

"A month later? I thought you said you'd all run down into the tunnels together?"

Bill shook his head. "No. We'd gotten separated when everything happened. My sister was still inside the Macy's. We'd gone out to take a look around. She wanted to get us something and didn't want us there when she bought it. When everything went to hell, she wasn't with us."

"How did it take you a month to find her? The Underground isn't exactly that big."

"Care to elaborate on your stubbornness?" Gary asked, his eyebrows lifting up his brow.

"After about a week, I decided I had to go check. So. I told Gary to stay with Simon, and I made my way, on foot, to her house in Pasadena." He shook his head, the image of tens of thousands of bodies in the streets, every square inch of freeway and surface street a mangled jumble of wrecked vehicles and bloody corpses flashing past. The drained husks of people and dogs, bodies eaten from within. He exhaled in a gust. "I made it, and she wasn't there. So, I gathered a few things of ours and made my way back to the underground. A month later, we volunteered for a work detail, securing the perimeter around Union Station. There is no way you could imagine the surprise, or absolute flood of joy I felt when I looked up and saw my sister staring at me, just bawling." He choked up, tears forming at the edges of his eyes.

Gary reached over, placing his hand on his thigh and squeezing gently.

He drew in a deep breath and let it out in a gust. "She's still there. Stubborn old goat." A smile escaped his lips. "She told me I was crazy, bringing my family on this trip." He shook his head solemnly. "But if there's hope for a place where we don't have to worry every waking moment about being killed by those *things*. It's a risk I was willing to take."

"We," Gary corrected. "A risk *we* were willing to take."

Bill smiled, placing his hand atop his.

"We."

"What about you, Dean?" Bill asked. "I don't think I've heard you even mention it once? How did you end up down in the tunnels?"

Dean drove the next few moments in silence, his mind working back to that first day. The attack, the accident. His son being drug away as he was helpless to watch. His brow furrowed as he swallowed, his voice making a soft *click*. "Same as everyone else," he said a beat later. His head shook almost imperceptibly. "Doesn't matter how." He looked at him through the rearview. "All that matters now, is getting north and surviving." A thin smile tugged at his cheeks. Looking back at the family through the mirror teased a bitter resentment in him, that single, echoing thought whispering, *why couldn't that be my family*. But seeing them together, being there as they struggled and fought to survive. Their strength. It offered him a thin sliver of hope. It was that that pulled the smile ever-so-slightly wider.

There was a silent agreement shared between them. It was about surviving. That was it. They had all one through an incalculable amount of pain and loss at the arrival of the insects. There was no scale for the grief the world had felt, the oceans of tears spilled. But people were surviving. They were doing as humanity had always done. They were adapting and finding a way.

Gary reached across Simon, placing his hand on Bill's leg. His hand came to rest atop his.

"Do you think it's ever going to go back to the way it was?" Bill asked.

The cab stayed silent while everyone pondered that question, a myriad of thoughts and feelings coalescing in a deep silence, the truck's tires pulling against the asphalt below and grumbling engine the only sound above their breathing.

"I think this is it," George replied after a solemn moment. "I think. We learn to adapt. Maybe one day we'll figure out a way to take the world back. But for now." He shook his head. "We just hide and hope they don't evolve alongside us."

That was the unspoken thought that terrified Dean the most. What if the bugs were also learning to adapt. They had no idea what they were, or where they came from. They had no idea if they had some, advanced genetic makeup that would allow for rapid mutations or, evolutions. There were frogs that could alter their sex in order to continue their species, fish that have adapted to living in the pitch black of caves and shifting from salt to fresh water. They knew nothing about these creatures. That was the thought that scared him the most. Sure. They could escape to the north, but how long would they be safe? Years, decades? They had no way of knowing. So, in that thought, he knew that even *if* they managed to survive the journey there, they would never truly be able to shake of the fear that one day they might wake up and hear the thrumming buzz of wings.

The night air moved past, a light scattering of clouds filtering silver overhead. The deserted roadside drifted past, darkened houses and empty swaths of agriculture laying bare in the dim moonlight.

"There's a town called Redding," George said, the light from his phone casting shadows on the roof over him. "Couple hours from here. I'm thinking we could probably stop there for the night, or we can push on into Oregon."

"How are we on gas?" Gary asked.

"We'll have to stop and syphon some off," Dean replied. "I'm guessing most of the gas stations are going to be like the one back there."

"That's what I was thinking," George said. "That's why I threw a length of hose and a gas can in the back."

"I think we should try and get as many miles in as possible before stopping," Bill added.

"You good with that?" George asked, looking at Dean.

Dean nodded. "Yeah. I'm good for another few hours," he replied. "I'll let you know if I need to pull over." He yawned softly, drumming his fingers on the steering wheel for a moment. Then he threw a quick glance at George, nodding toward the phone in his hand. "You got any other music on there we might like?"

George smiled. "I think I might have one or two albums."

Dean settled his gaze back on the road, watching the illuminated yellow lines drift past.

They drove like this, the empty world drifting past for the next three hours. When Dean felt the onset of fatigue, his back tensing and weariness tugging at the back of his eyelids, they pulled into a small rest area. George syphoned nearly three-quarters of a tank of gas from the cars left sitting in the lot, and they made their way back onto the road, Bill taking over while Dean caught a few winks in the back. The air outside had gotten noticeably cooler, a gentle chill now whispering on the wind.

-21-

It was a little after four-thirty in the morning when the truck crossed over the California, Oregon state line. Dean had awoken, but Gary and Simon were sleeping peacefully next to him. George was looking out the window, watching the trees drift by, when Bill's voice pulled him back.

"Great..."

George pulled his gaze from the towering pines and looked ahead, to where a large tractor trailer semi was parked across the length of the highway. "Slow up," he said, a gentle flutter of nervousness moving through him.

"Should we be worried?" Dean said, leaning over to look.

"What's going on?" Gary asked, stirring awake at the talking.

"I'm not sure," George replied as their truck slowed. "But something doesn't feel right." He scanned the road ahead as they drew nearer. "That truck was parked like that on purpose."

"What do we do?" Bill asked, slowing the truck to a stop a hundred feet away.

Then, as if answering the unheard question, two men spun around the blocking truck, rifles raised in their direction.

"Shit," George grunted.

"What do I do?" Bill asked, panic flooding his words.

A floodlight came to life, blinding them as it illuminated the truck and road around it.

"Shit!" George barked. "Back, back!" he shouted.

Bill slammed the truck's shifter into reverse and smashed the gas pedal to the floor.

The tires on the truck screeched to life and they lurched backwards as the truck peeled out, instantly gathering speed.

Ahead of them, the men near the truck began shouting. George watched as six more peeled out from behind the barricade.

Twenty yards behind them, another pickup emerged from the line of trees and pulled out onto the road, skidding to a stop directly in their path.

"Hold on!" Bill shouted, bracing himself as the back of their truck roared directly at the other.

A moment later, they were all thrown back into their seats as the sound of shattering glass and crunching metal screamed out into the night.

Gary screamed, hunching over and pulling Simon to safety beneath him. A moment later gunshots erupted from the direction of the blockade.

Bullets tore through the truck, the windshield exploding in a network of cracked webs.

Bill kept his foot on the gas, and a moment later, the truck which had pulled out in an attempt to block them, rolled onto its side and screeched across the pavement as it was pushed out of the way.

"Go!" George yelped, ducking as another volley of bullets rapped across the front of the truck.

Bill spun the wheel, nearly flipping the truck on the side as tires screeched against the road. Then he slammed the shifter into drive and smashed his foot down on the gas pedal.

They lurched forward, more bullets tearing into the tailgate and ricochetting off the asphalt.

"Go, go, go!" George screeched again.

The truck's engine screamed, the night air whistling past Bill and George through the holes in the windshield.

"Is everyone okay?" George asked, twisting in his seat. "Is anyone hit?"

Gary gently pushed Simon away, giving him a quick once over. "Are you hurt?"

Simon shook his head, staring back at him through wild eyes. He shook his head in a series of frantic motions. "I. I don't think so."

Gary looked at Dean who was now wide awake. "Dean?"

"No," Dean replied. "I'm good."

"We're good," he replied. "What the *fuck* was that!?" he burst, unable to control the reaction.

George glanced at the speedometer. Bill had his foot pegged to the floor and the gauge read a hundred and fifteen. "Ease up," he said, looking at Bill's white-knuckled grasp on the steering wheel. "Last thing we need to do is crash going this fast. That'll put a quick end to this trip."

Bill pulled in a deep breath, exhaling in a short series of shudders. Then he pulled his foot off the gas and let the truck begin to slow.

"What was that?" Gary asked again.

"Militia, maybe," George replied. "It doesn't matter. Whoever it was, we got away. All that matters is that we get off the main road and find a way around. There's gotta be some old forest roads we can use."

The truck slowed to a smooth sixty miles an hour before Bill put his foot back on the pedal. They could hear a metallic whining coming from the engine, and the smell of burnt plastic and scorched wires drifted in through the vents.

A few minutes later they saw an exit sign.

George pulled his face from the screen of his phone and pointed. "There. Forest road."

Bill slowed, taking the exit. The small, two-lane road led through a tall line of pine trees. The smell in the cab of the truck had grown stronger, and George rolled his window down. With the window open, the knocking sound he'd heard coming from the engine grew louder.

"That doesn't sound good," Bill said, his hands sweaty on the wheel.

They drove another twenty minutes before the engine shuddered, smoke billowing out from beneath the hood and they coasted to a stop.

"Shit," Bill groaned, pressing his eyes closed.

For the next few moments, they sat there, unspeaking as the truck's engine continued to click loudly.

Bill stood next to George, arms folded across his chest as they watched the tendrils of smoke rising into the air. The truck had been hit multiple times. One of the headlights was gone, and the radiator had multiple holes in it, the last remaining liquid puddling green beneath. The engine block itself had taken a direct hit, one of the rifle bullets having cracked straight through.

"Goddamnit," Dean hissed. "What the hell are we supposed to do now?"

"Dad," Simon said from behind, fear in his words as he watched. "I'm scared."

"I know," Gary replied. "Me too."

Dean lifted his wrist, checking his watch. "Shit," he hissed, seeing that it was already passing five in the morning.

"Did you see anything on the map?" Gary asked, looking at George, who was still staring in disbelief at the truck before them.

George pulled his gaze away.

"I thought I saw something," he replied, pulling his phone out. "Looked like some type of structure." He thumbed it open and zoomed in on the map. "Yeah. Right here," he said, turning it so the others could see.

"How far is that?" Dean asked, lifting his hand and rubbing the back of his hair. A piece of glass fell out, landing on the pavement.

"Not far," he replied, his expression changing.

"You hear that?" Bill said, catching the sound at the same time.

They stood there, listening for a moment, before the sound registered. Somewhere down the road, in the direction they had just come from, were the sound of engines, and they were approaching, quickly.

"We gotta move," George said. "Grab your packs. Let's go!"

They moved to the back of the truck and Dean passed their packs to them.

"Into the trees," George said, staring toward the woods a short distance away.

The group followed behind, feet crunching against the undergrowth. Behind them, the fading sounds of engines drew nearer.

None of them spoke. George had taken a quick mental picture of the map, and if they stayed on course, he calculated that they would reach whatever structure it was that he had found, in just under twenty minutes. He heard the approaching vehicle engines slow and the sound of car doors being shut. As they made their way further into the forest, the sounds behind faded away.

The two approaching vehicles slowed to a stop. Doors opened and six men carrying an assortment of firearms stepped out. They scanned the surrounding woods with their weapons as one of them started toward the truck.

"They couldn't have gotten far," the one in the lead said, moving around the truck to look at the smoking engine. "Fan out. Look for tracks."

"Yo, James," another of the men said, lifting his wrist and tapping his watch.

"I don't fucking care!" the man shouted back, fury in his gaze. "Laura's fucking bleeding out right now because they rammed her fucking truck. Start fucking looking!"

The other nodded, turning to the others. "Reggie, you and Carl with me. Benny. You take Kyle and Jose and to that way." He turned to the man by the truck. "We'll find them."

The other pulled his gaze away from the stalled-out vehicle, nodding in reply.

Back in the woods, George was making his way through the trees. He was doing his best to keep a linear direction. He didn't want to check his map for fear of the light giving away their location. He had no doubt that if whoever had given chase had tracked them this far, that they likely weren't going to just give up and go back the way they had come. He guessed that they were also likely back at the truck looking for tracks, and once they found them, which wouldn't take very long at all, they would be right on their heels. They had to keep moving, and they had to get to that structure quickly. Dawn was already beginning to caress the eastern horizon.

"Got em!"

James, the leader of the small group and husband to the girl Bill had crushed with the back of their pickup truck when escaping, made his way over to the other. He came to a stop and looked down at the clear impressions in the soil.

"They went that way," the other said, nodding into the trees.

James stared at the impressions for a moment. "Let's go."

"James," the other implored. "Dude. It's already five-twenty. The sun's coming up."

James reached out, grabbing the other by his jacket and yanked him close.

"Let the bugs get 'em," another behind said. "They ain't gonna get that far."

James pulled his pistol, leveling it at the man behind without taking his eyes off the one in his grasp.

"We're not leaving until I put a bullet into every one of those motherfuckers. You hear me? My wife is bleeding out on the side of the fucking road right now. And they're getting the fuck away. And I'm not going back to tell Andy we let these fuckers get away because you were afraid of bugs coming out."

The other swallowed and James locked his gaze on him. He shoved the man backward, nearly sending him to the dirt. "Now get your ass moving."

The other two men shared a quick glance, but the one who had nearly fallen backward turned, checking the tracks one last time before moving away.

George and the others were making their way through the dense trees, when he saw a break ahead. "I think I see a road," he said, his voice at a whisper.

They cleared the next thirty feet and emerged onto a small, single lane road.

"Which way?" Dean asked, glancing up at the lightening sky.

George pulled his phone out, thumbing it on and zooming in on the map. He turned his phone, watching the direction arrow shift. "That way," he gestured with a nod. He stole a glance up as well, seeing the coloration beginning to spread across the tops of the trees. "We gotta move."

They started quickly down the road, their pace nearly at a jog.

Coal trotted alongside Simon who was walking briskly.

"How's he doing?" Bill asked, looking at Simon, who was between George and Dean, and to where he had fallen back and was now walking beside Gary.

Gary watched their son walking quickly ahead. "I don't know," he replied.

"He's strong," Bill replied. "He takes after his father."

"Which one?" Gary replied with a smile, trying to inject some lightheartedness into their situation.

"We'll be fine," Bill said, his smile fading. "We just have to get to that house. I doubt they're following us. They probably headed back to wherever it was they had come from, and they'll wait until tomorrow night to come back. We'll be long gone by then."

"How?" he asked. "We don't have a car."

"I don't know," he replied, his tone sharp. "We'll figure it out," he added. "That's what we've been doing this entire time, right?"

Gary pondered that for a moment, nodding. "Yeah. I guess so."

George pulled his eyes from the map in his hand, looking up the road. The structure, which looked like a house, or a cabin of some sort, was only a half-mile away. His directions had gotten them within jogging distance of it, which was good, because as he looked up the road, he heard a distant trill rise into the air.

"We gotta move!" Dean shouted as the sound of the bugs rising in the distance flooded panic through his nerves.

As he shouted, a gunshot cracked from behind. The bullet whistled past his ear.

George spun, firing off three shots and watching as two men ducked back into the trees. "Run!" he shouted, the pistol leveled at the space the men had emerged from.

Another series of trills sounded out, the gunshots likely telling every bug in a five-mile radius exactly where they were.

Another of their pursuers leaned out, taking aim, and George fired two more shots, forcing the man back into cover. He turned, running after the others.

"Don't stop!" Dean shouted, seeing the small house fifty yards ahead.

The trilling sounds had grown. The gunshots had sounded out like a dinner bell, sending every alien insect in the surrounding hills in their direction. As they darted toward the house, another flurry of gunshots erupted. George spun, firing off three more rounds.

Two minutes later the group were crashing across the pebbled driveway toward the house. Behind them, the sun was just beginning to peek across the tops of the trees.

"To the back!" George shouted, spinning and sending another two bullets in the direction of the men who had ducked back into the trees. Overhead he could see a murmuring cloud of insects turn in their direction.

Dean spun around the edge of the house, rushing toward the back door. He reached out, his hand grasping the knob as his shoulder impacted against it. The knob held, and his shoulder cried out in pain. He leaned back slamming his shoulder against it once more. This time, the frame around the latch cracked, a small gap splintering apart. He gave it one more heavy impact, and the lock broke through the frame. The door swung open. "Inside!" he shouted as he stepped in.

A moment later, Simon burst through the door, Coal right on his heels. They were followed by Bill and then Gary. George had stopped and was firing around the corner at the approaching men. The seconds ticked by before he spun and bolted for the door.

Dean slammed the door shut as George stumbled in, nearly pitching forward.

Outside, the trilling had turned to a buzz and a swarm of the insects descended on the approaching men who were now running full speed at the house.

"Help me!" George shouted, rushing over and flipping a heavy dining table.

Dean made his way over and they hoisted the table up, carrying it to the door and propping it against it.

George moved to a heavy gas stove a few feet away and wrestled it from the wall. He got behind it and shoved with all his strength. It slid three feet and then stopped. He looked down at the gas hose connecting it. He could hear the approaching men shouting. They were almost at the house. He lifted his foot, bringing it down on the connecting hose. Two stomps later it broke free, a loud hissing filling the room. "Kill it!" he barked at Gary, shoving the stove toward the door.

Dean reached out, helping him maneuver the heavy object into position as Gary reached down and twisted the gas valve, stemming the flow.

As they shoved the stove into place, someone slammed into the door on the other side. The table and stove lurched forward, and Dean and George shoved it back into place.

Outside, a scream rose into the air, guttural and loud. A breath later another joined.

"Open the door!!" a panicked voice screamed as something slammed heavy again and again against the blocked door.

Another scream sounded out, the clicking buzz of insects now audible just outside.

Thuds sounded overhead as the giant bugs landed on the roof. Gary's gaze jerked up as a series of thuds sounded, moving in the direction of the back door. Coal began to bark.

"Let us in!!" the voice outside pleaded. It was followed by four gunshots that erupted through the door.

George yelped, barking in pain as he spun. His hand darted to the fiery pain in his shoulder.

The stove and table lurched inward again, and Bill darted forward, spinning as he dropped to the floor and slammed his back against the stove.

George collapsed to a seated position, eyes moving to the doorway. Coal hurried over, tail curled underneath him, ears flat. George groaned, leaning closer to the dog. "It's okay, buddy," he grunted. "It's okay."

There were another three heavy impacts with the door as another two screams rose up, followed by a series of gunshots. Then the door went still, and the screaming abruptly stopped.

"Get away from the windows," George grunted, looking over to where Gary had knelt. He was holding Simon tightly against him.

He nodded, scooting into the next room with his son.

Bill stayed pressed against the stove, Dean with his back against the wall a few feet away.

George edged his way into the space the stove had been and listened as dozens of the alien creatures skittered about outside, their clawed tarsi crunching against the loose gravel.

Heavy thuds sounded out above as more of the bugs landed on the roof.

One last thud impacted against the door, and then it fell silent.

The six of them sat there silently, listening as the insects searched the small house for a way in. The curtains had been drawn, so they weren't visible to the monsters hunting outside, but each of them knew that the bugs could smell them within, especially with George's shoulder bleeding from the gunshot wound.

They sat there in continued silence for the next three hours, while the bugs continued searching for a way in. George's shoulder was burning, and he could feel the onset of dizziness from shock. He forced himself to stay conscious, even going as far as to squeeze the wound when he felt sleep tugging him away. He scanned the interior of the house, grateful that whoever had left it had drawn the curtains. That was likely the only reason they were still alive. Had the bugs seen them through the windows, they would have broken through, and they would all have been killed. That single fact was the reason any of them were still drawing breath.

It was another two hours before the bugs finally gave up their attempts and made their way in search of a different meal. They wouldn't likely have to go very far, as the woods were abundant with all manner of deer and elk, wildcats and coyotes. It was that fact alone that kept a large population of the insects in the mountains. They would burrow into the ground at night and emerge to feed on wildlife in the day.

"Let me see," Gary said, edging his way to where George was seated.

George scooched sideways, wincing as he did.

"This is going to hurt," he said, grasping the collar of his shirt and pulling it away. There was a wound that started near the middle of his shoulder and ended with a slightly larger hole at his back.

It did hurt, and George grunted in pain.

Gary breathed a sigh, looking from the front to the back. "It went through," he said, letting the shirt go and leaning back. "But we're going to have to clean and dress it. And it's going to need stitches."

"I have a kit in my bag," George replied, shifting his weight. "Oh, shit..."

"That was too close," Dean said, still pressed against the wall. His wrists were resting on his knees, and his gaze was locked to the ceiling above.

"How did they find us?" Bill asked.

"They're probably local," George replied. "They probably know every back road and highway in the county."

"So, what are we going to do?" Bill asked. "We can't stay here. They're just going to come back when the sun goes down and finish what their friends started."

"I'm thinking," George replied, watching as Gary fished out the medical kit from his bag.

"Okay," Gary said, kneeling back in front of him. "I've never done this before."

George nodded. "Well. You didn't have to tell me that. I was hoping that you were going to tell me you were a surgeon before all this."

He chuckled nervously. "Sorry," he replied. "I was in marketing." He paused. "If you want to create an ad campaign and a really cool story to go along with that," he said, gesturing to the bleeding wound with a nod. "I'm your guy."

"Great," George scoffed, taking a deep breath and sighing. "It's fine. I'll walk you through it," he replied.

"Simon," Bill said, yanking the boy's attention to him. "Why don't you go on into the other room. I'm sure the couch is a lot more comfortable than the floor."

"Is it safe?" the boy asked, his gaze moving to George.

George nodded. "Yeah. They're gone," he said. "Just. Keep the volume down."

Simon nodded, looking at Bill.

"Go on," Bill assured. "You don't need to see this."

Simon nodded, making his way into the other room.

"Go on, boy," George said, looking at Coal. "Go with Simon."

Coal whimpered lightly, but obeyed, following behind the boy.

"Alright," George said, dragging his gaze back to Gary. "Let's get this over with."

Gary spent the next twenty minutes cleaning, stitching and dressing the wound. With no local or topical anesthetic, it was nothing more than stiff whiskey and pained grunts that got George through the procedure. When they were done, Gary and a freshly bandaged George made their way to the living room.

"Thirty minutes," Dean said a short time later, answering the question Gary had asked regarding how long it had taken them to reach the house from the truck.

"And you're sure you can get us back there?"

George nodded. "Getting back will be easy," he replied. "Just gotta follow our tracks."

"And you're sure their cars are going to be there?"

George nodded. I didn't hear them drive away. I think they're all dead out there. Or worse..."

"So," Dean said. "When do we leave?"

"I'd say we catch the tail end of daylight and use that as an advantage. We just need to get a working vehicle, and we can backtrack down the 5. We can cut across to the coastline and take the One up." He paused, his shoulder sparking in pain. "It's gonna add a half day to our journey, but that'll get us up and around the group. I think the extra drive's worth cutting out that risk."

"Why did they attack us?" Gary asked, the question bordering on rhetorical.

"That's just how the world is," George replied. "It was like that before. It's probably gonna get worse before it gets worse."

"That's comforting," Bill said, shaking his head.

"It's how it is."

"Okay," Gary said, looking at Simon. "We get back to the coast. What then?"

"Same as before," Dean replied. "Nothing's changed. Just the route." He paused. "But I think it would be best if we at least tried to get a few hours of sleep before we leave. We're all exhausted and need to be alert tomorrow."

The small house had two bedrooms. George took one, Gary forcing him to take the bed because of his injuries. The second bedroom had a bunk bed and Simon took the top, Gary taking the bottom. Bill fell asleep in a chair in the living room and Dean took the couch. Coal curled up at the foot of George's bed and was snoring just moments later.

The hours filtered by; one making way for two, and the second and third phasing into late afternoon. By the time the sun had begun to crest down the edge of the horizon, each of them had managed to pull in a

FINAL DAYS

few hours of much needed sleep.

-23-

Gary awoke with a start, flinching back at the sensation of someone looming over him.

"Hey," Bill said, pulling his hand back. "It's just me."

A short moment passed as wakefulness took hold.

"Time to go," Bill said.

Gary looked at him for a moment, reaching out and taking Bill's hand.

Bill leaned down and pulled him into a hug. "I love you."

"I love you too," Gary replied.

"Okay," Bill said, pulling back. "I'll get our things. You go get sleepyhead out of bed."

"I'm awake," came a tired voice from above.

"Okay," Bill said, a smile tugging at his cheeks as he looked up to where Simon was laying. "It's time to go."

In the living room, George was getting to his feet. He winced, grunting as the movement pulled at the wound through his shoulder.

"Here."

He turned to see Dean holding his hand out. "Tylenol," he said. "The good ones."

George took the pills and popped them into his mouth, swallowing.

"You don't need water?"

George looked at him. "I stopped needing water twenty years ago."

Dean chuckled lightly, bending down and hoisting his pack up over his shoulder. "You going to be able to carry that?" he asked, gesturing toward George's pack with a nod.

George cocked his head to the side, sighing. "It's only the one shoulder."

Dean nodded. "Well. Let me know if you want me to take it for a while."

George smirked. "I'll manage. But thanks."

Bill stepped back into the room. A moment later, Gary and Simon followed.

"Morning," Dean said as they stepped in. "How'd you sleep?"

Gary shrugged and Simon smiled. "Okay."

"Good," Dean said, looking between them and then at the yellow light filtering in from around the curtains. "We ready?"

"Is it clear?" Bill asked.

Dean nodded. "I think so. I haven't heard anything for a while."

They made their way to the front door and Dean opened it, peering out. Lying a short distance away were two of the men from the night prior. One of them lay face up, hands splayed to the side. There was a large, sunken cavity where his stomach was, and the torn shirt and jacket were caked with dried blood. The man lying a few feet away was facedown, a thin, viscous fluid coating a large puncture wound in his back. Dean watched him for a moment, seeing the gentle rise and fall of his chest. "Shit," he muttered to himself as he shifted his gaze to the treetops above. The gradient pattern of coral-colored sky was pulling down on the skyline, and a twittering of birds making their way to their nests for the night drifted through the trees. "We're clear," he said, pulling his head back in and glancing at Simon and then Bill. "There's uh, two of the guys from last night."

Bill caught the intonation and nodded, looking over to Gary. He nodded in return, understanding.

Dean stepped out onto the small porch and crossed the space between the cabin and the paralyzed host. He stepped up, pulling his pistol and looking down. The man's face was turned to him. He saw a tear working its way to the corner of his eye, gravity pulling it down his cheek. He had heard from one of the surviving members of the underground, who prior to what they had referred to as the *invasion*, that the neurotoxin the alien creatures used to paralyze their hosts did nothing to sedate them and had no effect on pain receptors. In essence, once you were implanted, you were alive, feeling the growth of the larvae until the moment they fed their way out.

George stepped up, looking down at the man. There were tiny ripples of movement beneath the man's flesh. One of the small lumps twitched against the skin just below the man's neck. Another tear formed, falling to the dirt below.

Dean looked over to see Gary approaching with Simon. "Go on," he said, nodding toward the road. "You guys get a head start."

Gary nodded, putting his hand on Simon's shoulder. "Come on," he said, giving him a gentle nudge.

Simon looked down at the man as he passed.

When the pair were a few dozen paces away, Dean looked down. Another tear fell down a paralyzed cheek. "All you had to do was let us go," he said. "But you didn't deserve this. I'm sorry." He brought the pistol out and pointed it at the side of the man's head. It lingered there for a moment before he pulled back on the trigger, sending the contents of the man's skull splashing out across the gravel.

The three of them stood there, watching as the movement beneath the man's skin slowed to a stop. Then they turned and started down the road.

George was right, and it taken them less than thirty minutes to make their way back to where they had left the truck. Just behind it were the two vehicles the others had arrived in. They spent a short while transferring as much of the truck's contents into the trunk of the car hurrying in what little time they had. Ten minutes later they were back on the road and making their way back in the direction of the main highway.

By the time they pulled out onto the asphalt, George's shoulder was throbbing badly.

The group dropped south and drove another twenty minutes until they reached the road that would eventually connect them with the Pacific Coast Highway. From there it was a straight shot up the coast. By midnight they were already working their way north.

"I woke up," Dean said, watching the headlight illuminated lines moving past. "I was still upside down. Just. Hanging there in my seatbelt."

The clouded sky overhead filtered moonlight across the quiet ocean to their left. The group had made their way from the 5 freeway to Highway 1 and had been working their way up for the last half an hour. Simon sat between Bill and Gary, immersed in his game, the dim lighting illuminating the back seat. George sat in the front, watching the ocean waves rolling past as Dean spoke. For the first time since it had happened, he was telling the story of the moment it had all begun.

"I couldn't feel my left arm," he continued. "The seatbelt had cut off all the circulation." He took a deep breath, exhaling heavily. "When I did finally manage to get it free, I fell to the roof. I think I might have passed out again. I had hit my head pretty hard when our car got hit." He remembered back to crawling out and seeing the panicked chaos. "Those things had drug my son away." His brow furrowed as he swallowed hard. "There was nothing I could do. I watched one of those things drag him screaming from the car. I couldn't do anything." He winced. "Just. Fucking helpless."

A somber moment of silence filled the car.

Dean exhaled in a sigh, his brow knitting together. "I think I made my way back to our house. Eventually. I just remember not being able to believe what I was seeing. It was like being in a movie. People were running and screaming. There were cars crashed and burning. Smoke. And the bugs." He scoffed lightly. "The fucking bugs..." Another beat passed. "It took me almost an hour to get home. I remember. I just kept trying my wife on the phone, over and over. It just kept ringing and ringing and then going to voicemail. I could only imagine how things were at the hospital." Another few moments went by in silence. "I waited until that night for her to come home. Then I made my way there." He paused. "I think it was like, day two or three that people started to realize the bugs only came out in the daytime. I remember not caring. I had already lost my son. I'd watched..." He choked back a sob, Gabe's pleading face flashing past, warped with a fear he'd never seen it wear. "I found my wife. Anna. There." His gaze dropped to the vehicle emblem on the steering wheel for a moment, a barrage of emotions constricting his chest. "She'd, uh..." He cleared his throat, sniffling. His hand came up, wiping the moisture that had formed in his nostrils. "Whoo," he sighed.

"It's okay," George said, nodding softly. "You don't need—"

"No," Dean interrupted. "No. I do." He fell silent for another few moments. "She'd been uh. What did they start calling it? Before everything collapsed? *Phoresied* or something like that. When an insect uses another creature as a host for its young." He paused again, trying to remember the right word the scientists had used. "I remember just standing there. All the noise and screaming and codes being shouted over the intercom just fading away. I stood there, I don't know how long, just looking down at my wife who was lying there on that stretcher. I watched those things crawling around, moving under her skin. It was the second time in two days I had felt that helpless." His eyebrows drew together. "Useless. Just. Absolutely helpless." He shook his head, taking a deep breath and exhaling through slightly puffed cheeks. "I stayed there with her, holding her hand, until the end. Then I watched those fucking things claw their way out."

The car stayed silent, the sounds of the road passing beneath the only thing heard.

"I don't know if it's going to be safe, up north," Dean continued. "But at least I won't be in that goddamned city anymore. Every single thing. Every store, every restaurant, even that goddamned Hollywood sign was a reminder of everything I've lost." He paused for a moment, smirking. "There were so many times that I just sat there, pistol in my hand." He scoffed. "So many times..." A long moment passed. "Then I heard somebody saying they were headed to the subway in downtown. People had turned it into some, makeshift survival shelter and people were flocking there by the dozens. I figured I'd give it a shot. And my wife would have kicked my ass if I'd have taken the easy way out. *The coward's way*, like she used to call it." He nodded, drumming his fingers on the steering wheel for a moment. "That's how I ended up in the underground. And now I'm here."

"I'm sorry," George said, looking across at the man driving stoically.

Dean smirked again, glancing in the rearview mirror at Simon for a moment. "Now I'm doing what I can to ensure no one else has to go through what I did."

This brought a smile to Gary's face, and he reached out, placing his hand on Simon's leg.

"So," Dean asked after a moment, sniffling lightly as the painful memories gently dissipated back to that dark space in which they resided. "What's the story with Coal?"

George smiled.

"Was he yours before all this?"

A small pileup drew closer, and Dean slowed their car as they passed. As they did, George looked out the window, peering at the desiccated corpse of an older woman in the driver's seat of a crumpled sedan. "Yeah," he said, seeing another body lying a dozen feet away, clothing weather beaten and tattered, hanging in strips. Most of the flesh had been torn away, likely eaten by scavengers over the past months. "I've had that guy since he was a baby." He chuckled. "Got him from the shelter, right after his eyes had just opened." He smiled again at the thought. "Lucky, the dog I'd had before Coal had passed a few years prior to getting him. I'd thought it was time to fill the hole he'd left. That's when this guy came into my life." He smiled again. "I just remember walking into the shelter, no expectations. And then I see this little black puppy lying there on the concrete. And it looks up at me with these big black eyes and I see that tiny tail thump twice against the cement." His smile grew. "He came home with me that day. He's been my best friend ever since."

"He's really well behaved," Gary said from the back. Looking down at Coal, who was curled up between Bill's feet.

"You could thank my sister for that. Murietta owned one of those, K-9 training and boarding kennels in Jersey. She used to watch him when I'd take on side jobs for spare cash." He shook his head at the memory. "I did private security after I retired from the military. Paid well enough. And you know what they say. Nothing brings death faster than retirement."

"You were in the military?" Bill asked, piquing up. "My uncle was in the Marines."

"I'm sorry to hear that," George replied with a grin.

A moment passed.

"I was Army. Seventeen years."

"How was that?" Bill asked.

George scoffed. "Worst seventeen years of my life."

"Oh," Bill replied unexpectantly.

"It's a different military now than it was when I joined. Before, they'd drop you out of a helicopter thirty klicks into enemy territory. You'd make your way to your objective. Complete the mission and hike your ass back out for extraction. Now. Well. Before this. They'd just send in a strike drone." He paused. "It took all the magic out of it." He paused. "In the end it was a lot of *hurry up and wait*." He sighed. "But hey. At least I got to enjoy a few years of retirement before the world went to shit."

"Bill's father refused to retire," Gary said, shooting Bill a glance. "Same reason. He said, if I stop working, I'm just going to wither away and die. *Ain't no sense sitting around waiting for the good Lord to take me away.*"

"Sounds like a smart man," George said.

"He was," Bill replied, a soft sadness in his tone.

"Oh," George said, catching the tone. "Before or after?"

"Before," Bill replied. "My mom too. Three years ago, next month." He took a moment, remembering the smiles on their faces and the better of the memories. "Drunk driver sideswiped their car doing eighty through an intersection. They never saw it coming."

Gary reached over, placing a hand on his shoulder.

"But at least they didn't have to see this."

"That's a good way of looking at it," George replied. "My dad passed away when I was just a kid. He was military, like me. I'm pretty sure that was the reason I joined. My mom passed eight years ago. Lucky for the bugs, because she probably could have taken them all out, single handedly, with a rolling pin in one hand and a chancla in the other." He chuckled to himself. "She was a strong woman. All the fire of Quetzalcoatl in that one."

Gary's gaze drifted out the window to the passing waves. His mother had been suffering from Dementia for the past six years prior to the invasion. She had been living in an assisted living facility in San Diego. She had been there when the bugs had first arrived, and he had been left to only be able to assume the worst. There was no way he would have been able to check on her, and even if he could, she wasn't capable of taking care of herself. And in a world filled with alien creatures... He pushed the thought away, exhaling softly, when Bill's hand grasped his and squeezed. He wrenched his gaze from the window and shifted it to meet his husband's. Bill smiled softly. Gary nodded gently in reply.

Gary cleared his throat, bringing his hand up to wipe the tears from his eye. "So. What are we going to do when we get to Alaska?"

"The way I figure," George replied. "First thing, we should see if our theory holds true. We need to make sure it isn't the same up there as it is down here. If it is, I say we keep going north."

"Past Alaska?" Bill asked. "What's above Alaska? The Antarctic?"

"If it isn't," George continued, ignoring the question. "I suppose we introduce ourselves and see if we can't integrate. I'm sure we all have some strength or occupation we could bring to the table."

"And what if it's more people like the men from the roadblock?" Gary asked.

"I've been putting a lot of thought into that," George replied. "Alaska's a big state. I'm sure we'll find somewhere to call home."

Gary shot a concerned glance at Bill, who offered a slight shrug in response. They didn't exactly have a better option, and like George had said, they would have to cross that bridge when they got to it.

The car fell silent once more, and Gary shifted his gaze back to the window. Bill went back to reading from a small paperback; a science fiction story about a post-apocalyptic group of survivors living in a society above the clouds, and the group of Hell Divers that scavenged the radiated surface in search of supplies. Simon continued unphased by the adult's conversation, console in hand.

They drove another thirty minutes before Dean took his foot off the gas and the car slowed to a stop. A massive wreck was blocking both lanes of the highway, cars piled all the way up the slope of the embankment, and over the railing into the ocean fifty feet below on the opposite side.

"Well," Dean hissed. "Damn."

"Give me a minute," George said, pulling his phone out and thumbing it open. Wincing as the motion sent pain shooting out through his shoulder.

Dean looked at the burned wreckage, wondering what it must have been like for those rotting in the crumpled vehicles. He assumed it was very similar to what he had experienced.

"If we go back a few miles," George said, pulling Dean's attention to him. "There's a small access road that goes up and around. It connects a few miles further."

"Alright, Magellan," Dean replied. "Show us the way."

Dean turned the car around, making their way back to the road George had found. They traveled the next thirty minutes up and over the rise, dropping back down in a series of twists and turns to the highway. Dean turned left and pulled the vehicle out. For the next twenty minutes they drove in silence.

"Is everything okay?"

Dean smiled, glancing at George for a moment as he slowed the vehicle.

"Figured we could get out and stretch our legs for a bit," he said, pulling the car off onto the shoulder of the highway.

Just beyond was a long, sandy beach running for miles up the coast.

He pulled the car to a stop and put it in park, shutting the engine off. Then he leaned around to look at Simon. "Want to go get your feet wet?"

Simon looked at him for a moment. "The water's going to be cold."

"Oh, don't be a sissy," Dean said, reaching out and opening his door. "I'll race you there."

Simon smiled, nudging Gary to move.

"Okay," Gary smiled. "I'll get out of the way."

Gary stepped out of the car, looking in both directions out of habit. A moment later, Simon emerged, making his way quickly toward the edge of the road. Coal was right on his heels.

Gary sat there a short time later, his shoulder pressed against Bill's as the waves rolled in, breaking against the shore. There was a chill in the air and the breeze that ruffled through their hair, flipping it about, had a hint of what felt like fall in it. A little ways away, Simon was running barefoot in the sand, Coal jumping and chasing behind as they dodged the incoming waves. Dean sat a short distance down the beach, soda can in hand, watching the moon dance off the rolling waves.

"Here you go."

Gary twisted to see George walking up, two bottles in hand.

"Oh," Gary replied, reaching out.

George handed him one of the bottles and he turned the label to him.

"Can't sit at the beach and not drink a beer," George said, smiling as he handed one to Bill. He looked over to where Dean was seated. "Dean," he called out, grabbing the other's attention. "Quieres una cerveza?"

Dean smiled. "I'm good," he replied. "Gracias."

George smirked. "Suit yourself," he said, turning and making his way a short way down the beach before taking a seat in the sand. He lifted his bottle in a silent salute and brought it to his lips, taking a sip of the warm brew. He sat there, sipping his way through his beer and watching Simon and Coal chase each other at the edge of the water.

"I would actually recommend against mixing alcohol and painkillers," Gary called out, eliciting a backwards glance from George. "Not sure that's the best thing to be doing."

George looked at him, raising the bottle in toast. "I think we've got bigger things to worry about these days." He turned, taking another sip and letting his gaze rest on the moonlight dancing across the waves.

Gary shook his head. "Stubborn goat."

Bill smiled, lifting his own bottle to his lips.

"We should probably be getting on our way," Bill called out a good while later.

Simon and Coal had exerted the last reserves of their energy and were sitting near the edge of the water, both digging contentedly in the sand. George had lain down and was watching the stars flicker above. He slowly sat up, looking at his watch. Then he stood and started his way toward them, reaching down and brushing the sand from his pants.

Five minutes later they were back in the car and headed north.

-25-

It was almost five in the morning before their vehicle pulled into a small motel parking lot in Crescent City. They had pushed the limits of their travel, circling around and nearly making it back to the Oregon border. They had decided, after a much deliberated conversation, to settle on a cheap roadside motel, versus taking the time to locate and inspect any of the local homes. They were already starting to push it, with the tickle of light edging up the distant horizon.

The car pulled to a stop and they stepped out. "I'll check the office," George said, turning and making his way away. "Gonna need keys."

"We should unload," Dean said, eyeing the two rooms closest. "201 and 202," he called out.

George lifted a thumb in the air, not looking back.

Dean could feel fatigue already sapping his energy. He'd driven the entire night, only taking the short rest at the beach, and once more after to stretch his legs. All he wanted to do was get inside, tape the curtains closed, wet towel the base of the door and go to sleep in a comfortable bed. Maybe after that, when he eventually woke up, he'd take a long, hot shower. As he pondered that thought, he found himself praying that the hot water was still on.

Gary stepped out of the car, making his way to the trunk to gather their bags. He looked up as Bill approached. "Want to let Simon have his own room?"

Bill smiled, the innuendo warming him. "As much as I love that thought, I'm sore, exhausted and I smell like your aunt Theresa's hamper."

"That's oddly specific," Gary replied with a smirk.

Bill lifted his left arm, leaning his face to the side and pulling back with a look of disgust. "It's an oddly specific smell."

Gary smiled. "You can just tell me you're not in the mood."

Bill looked at him, the smile fading. "Yeah. Sorry."

"It's fine," Gary smiled, reaching out and grasping Bill's forearm. He held it, squeezing lightly as he looked into his eyes. "I love you, no matter what." He paused, pulling his hand back. "And I know you're good on your rain checks."

This brought a smile to Bill's lips.

"Oh," Gary said as Simon crept around behind Bill. "Here you go." He handed Simon his backpack.

"Which room is ours?" Simon asked, looking over to the row of doors.

"Um," Gary said, looking at the numbers. "202?"

"Oh," Simon replied, his words lingering on a question. Then he looked between the two of them. "Can I have my own room?"

Gary smiled, his gaze turning on Bill, who returned the smile, a gentle shake of his head accentuating the gesture.

"Are you sure?" Gary asked.

Simon nodded, his nose wrinkling. "Daddy Bill snores too loud."

Gary snorted, trying to stifle a laugh. It lasted just long enough to make eye contact with his husband. Then he broke into laughter.

"So do you," Bill remarked flatly. He leaned in. "And you fart while you sleep."

"I do not!" Simon burst. "Take that back."

Bill blew a loud raspberry, drawing the sound out. "Yep. Just like that. All night long."

Simon grunted, turning and making his way over to one of the doors.

Bill turned to Gary, reading the look in his eye. "I'm showering first." He paused, eying his husband up and down. "We're *both* showering first."

The smile on Gary's face widened.

"Everybody ready?"

Bill turned to see George walking up, keys in hand. "Where'd you find those?" he asked as George walked up. "Apparently, Simon doesn't want to sleep with his parents." He hesitated a breath before adding. "The common consensus is that I snore too loud."

George smiled. "Well, I'm glad he said it, not me."

Bill's jaw dropped with a scoff.

"In the office," George said with a smile. "Behind the desk on the left."

Bill shot them each a disapproving smirk and turned to make his way to the office.

Gary hoisted Bill's bag and carried it over to the room next to Simon's, setting it down and unslinging his own to the ground beside it. He turned to Simon. "You're sure about this?" he asked.

Simon nodded.

"Okay." He reached out, slipping the key in the lock and opening the door.

Every roadside motel room has a distinct odor: linens washed too many times in not enough detergent, those grimy spots housekeeping can never truly reach, old wallpaper and stale body odor. The smell that drifted out to greet Gary was exactly that. He eyed the room, reaching in and fumbling at the wall for the light switch for a moment. He found it and flipped the tiny plastic lever up. The single light in the ceiling illuminated, casting a dull glow through the room. "It's nice," he said, stepping in. "Quaint."

Simon made his way in, crossing the room to the single chair it seemed every roadside motel was obliged to have. He dropped his backpack on it and turned, climbing atop the bed.

"You're sure?" Gary asked one last time.

Simon smiled and gave another nod.

"Okay," Gary replied. "But the same rules apply. No staying up all night playing video games. And no volume."

"I know," he said, offering an exasperated look.

"Okay. It's my job to remind you." He turned, examining the room further. "Why don't I help you with the curtains," he said, flipping the door latch so that it wouldn't shut behind him. He made his way out to his pack and grabbed the roll of duct tape. Then he made his way back in the room and went to work taping the curtains to the wall. When he was finished he made his way back to the door. He turned to Simon. "What am I forgetting?"

Simon looked at him quizzically for a moment. Then he looked from the taped curtains back to the door. "Wet towel," he replied.

Gary nodded. "Okay. Maybe you do have this."

Now, if you get scared, or need anything, just tap very lightly on that wall," he said, pointing at the room he and Bill would be sharing.

Simon nodded, turning his game console on.

Gary smiled, watching the boy for a moment. Even at ten years old, he was still surprised nearly every day how well he and Bill had managed to raise him. He was light years smarter than he had been at his age, or at least that's what his paternal memory told him. As he closed the door to the room, he felt a warm sense of pride glowing in his chest.

"We're sure about this?"

Gary turned to see Bill standing there.

Gary pulled in a heavy breath, holding it for a moment and then releasing it in a gust.

Bill lifted his hand, dangling a key by the hotel logo keychain. He gave it a little shake and smiled.

Gary stepped toward him and he put his hand out, pushing him back a step. "Shower," he said, his eyebrows lifting.

Gary grunted, holding his gaze.

Dean had prepped his room, sealing the windows and wet-toweling the door, something they did to help mask their smell. Basements, which were the preferred location to lock in for the day were generally self-contained. First floor rooms and above, however. There were plenty of gaps in doors and windows to allow their scent to pass through. All it took was a single papercut on a book, or piece of broken glass, and every bug within a three mile radius would be drawn to them like moths to a flame. It had only taken a handful of times of that happening in the beginning to make door-toweling a commonplace survival technique. Some people even went as far as to carry sage and strong spices with them, which they rolled inside the towel, or blanket, or whatever object they had on hand. On more than one occasion, he had been reminded of a quote from a book he had read as a teen involving a man hitchhiking across the galaxy and the importance of never, ever, forgetting to bring a towel.

He lifted his wrist, checking his watch. Just after five. He calculated the amount of time it would take to shower and made his way to the bathroom.

As he was undressing, he heard the water flow shake the pipes in the wall. It appeared someone else had already beat him to the idea. He smiled, shaking his head as he stepped out of his underwear and allowed them to drop to the floor. He stood there, naked, looking at his skinny frame in the mirror. He was nearly thirty pounds lighter than he had been at the beginning. He was still lean and muscular, but the pudginess his gut and thighs had taken on was gone the years prior was now gone. He lifted his gaze to his face, turning it from side to side. The scruff growing out was almost an inch thick. He'd been chewing on his moustache the past few weeks, procrastinating shaving. He sighed, reaching out and kicking on the hot water. Then he made his way back to his bag and fished out his shaving kit.

By the time Dean stepped into the nearly scalding hot shower, a large pile of hair was clogging the bathroom sink, a scattering of hair on the floor around.

Dean had just fallen asleep when the sound of an engine caught his ear. He lay there for a moment, the distant rumble registering. Brow furrowing, he reached out, lifting his watch from the bedside table. He maneuvered it so that he could read the black dial. It read six forty-five. He held it there, watching the secondhand tick by as the vehicle engine grew louder. Then, in one fluid motion he had slipped the watch on his hand, brought himself to his feet and was slipping into his pants.

The engine sound drew closer. He could tell by the high revolutions that whoever it was, was coming fast. By the time he had slipped his shirt on and grabbed his rifle, the outside car was nearly at the motel.

He tensed, his fingers grazing the edge of the duct tape as he listened to the vehicle approach. Then, as quickly as it had arrived, the engine roared past, continuing down the road. Two blinks later he heard the clicking screeches as a swarm of insects trilled past, following after the racing car.

He stood there, listening as what had to have been dozens of the creatures flew past. A buzzing swarm sounded, trailing off only after a very long minute. Then the road fell silent again.

Dean pulled his fingers away from the duct tape, standing there for a moment, listening. Another five minutes passed before he set the rifle back against the doorframe and made his way back to bed. This time though, he didn't bother undressing.

Dean stepped out of the room, glancing over to see Bill stepping out, pack already slung across his shoulder. "Morning."

Bill looked out at the fading twilight. "Do you think we're ever going to adjust that colloquialism?" He paused for a moment, a puzzled glance working his eyes. "You shaved?"

Dean nodded.

"Looks nice," Bill added.

"Thanks," Dean replied. And to answer your question. I doubt it." His gaze drifted out over the coastline a short way away. "Morning implies waking. Night implies sleep. I don't think the expressions correlate to a time of day. Just an expression."

Gary made his way out, hair still wet from another shower he had snuck in early. "Morning," he said, stepping out. He paused. 'You shaved."

"Yep," Dean said, his eyebrows lifting.

"Hmph," Gary replied, not offering anything further.

Dean looked at Bill and smiled, his eyebrows lifting.

Bill smirked agreeingly.

"Is Simon up?" Gary asked.

Bill shrugged, making his way to the next door and tapping lightly. He looked back at Gary. "Probably up all night playing his video games."

No sooner than the sentence had punctuated than the door opened and Simon stepped out, pack on his shoulders and ready to go.

Bill gave him a puzzled look.

"Morning," Simon said, offering him the same expression.

"Huh," Bill smirked as Simon stepped past.

George was the last to make his way out, Coal just on his heels. "We ready?"

They nodded and spent the next few minutes loading their packs into the trunk. Three minutes later they were back on the road driving north.

"How are you doing?" Bill asked.

George moved his shoulder, wincing. "I'll live. The pills are helping."

The last of the daylight was fading away as they traced the coastline up, the shifting corals and pinks making way for a light misting of peach, followed by the azure and eventually the dark denim night. The sky was cloudless, the sliver of a moon just visible at the edge of the eastern sky. Beyond, a dazzling array of stars sat motionless across.

"You think we're ever going to come back from this?" Gary asked, breaking a long spell of silence. "People?"

Another long moment passed in quiet contemplation.

"We'll survive," Dean said after a moment. "But back to the way things were. I find that hard to believe." He paused, eyes watching the lines on the road drift past. "Unless we find a way to eradicate the insects. I don't think we will."

"We will," George countered, allowing another silent moment to pass as he contemplated his words. "We've suffered catastrophic losses before and survived. As a species. You all know I'm not an incredibly religious man. Especially not now. But even the Bible has the story of the great flood. It's a story of perseverance. I believe humanity was around during the time of dinosaurs. Maybe not in the iteration we are now, but in some form. That means we survived the asteroid that wiped nearly all life off the planet. We survived the Spanish Flu, the Plague." He scoffed. "The Spanish conquistadores nearly eradicated my ancestors. And they nearly succeeded. An entire culture was wiped from the face of the earth. And I find it hard to believe it was the first." He paused again. "Did you know that the slaughter of my people was so great that it can be traced by the carbon print it left?" He shook his head. "But, here I am."

A long moment of quiet filled the car.

"I think that some species won't make it. Too much has been altered. The butterfly has already flapped its wings." He pondered that statement for a breath. "But most will. We will. We're like cockroaches."

"That's romantic," Gary remarked flatly.

"It's true," George replied.

"I don't think we lived alongside the dinosaurs," Bill said after a moment. "We hadn't evolved yet."

"There's scientific evidence of our existence pre-dating the ice age," George rebutted. "There are hieroglyphics and carvings depicting us alongside stegosaurus and brontosaurus. We have saber tooth cat paintings on cave walls." He glanced back at Bill. "Don't tell me you believe those just popped up a few thousand years ago. What about that underwater cave in France? Or the megaliths?"

Bill pondered the thought quietly.

"I think we were here before dinosaurs," Dean said, breaking the stillness. "There is proof of long lost civilizations. Stories like Atlantis, and evidence and findings that support the theory. Think about it. The Earth is always shifting, right? We have tectonic plates that are shifting and moving along the crust. Continents move over and under each other. Liquefaction and subfaction. That means that any evidence predating Pangea would be lost, buried beneath, Asia, Africa, the Americas. There could have been a vast, worldwide civilization matching even the one we have today. *Had*," he corrected. "We wouldn't have a clue." He paused for a breath. "You know what I think? I think we didn't come from here. I don't think we evolved at all. I think we come from out there," he said, pointing at the roof of the car. "I think we came here, probably after destroying whatever world it was that we were living on out there, and tried starting over. Maybe we did. Maybe we were successful. But I think that all of that was lost to time as the world shifted. It's still shifting and changing as we speak. And

I think that a tiny amount of that knowledge was kept, passed down through the ages. I think we did what humanity has always done, and broke into factions. Part of that became what we refer to as *cavemen*, and the rest became humanity as we know it now." He paused. "Think about it. Look at how fast our species has evolved. We went from rubbing sticks together to create fire, to sending people to space in what? A blink in our planet's existence. Hard to believe it was the first time."

The car fell silent.

"That is a very compelling belief," George said.

"So, then, no God? No higher power?"

Dean glanced at Bill in the rearview mirror. "I believe we *are* that higher power. We *are* the gods our ancient ancestors spoke of and worshiped. I believe they were simply paying homage to their ancestors. Find me a better explanation of the constant fascination with the stars and constellations, since the dawn of time."

Another moment passed.

"Boredom," George said flatly.

Dean looked over at him, a puzzled smile growing on his face.

George shrugged. "They couldn't hunt at night, couldn't farm, or gather. All there was to do was sit there and look up at the ever-shifting sea of stars above. Now imagine it with zero light pollution. Imagine seeing a shooting star for the first time, or a meteor shower, and having no clue what it was... I can see how they thought there were gods. Or at least, other existence. Our species needs to believe there is purpose. I think we created a story for just that." A beat passed. "I think we'll come back from this. Just like we have always done. But I don't believe we will see it in our lifetime..."

"That's what scares me," Gary said, looking down at Simon.

"We'll be fine," Bill said. "We just need to get to where it's safe."

Gary held his tongue and buried the question that raged just behind his lips. What if it wasn't safe? What if there was nowhere that was safe? What then? How then, would they raise their son? And what kind of life would that give him?

The next long while went by unspoken. Each had fallen into their own pit of contemplation. It wasn't until an hour later that George broke the silence.

"Hey, slow up."

Dean took his foot off the pedal, allowing the car to coast. As it slowed, he saw a vehicle parked at an angle, the front half off the side of the road.

As they drew closer, he realized that it wasn't parked, it had crashed.

"It looks fresh," George said as they slowly approached.

"How can you tell?" Bill asked.

"No dust," George replied.

They approached slowly, Dean giving a wide berth to the wrecked vehicle, and two bodies lying visible in the dirt just outside.

The expensive sedan sat with its front end wrapped around a tree. The driver and passenger in the front were both dead, from what looked to have been the impact. By the damage, George guessed they had to have been going at least a hundred miles per hour. One of the corpses lying a few feet away was drained, the husk completely desiccated. The other lay a few feet beyond that, multiple lesions across the visible skin, where dozens of larvae had ripped their way free.

They drove slowly past.

"Do you think it's the car we heard last night?" Gary asked.

"Pretty sure," George replied, eyeing the riddled corpse as the last of the vehicle's headlights peeled away.

"I thought those things took longer than that to gestate," Dean said, his gaze narrowing.

"Might explain the accident," George responded, glancing from the dead woman to the vehicle and back. "Maybe they were trying to get her somewhere, and those things started coming out." He paused, glancing at Dean. "I could see how that could very easily cause an accident."

"Especially if they were doing over a hundred," Dean agreed.

Gary shared a silent exchange with Bill, and Coal whined quietly between their legs. Gary reached down and rubbed the dog's head. It quieted, laying its head back across its extended paws.

Three hours later they stopped again, taking up residence in an abandoned house in a small town called Crescent City.

They rested the night, shut tight in the house's secured basement. Gary had changed out the dressing on George's shoulder, replacing the homemade belt sling with a proper one gathered from a drugstore they had stopped at on the way in. They had stocked up on a large number of medications, including antibiotics that Gary had insisted George start taking straight away. The next night they made their way out and continued north.

The next seven hours drifted past, a blur of shadowed woods and filtered rays of moonlight peering through in cracked streams. The air had grown noticeably cooler, and the smell of forest and pine was nearly overwhelming. They had driven with their windows down for a portion of the evening, only rolling them up in the early hours. Now, with dawn just a short time away, their thoughts had shifted to shelter.

"There's a couple small towns coming up," George said, grunting as he instinctively reached to slide his thumb across his phone. He repositioned it to work it one-handed. "Looks like Warrenton, Union Town or Astoria." He looked at the map, trying to zoom in with his thumb and forefinger. Frustrated, he set it down in his lap, pressing the button on the side to turn the screen off. "We could stay at either."

"Which is the closest?" Bill asked.

Bill had taken over driving a few hours prior, George's rotation being skipped on account of his shoulder. Though, he's stubbornly tried to argue the fact it only took one hand to drive. They had all decided it was best if he focused on healing and put as little strain on his shoulder as possible.

"Warrenton," George replied.

"Warrenton it is then," Bill said. "Let's hope there's a working gas station. I'm still trying to get the taste of gasoline out of my mouth from the last time."

"But it worked," George said.

"And technically you can survive off of filtered urine," Bill replied. "But that doesn't mean I want to."

"Point taken," George replied, grunting softly as he adjusted his shoulder.

"How far?" Dean asked.

"About twenty minutes," George replied.

"I have to pee," Simon added.

"Me too," George said. "Think I've been holding it for the past hour and a half."

"You could have said something. I would have pulled over," Bill said, throwing him a glance.

"Eh," George remarked blankly. "We'll be there soon enough."

A little less than twenty minutes later they reached the outskirts of the small town. They made their way a few blocks in and decided to find a place to stay. They had enough gas that it wasn't an emergency, and with what seemed like a constant occurrence, dawn being on the horizon, they felt it best to spend their valuable time finding a comfortable place to stay, and worry about gas when they woke up.

Bill turned the car into a small residential neighborhood just off the main highway. They passed a small marina, where a handful of boats were still moored at the docks. As they passed, George noticed that three of them had sunk, only their main and mizzenmasts visible above the water. One lay off-kilter to its side, resting against the dock. Moonlight reflected off the still water.

"That one," Gary said, tapping Bill on the shoulder and pointing at a two story, Victorian house with rounded turrets at the front corners.

"Shopping?" Bill asked with a smile.

"You know I always liked Victorian," Gary replied, eyeing the house as they approached.

Bill pulled the car into the driveway and put it into park. For the next few moments, they stood there, watching the dark windows.

"Vámonos," George said after a moment, opening his door and stepping out.

The others followed suit, each stepping out and scanning the neighborhood around them.

"Bill..."

Bill turned to Gary, something about the tone in his voice prickling the hairs on his arms.

Gary nodded down the street at a house a short distance away.

"George," Bill said, nodding as inconspicuously as possible.

Six houses down the block, a single, dim light illuminated a window. It was no more than a sliver, and when the group turned to look, the curtain closed quickly, snuffing the light out.

"I saw it on the way in," George said. "I wouldn't be too worried about it. But, if it makes you feel safer, I'll string up a perimeter alarm once we get inside."

Gary nodded, looking at Bill and then him. "Please."

George smirked, glancing one last time at the dark house. "Well. Let's get settled in then."

The group pulled their bags from the trunk and made their way inside the house. After calling out and receiving no response, they located the basement and made their way down.

George spent the next short while, with Dean's help, setting up trigger warnings. He placed glassware at precarious angles along the windows, so that if any were opened, the glass would fall and shatter, alerting them to the breach. He placed a butterknife in the gap atop the front and back door, placing empty wine bottles atop both. If the door opened, they would know. He went through the house, ensuring all the windows were latched and then set up one last alarm on the basement door before making his way down for the night.

"I think one of our best memories," Gary said a short time later, answering a question Dean had asked regarding the moment that Gary and Bill knew they were going to be together for the long haul. "It was when we had just started seeing each other. We had met on an app, of course. And it was like, our third or fourth date. Anyways. We were at this swanky restaurant, again." He shot Bill a smirk.

"I'm guessing Bill didn't order wine this time?" Dean asked with a grin.

"No," Bill answered. "I only needed to learn that lesson once..."

"Anyways," Gary continued. "Bill and I were sitting at the table, and he points out that this guy keeps looking over at us. He's snickering and laughing with some girl he was with." He paused, sighing. "Flagstaff has always been pretty LGBTQ friendly, but there's always one." He smiled at Bill, who had a big grin on his face. "Needless to say, the guy who was doing the snickering, had hooked up with *my* ex two years prior. And his Grindr profile was still active..."

"Oh, shit," George said.

"Oh, shit, indeed," Gary said, lifting his glass of wine to his lips. "So, we enjoyed our dinner, even had dessert. And right as we were getting ready to leave, I found his old account." He smiled at Bill, then looked back between George and Dean. "I walked over to the table and asked, whatever his name was, I don't remember at this point, but *hey... you're whatever your name is, right? How's Toby doing..? He says you never called him back after that amazing night you two had. I think he misses you.*" The smile on his face spread wide. "The guy's face went just white..."

"And then he pulls out his phone and puts it in front of the girl's face," Bill adds, smiling at Gary.

"And then I put my phone in front of her face. *Wow*, I said. *That sure looks like your boyfriend.*" He gasped, bringing his fingers to his lips. "On Grindr..."

His smile spread ear to ear. "You should have seen the look on that..." He looked at Simon. "Cover your ears..."

Simon smirked, placing his console down and covering his ears.

"Bitches face," Gary continued, giving Simon the all clear thumbs up.

Simon uncovered his ears and went back to his game.

"That was the moment I knew I was going to spend the rest of my life with this man," Bill said, reaching out and placing his hand on his leg.

"And he still hasn't given up," Gary said, smiling.

"Wow," Dean said. "That's funny."

"I wonder how that guy's night ended," George said, lifting his glass and taking a sip.

"Not as good as Bill's," Gary said.

George pulled the glass away and chuckled.

Dean lifted his watch, glancing at the time. "I think I'm going to turn in."

"Yeah," George added. "I'm going to chase this wine with a Tylenol and then I'm right behind you."

Gary reached out, tapping Simon on the leg. "Time to get ready for bed."

Simon turned off his console and yawned, not realizing how tired he was until he had pulled his eyes away.

"Go brush your teeth," Bill added.

Simon groaned, getting up and making his way to his pack, where he pulled his toothbrush and paste out. He made his way to the small utility sink and brushed. Then he made his way to the small couch and curled up. A breath later, Coal climbed up and curled at his feet. It was only a short time later before the house was quiet, and the group was sleeping peacefully below.

-29-

Dean opened his eyes to the soft sound of snoring. He lay there, listening to the rhythmic grating for a moment as his eyes adjusted to the dark. He heard a sniffle, followed by the quiet rustling of clothes as one of his sleeping companions shifted where they lay. He lay there for the next few minutes, sleep gently releasing its hold. Then, he craned his neck to both sides and brought himself to a seated position. He had slept on the floor, his light sleeping bag the only padding against the cold concrete below. Before he even stood, he could feel the light bruising on his hip. The age old adage, *I'm too old for this shit*, ran through his head. Then, he did force himself up.

Dean climbed over George who had taken up his sleeping space a few feet away, and made his way to the stairs. He checked his watch. 6:45. Still too early to get going, but he was already awake, and knew that when he got back from going pee, there would be no way for him to fall back asleep. Especially not lying on that hard-ass floor. So, with that thought, he resolved himself to prepping his morning, which started with a quick trip to the upstairs bathroom, and then the kitchen.

When he had finished relieving himself, he made his way back downstairs. He crept over to the living room window and inched the thick drape back. It was still light outside, but a thin layer of fog hung in the air.

He worked his gaze to the house they had seen the light in earlier in the night. Only sealed curtains peered back. He stood there, feeling the day's warmth coming off the glass, and then let the curtain go, stepping quietly through the house to the kitchen.

The house, a two story Victorian, had to have been built in the early twenties. But as a testament to the craftsmanship of the day, not a single floorboard creaked. He smirked to himself as he crossed the wooden floor, impressed with how solid it felt beneath. He crossed the living room into the kitchen, navigating the dark. When there, he slid a track style door closed and made his way to the cupboards. Opening them one by one, he took a quick inventory of the useful goods contained within. There were jars of peaches and preserves, dozens of cans of food, most not yet swollen. He found an entire bushel of pasta and three bags of ground coffee. He pulled one out and made his way over to the coffee pot on the counter.

George awoke a short time later, bringing his hand up to check his watch. He lowered his arm and lay there for a moment. Someone was snoring loudly and he remembered back to the comment the boy had made the night prior. He smiled, shaking his head slightly and then brought himself to a seated position. His entire body hurt from sleeping on the solid floor. His sleeping bag was cold-weather rated, down to thirty-two, but as far as padding, not so much. He stretched his back, wincing as pain shot from his shoulder out, like a thousand tiny lightning bolts of fire. Then he brought himself to his feet and stood there, waiting for the searing in his shoulder to subside. He shifted his gaze to where Bill lay, his chest moving up and down, the chainsaw in his throat revving with each breath. Then a faint odor tickled at his nose. He sniffed, drawing in a deep breath and started toward the stairs.

Dean was seated at the dining room table, an old hardback novel folded out before him when George stepped into the room.

"Morning," he said, gesturing toward the counter with a nod. "Made coffee."

"Yeah," he replied. "Followed the smell up the stairs like Toucan Sam."

Dean chuckled. "Don't date yourself that far back, old man."

George smiled, walking over and opening two cupboards before finding the one containing the mugs. He closed the door and made his way over, filling his cup. He took a sip and turned, a gentle sigh escaping. "How's it look out there?"

"Bright," Dean replied, not taking his gaze off the page.

George scoffed, making his way to the table and taking a seat. "I think we're doing pretty good so far," he added, taking another sip.

Dean lifted his gaze, watching the steam waft out of the older man's mug. "All things considered," he said, eyes moving to the bandage on his shoulder. "I'd say we're making pretty good time. And other than that." He nodded to the bandage, eyebrows lifting to accentuate. "I'd say I agree."

George looked down at the wound, shifting his shoulder to test it. A stab of pain lanced through. "It's going to be tender for a while."

"You're lucky," Dean replied, locking eyes with him. "Four inches to the right..."

"I survived Iraq," George replied. "A handful of pot farmers sure as shit aren't going to take me out."

"I'd say they came pretty close," Dean replied, glancing again at the bandage.

The sound of footsteps pulled their attention to the doorway.

"Oh, my God," Gary said, stepping in. His eyes closed and he lifted his chin, sniffing the air. "Coffee..."

George smiled, lifting his cup and wafting his hand back and forth across the top.

Gary smiled, making his way to the cupboard and repeating the process George just had, pulling a mug out and filling it. "So. How'd you sleep?" he asked, leaning against the counter as he took a slow sip from his mug.

"You ever hear that story about the princess and the pea?" Dean replied. "Well. Imagine if the whole mattress was filled with them..."

Another grin tugged at Gary's lips as he pulled in another sip.

"I want to know how you can sleep without earplugs," George added. "Simon wasn't joking..."

Gary chuckled lightly. "Yeah. That took a little getting used to."

"A little?" George replied. "It's like sleeping next to a wood chipper."

This brought a laugh from Gary and Dean.

"Morning."

The three of them looked over to see Bill stepping into the room.

"Hey," George said, "Ears ringing?"

Bill shot him a puzzled glance.

"Coffee?" Gary asked.

"Please," Bill said, stepping in. "I don't think I got any sleep last night." He moved his hands to his hips and flexed, wincing as he did.

"Sounded like you did," George mumbled under his breath.

Bill glanced over his shoulder at him, shooting him a grumpy look.

George smiled back, raising his coffee mug in toast.

Bill reached up and started pulling open one of the cupboards.

"Here, Babe," Gary said, opening the one with the mugs in it and grabbing one for Bill.

"Thanks," Bill said, taking the mug and moving to fill his cup.

"So," Gary said, looking between them. "What's the plan for the day?"

"Avoid any unnecessary run-ins with militia rednecks and put as many miles between us as possible," Dean replied.

Gary smiled. "So, same thing we've been doing since we left."

George nodded. "Same thing we've been doing since we left."

Gary sighed, his gaze drifting around the room. "I love this house."

Bill reached out, brushing his arm lightly. "Well. Maybe we'll find one in Alaska."

"Ugh," Gary grunted. "Imagine..."

Simon was the last to make it upstairs. By the time he did, the sun was already lowering on the horizon. Bill and Gary had taken a tour of the house and George and Bill had spent a short time going over the map, plotting their best course. The drive would bring them across a short bridge from Astoria, past a place called Cape Disappointment, which had elicited a chuckled scoff from both of them. From there, they planned to cut across and make their way around Seattle. Both of them doubted they would be able to cut through. Jammed roads would likely send them miles out of their way, so they chose a route that circled down and around. From there it was a short shot up into Canada. They both figured Roads would be wide open after that, and they would be to Alaska in a few short days.

"We all packed up?" Bill asked, watching as Simon stepped into the room, pack slung across his shoulders and Coal standing beside, tail wagging.

George looked over at the dog, smiling. "Traitor…"

Coal's tail wagged even more.

"I think it's safe to hit the road," Dean said. "I think we could have left an hour ago to be honest."

"Better safe than sorry," Gary replied.

"Fair enough."

They made their way outside and piled their packs into the trunk. Two minutes later they were pulling out onto the main road that would lead them through Astoria.

"This is a long bridge," Simon said, looking out at the ocean on his left and the vast inlet on his right.

"Yes, it is," Bill replied. "You remember when we walked across the Golden State Bridge in San Francisco?"

"Yeah," Simon replied. "That was pretty scary."

"Scary?" Dean asked, looking back through the rearview. "Why was it scary?"

"Because," Gary replied, looking over at Bill. "Someone had let him watch a little *disaster movie* called San Andreas, and the entire time we were walking across, a certain little boy, who shall remain unnamed, kept staring at the ocean and waiting for a giant tsunami to come wipe us out."

"It was a good movie," Bill replied. "And it had the Rock…" There was a gentle innuendo in the addition.

"Maybe so," Gary replied. "But also, a little bad on the timing."

"How was I supposed to know," Bill replied.

"It was the main part of the trailer…?" Gary responded.

Bill smirked.

Dean smiled, glancing into the rearview mirror again. Then, movement caught his eye and the smile instantly faded. "Shit," he hissed.

George looked at him and then into the side mirror. "Just keep going," he said. "Nothing we can do about it now."

The bridge they were driving across was nearly five miles long. A straight, two-lane shot from one end to the other. Even if they did turn around, they would be blocked if the following vehicle pulled sideways.

George reached across his waist and pulled his revolver free, checking the cylinder out of habit. He rested it in his lap.

As they group continued forward, the car behind was joined by another. They pulled side by side and kept a safe distance behind.

"I don't have a good feeling about this," Dean said, watching the vehicles draw parallel.

"What are we going to do?" Gary asked, reaching across Simon and clasping Bill's hand.

"Just keep going," George replied, still watching the pursuing vehicles in the side mirror.

"Oh, great," Dean sighed.

George shifted his gaze out the windshield. A mile away, vehicles were pulled across the bridge, completely blocking any exit onto the intersecting highway just beyond.

"Just keep cool," George said. "We still don't know what they want. Could just be a checkpoint."

As they drew nearer, four men stepped out from behind the vehicles, rifles held across their chest. One of them stepped forward, holding a hand up, signaling them to stop.

Dean slowed the car to a stop, his foot on the break.

The man in front studied them for a moment, eying the car. George could see three of the men behind exchange a quick conversation. Then the man in the lead started forward.

Dean rolled down the window as the man approached.

"Remember what I said," George said. "Just keep cool."

The man approached, leaning down and scanning each of their faces individually. He hesitated on Simon for a moment. Then his gaze shifted to the gear shifter and back to Dean. "You mind putting it into park for me?"

Dean glanced in the rearview, watching as the other two vehicles pulled to a stop, blocking any chance of escape. He exhaled slowly and put the car into park.

The man studied him a moment longer, glancing at the pistol in George's hand. "Where are you all headed?"

"North," Dean replied, doing his best to keep his composure relaxed.

The man smirked, eyeing the pistol in George's lap once more. "You mind doing me a favor?" he asked. "That pistol isn't exactly evoking a sense of trust. Mind putting that up on the dash for me? Nice and slow like?"

George held the man's gaze for a moment and then smirked, nodding. "Sure," he said, taking his time to lift it up and set it on the dash.

"Alright," the man said. "That's a little better. Guns make me nervous." He paused, glancing into the back. "Where are you all coming from?"

"L.A." Dean replied.

The man nodded again, glancing through the car.

"We're just making our way north," George said, drawing the man's attention to him. "That's all. We aren't looking for any trouble, and we don't have anything worth value. Just our packs in the trunk."

"Oh," the man said, leaning back and looking the vehicle over from one end to the other.

At the same time, two of the men near the blockade brought their rifles up slightly. "I'd say, on the contrary." He stepped back, leaning down and peering across Dean at George. He lifted one hand waving the men closer.

George glanced forward, watching as two of the men started toward them, rifles now at their shoulders.

When George looked back, the man was holding his gaze. There was fire behind the man's eyes. "See. That's my brother-in-law's car you all are in. And I don't see him in there with you." A beat passed. "Or Reggie, or Carl." His gaze drifted between George and Dean.

The other men stopped just in front of the car, weapons raised.

"Matter of fact, we're missing two other men from checkpoint Five as well." He sniffed, clearing his throat as he glanced back at Gary, Simon and Bill. "You wouldn't happen to know anything about that would you?" His face tightened.

George stared at him, waiting for his gaze to return. When it did, he spoke, choosing his words very carefully. "We found this car on a back road just over the border between Washington and Oregon. We'd been taking the 5 up, but our truck threw a rod. We found this car parked near two others. We just assumed it was abandoned, like everything else." He paused, gauging the man's reaction, which was non-existent. "Look. If this vehicle has sentimental value to you, we'll gladly get out and continue on foot. There are plenty more cars to choose from."

The man stared at him, his gaze drifting to Dean. His head slowly began to nod. "Yeah," he said, gaze slithering back to George. "I think that's a good idea. How about you get out of the car. All of you. And nice and slow. My friends here have a heavy finger." He paused. "Leave that sidearm on the dash."

In that instant, George caught the phrasing. Law enforcement or military.

"Nice and slow," the man said, taking two steps back.

"What do we do?" Bill asked, trying not to move his lips.

"Do as he says," George said, reaching out slowly to open the door.

The five of them stepped out, standing where they emerged. Gary pulled Simon close, wrapping his arms around the boy's chest. Coal climbed out stopping just beside Simon.

The man eyed Coal for a moment, some terrible decision being weighed behind his eyes.

"Sit, Boy," George said, glancing at Coal.

Coal released a soft whimper and dropped to his haunches.

The moment Coal's butt touched the ground, the man turned his gaze on George, fury now worn freely. "Where the fuck are my men!?" he shouted.

The others tensed, the men with rifles leveled at them inching forward.

"I don't—" George began, his words being cut off as a boot rose up, impacting directly into his crotch.

George doubled over, dropping to the ground as his legs buckled beneath him.

In a flash, Coal lunged forward, teeth bared in a snarl.

The man kicked out, his boot impacting into the dog's face, sending it dropping to the ground with a yelp.

The man reached down, pulling his pistol free from the holster at his waist.

"Coal!" George grunted in pain. "Go!"

Coal leapt up, rushing behind the man in the direction of the bridge's edge.

The man spun, firing off three shots that ricocheted off the concrete just inches past his rear paws.

Coal reached the edge and leapt, his paws touching the railing briefly before he took to the air. A moment later there was a splash.

The man turned his anger back to George, who was lying on the ground, tears coming from his eyes. He shifted to Dean. "I'm not going to ask you nicely," he said, lifting his pistol at his face.

"No!" Gary burst, putting his hands over Simon's eyes.

"They're dead," Dean burst. "They're dead."

The man stared at him.

"It wasn't us," Dean continued. "It was the bugs. They got them. The bugs."

The man held the pistol leveled at the space between Dean's eyes.

"We were just going north," Dean continued. "We came across their roadblock and got scared. We turned around and drove off. They shot at us. The truck we were in got hit. We made it a few miles up a back road before the engine gave out. We heard them coming and ran." He looked at the man. "We didn't know who they were. All we knew was that they had blocked the road, and had shot at us when we tried to leave. We've got a boy. We're just trying to survive." He paused again, glancing at George who was still cradling his crotch with both hands. "We ran through the woods. We made it to a house about a half an hour later. By then the sun was already coming up. Your men were killed following us. There was nothing we could do." He paused again. "That's the truth. I swear. We didn't kill those people. We never even spoke to them."

The man stared at him for a moment, his gaze lifting to the headlights now shining behind. "Is that true?" he said, raising his voice.

A response came back a moment later. "Yeah. But they're leaving out the part where they plowed into Laura's truck while trying to escape and sent part of a door panel through her side." There was a momentary pause. "She bled out in the middle of the road, Andy. I watched it happen."

The man's jaw jutted out as he lifted his gaze to the fading twilight. There was ice in it when it lowered back to Dean. "Is that true? Did you kill my sister?"

Dean stared at him, his mind racing to formulate the safest response.

"My sister!!!" the man screamed, cocking back and swinging out, the pistol in his hand impacting against the side of Dean's face.

Dean dropped to the ground. As his vision faded, he heard the sound of Gary screaming, and Bill's panicked shouting. Then his world went black.

One of the men that had been following them grabbed Gary from behind, wrapping his arm around his neck.

Gary tried to scream, but the sound was choked.

Bill moved to intervene, but felt the cold steel of a pistol press into his cheek.

"Don't fucking move!" a voice shouted, stopping him in his tracks.

"Somebody grab the kid," the man the other had called Andy said.

Gary let out a choked scream as another of the men approached, grabbing Simon by the arm and yanking him away.

"Please," Bill begged as he was shoved forward. "It was an accident. Please."

The main militia man leaned down, looking at George. "You should have gone south..."

George was grabbed under the arm and yanked to his feet. He looked to where two more men were lifting Dean up and dragging him by the arms toward the blockade.

"Dad!" Simon shouted, trying to yank free of the man's grasp.

"It's okay," Gary shouted. "It's okay."

The man holding Simon's arm jerked him forward, sending him staggering. He tripped, but the man swung him back to his feet by his bicep.

"Leave him alone you fucking asshole!" Gary barked, his voice cracking.

The man walking beside them swung his rifle out, the stock slamming full force into Gary's stomach. A sound escaped like a squeaking belch and he dropped forward.

"Stop!" Bill shouted, half to their captors and partially to Gary. "Please."

Dean felt the pain in his head even before he opened his eyes. There was a dull throbbing thump that drove like a nail into his skull with every beat of his heart. Slowly they opened, a solid blur making way for dim light and shapes. A handful of painful thumps later those blurred shapes formed into a group of men standing just a few feet away. Headlights bathed them from behind, casting them in dark silhouettes. He grunted, beginning the motion of putting his hand to his head, but as he lifted, he felt the constraints holding them both behind his back. He could feel the sharp plastic edge of a thick zip tie digging into his wrists.

"We were waiting for you," the man who had approached their vehicle said, looking down at him.

Dean looked up. He could feel the dry flaking line running down his cheek. Then he looked from his right to his left. Each of his companions were seated on the ground, hands bound behind their backs. Their binds were attached to a long running pole, and in that moment, he realized that eyelets had been screwed into a downed light pole and that they were all securely attached to it by their restraints. He shifted his gaze back to the man, the pounding in his head, which he was quite sure was a concussion, grew stronger.

"You let our friends die," the man sneered, staring down at him as a squint flashed through his eyes. "You killed my sister. And you left my men... Men with wives and children, to die." He clenched his jaw. "A year we have survived those fucking things. For over a year we have survived. And in a blink, you fucks come along and wipe out six of our best men, and my sister..." He stared at him, his gaze narrowing. "Now we're going to return the favor." The man drew a deep breath, exhaling slowly as he shifted his gaze between them. Then he leaned down, grasping Dean's face in his rough grasp and leaning in closely. "You're lucky I don't cut your fucking hearts out." He stared, squeezing to the point of drawing blood. Then, he shoved his face back and stood. "But I have a better idea though." He looked at one of his men and held his hand out, curling his fingers in. "Knife."

The man pulled his knife from its scabbard and walked over, handing it handle first to the man.

He turned, lowering down and placing the blade against Dean's throat.

"Please," Gary whimpered. He pressed his eyes closed.

The man held Dean's gaze for a moment and then shifted the blade to his shoulder, dropping it down and dragging it through his flesh.

Dean grunted in pain as the blade sliced through cloth and flesh.

The man stood, making his way over to George, who sat staring up at him defiantly. The man lowered his gaze to the dressing on his shoulder and then reached out, jamming his thumb into the healing wound.

George grit his teeth, trying not to cry out. Then the man shoved his thumb in the wound and the scream escaped.

"Stop it!!!" Gary roared, voice again cracking into a near falsetto.

The man pulled his thumb out, wiping it on the front of George's shirt and stood. "I want the last thing you see to be one of those things pumping you full of eggs." He let his gaze wash over each of them. "I hope every one of you dies that way. And I hope you're alive to feel them crawling beneath your skin before they tear their way out." He looked from Simon to Gary. "And I hope they kill the boy first, so each of you gets to watch. Maybe then you'll feel a little of what I felt."

"He's just a child. He didn't do anything." Gary whimpered.

Bill tried to reach out, twisting so he could clasp his hands, but the restraints kept him from doing so.

"My sister was a child," he said, staring down at him. "Thirteen." His gaze filled with ice. "Tell me how it feels."

Tears fell from Gary's eyes, rolling down his cheeks as he sobbed.

"All you had to do was stop," the man continued, turning his gaze back on Dean. "That was it. Just stop. Answer a few questions and all of you could have been on your fucking way." He scowled at him. "But instead, you killed my sister and four of my closest friends." He leaned forward, the knife held white-knuckled in his grasp. Every fiber of the man's being wanted to drag the sharpened steel across his throat. "They say they're like sharks," the man said, loosening up. "They can smell blood from miles away." He straightened, handing the knife back to the man, who wiped the blade on his pantleg before sheathing it. "I guess we'll see." The man lifted his wrist, eyeing a watch. Then he turned his gaze back to Dean. "I hope you die slow."

The man turned, walking back toward the parked blockade. The others turned to follow. After a short conversation, the men got into their vehicles and started north up the road Dean and the others had been planning to take. One vehicle remained behind, two men sitting inside. Headlights shined across the group as the man sat watching through the windshield.

"What's going to happen?" Gary blurted, punctuating the question with a sob.

"Shh," Bill consoled. "Baby. Sweetheart. I'm so sorry."

"Can you snap them?" Dean asked, glancing to George.

George looked at him, pain still flooding his eyes. Blood now flowed from the bandage. "No. Not with my shoulder like this. Fuck!" he barked, his breathing growing heavy.

FINAL DAYS

"What the hell are we going to do?" Dean asked, thoughts pummeling their way through his head like a thousand bulls in a China shop.

"We wait for those two to leave. Then we get the hell out of these and figure it out from there."

▬32▬

The next three hours passed with tepid slowness. The sky overhead shifted from black to denim with a gentle breath of pastel just at its edge, heralding the coming dawn. Eventually the men in the truck started the engine and pulled away, assumedly believing that even if the group did somehow manage to get free, there was not enough time for them to make their way back across the bridge, or to find any feasible shelter from the coming swarm.

Gary had nodded off at some point, his head slumped against his chest. Stress and fear had sapped all the energy he had had.

"Dean," George grunted, the pain in his shoulder flaring as he shifted to look down the line at the others.

Gary awoke with a start, jerking his hands and struggling against his restraints.

"Try and snap them," George said. "Turn your wrists in opposite directions and use the leverage to try and break the plastic.

Dean tried, but the plastic just cut into his wrists.

He looked over to where Gary, Simon and Bill were doing the same.

"Shit," he grunted as he felt the sharpened edge cut through his skin.

A moment later, Gary yanked his hand free, twisting the tie and pulling the other out.

"Oh, shit!" Dean barked, his face lighting up.

Gary held his hands out, folding his thumbs in. "Double jointed," he said, the faint whisper of a smile on his lips. His gaze lifted to the treetops behind him. "Oh, shit," he said, seeing the pale glow in the sky.

"Find something sharp," George blurted. "A sharp rock. A piece of glass. Anything!"

Gary spun, searching the immediate area frantically. There was nothing but gravel and loose forest detritus. He started toward the bridge, eyes scanning the ground in a panic. Then, a faint flicker of light caught his eye and he rushed over to see a bottle sticking out of the dirt. He bent down and yanked it free. "Yes!" he shouted, turning and holding the bottle up triumphantly.

"Perfect," George called out. "Break the bottom off of it and come cut these ties."

Gary brought the bottle down against the ground, but it just thunked off. He tried again but nothing. He was afraid of shattering it and the glass becoming unusable. Then he saw the bridge's guardrail. He stood making his way quickly over and turned the bottle in his hand, taking it by the neck. He swung out, smacking the bottom against the steel rail. There was a loud pop, and the bottom of the bottle shattered away. He was left with a jagged crown of glass in his hand.

Gary rushed back, starting first with Bill. In a flurry of movements, he cut the zip tie holding him to the steel cable running through the eyelets. Bill leaned in, kissing him. Gary spun him around and worked at the restraints. A moment later he was free.

Gary worked his way down the line, cutting Simon free next, then Bill and finally George.

As he was cutting through George's restraints, the sky overhead was quickly beginning to lighten. "I don't mean to rush you, but..."

Gary's hand slipped and he felt the sharp glass slide across his thumb, drawing a deep line through it. He jerked back. "Ow!" He held his hand up in a fist. "Shit!"

"Gary," George reiterated.

"I know!" Gary barked, turning his angered gaze on him.

"Okay," George replied, craning his neck to look at the sky behind them.

Gary turned his focus back on the restraint. His finger was freely pouring blood. A moment later the glass cut through the restraints and George nearly leapt to his feet. As he did, a low trilling sound rose up from the woods behind them.

"Fuck," George hissed, looking across the bridge to where the first strands of insects had begun to rise up, swirling and braiding their way into the sky before turning and starting in their direction. "We have to move!" he shouted, looking to the small pebble beach a short jog away. "Get to the water!"

George started forward, his shoulder crying out as he turned a jog into a run. The others followed behind.

The trilling screech grew louder, echoing clicks now audible through the dense thicket of trees behind.

"Run!" George shouted, putting on as much speed as he could conjure.

The murmur of insects fanned out, darkened spots drawing nearer. They were crossing the channel and had already targeted in on them.

By the time George reached the beach, the insects were nearly upon them. The buzzing trill of their wings filled their ears, and the hungered clicking were snaps and pops. George hoisted Simon up mid-stride and hefted him over his shoulder, crying out in pain as he did so. Ten steps later his feet were kicking against the pebbled stones on the shore. Ocean waves broke, lapping against the shoreline. "It's going to be cold," George shouted to Simon. "But when we get to the water, I need you to hold your breath for as long as you can. You understand?"

He didn't see Simon nodding, the boy's terrified gaze locked to the approaching swarm of insects making their way over the forest canopy three dozen yards behind.

George hit the water and stumbled, nearly dropping Simon as the waves crashed frigidly against his legs. Five steps later he was up to his waist.

Insects swarmed down at the group, talons reaching forward, venom dripping at the end of their two foot proboscis'.

George threw Simon from his shoulder, plunging him into the cold water as he dove forward. Behind him, Bill and Gary were charging down the shore.

Bill reached the water's edge and leapt forward, taking huge bounding strides toward the water. As he was diving forward, he caught a glimpse of Gary pitching forward. He had caught his foot on something and had tumbled to the rocks.

"Ga—" Bills shout was cut off as the first wave splashed against his face. He twisted, another wave shoving him forward as he struggled to get his feet under him. Then, as another wave was hitting from behind, he saw a blur of movement and heard a familiar sound over the insect buzz.

The first of the monsters hit the ground with a wet, crunching thud. Its claws tore furrows in the rocks, mandibles snapping, venom dripping in thin ropes.

Gary had felt the branch grasp at his ankle and had known he was going down. He'd tried to pitch forward, digging into his old gymnastics training as he tucked into a roll, but the hard stone beach impacted against his back and sent the air from his lungs. He rolled up, trying to get to his feet but staggered again. In that flash, the first of the bugs landed, its clawed tarsi shoving him to the ground.

Gary lurched to the side, avoiding the long, bony tube that jutted forward, again and again. Then, he heard a loud bark, and Coal seemed to materialize out of nowhere, grabbing one of the bug's hind legs and shaking it violently.

The insect turned its attention on the dog, and Gary broke free, scrambling backward and managing to get his feet underneath him as another twelve of the bugs dropped to the stony beach. He turned, darting toward the water as they quickly skittered after. He could hear their legs rushing across the rocks behind and when he was four leaps into the water, he dove, the cold a brutal shock that stole the breath from his lungs. He swam under the first wave and grasped at the rocks below.

On the beach, Coal tore at the creature's leg, the tiny bones snapping in his grasp. The bugs that had landed rushed toward him expectantly. He twisted, baring his fangs and preparing another attack, when a thin tube pierced the flesh of his hind quarters.

George had surfaced, watching in horror as a cluster of bugs surrounded his dog. Then he saw one lunge forward and heard Coal yelp. A moment later a dark shape swooping down from above, forced him to take a deep breath and plunge back beneath the surface.

The water was freezing, and he could feel his lungs begging for breath. His fingers were already numbing and in the short time he had been in the ocean, he was beginning to lose feeling in his hands and feet. They had come up, sporadically, taking quick breaths and scanning the shore, before plunging back under.

Hours had passed before George allowed the rolling waves to drag him to shore. His time in the water had numbed his limbs and had left him feeling almost hypothermic. At one point he had hoisted Simon atop him and held him in order for him to keep his face above water.

As he felt the gentle surge of waves, he heard a cough behind him. His gaze scanned the shoreline, lifting up to the canopy of trees beyond the road and out over the bridge. They sky was clear, the insects that had swarmed them hours prior, having made their way off in search of new food and hosts. He looked from right to left, searching for any sign of Coal, but the beach was empty, save for a small spattering of what looked to be blood. Any hope of a trail was lost to the loose gravel that lined the beach. Gravel crunched beneath him and he pushed himself to a seated position. Sloshing sounded behind him as Gary walked out of the surf, moving past to the pebbled beach to where he collapsed into a seated position.

"We need to... move," Bill said, teeth chattering.

The sun was overhead, the warm light melting away the frigid cold that permeated them.

"I saw an RV park just up the road," Dean said, shivering. He swallowed, wiping saltwater from his face.

"Okay. Yeah," George said, looking up and down the beach again. He had heard the yelp, and from the moment he had been forced beneath the waves, he couldn't get that sound out of his head. He wanted to stand and shout, to call and whistle. Then, as if falling in tune with his thoughts, a chattering voice spoke up from behind.

"Where's Coal?"

George looked over at Simon, who was also scanning the coastline in both directions.

"I think he ran off," Gary said, hands wrapped across his chest. "He's a smart dog." He stood there, water dripping from his saturated clothes. "I'm sure he got away."

George wasn't as sure. He'd heard the yelp, and with the bugs, that only meant one of two things.

"We've got to go," Dean said, placing a comforting hand on George's shoulder." He took a shivered breath. "We need to get out of the open."

George nodded, taking the extended hand and rising to his feet.

The group made their way back up the small embankment to the road. Dean was right. Just a few hundred yards up, was a small RV park.

Wet feet sloshed across pavement as the group made their way quickly to the park. When they were a few hundred feet away, a familiar droning buzz rose into the air.

"We've got to move," Dean said, stealing a glance behind him to see a swarm of the things rising into the air.

They put on the speed, numb legs carrying them as fast as they could. Gary stumbled and Dean caught him, hoisting him up and shoving him forward.

By the time they reached the RV park, the bugs were honing in on them, already swooping down from the sky.

Dean grabbed the door handle to the first RV. It was locked. He cursed, moving to the next. As his hand grasped the parallel handle, it clicked. "Here!" he shouted, yanking the door open and moving aside so that Bill and Simon could clamber in. Gary followed moments later, and George after him.

Dean climbed the two stairs and yanked the door closed. Seconds later they heard three of the things drop onto the roof.

Steps clattered, heavy skittering as the insects scrambled to find a way into the large, motorized home.

Gary and Bill made their way to the small kitchenette area and dropped to a seated position on the floor. They both had their arms huddled around Simon, who sat between them. George took a seat in the small hallway just beyond. Dean stood there, hand holding firm on the door handle. It was locked, but he wasn't taking any chances. He'd made sure to lean as far against the wall as possible, obscuring his view from the spanning windshield. More and more of the things landed atop the RV, thin tubes piercing the roof. Simon screamed as one plunged through, nearly skewering Dean's shoulder. He jerked away, heart hammering, as the tip withdrew, leaving behind a glistening smear of venom.

The bugs began to circle, their claws scraping and clicking, searching for a weakness. Shadows flickered past the windows, wings beating against the glass, leaving streaks of viscous fluid that oozed downward in slow, trembling lines.

"They're going to get in," Simon whimpered as another impact struck the door, lurching Dean back for a breath.

"No, sweetie," Gary lied, his own voice barely steady. "They can't get in." But his eyes darted to the windows, to the thin seams of the door, to the blood staining the sliced shirt at Dean's shoulder—a scent that could potentially draw more.

For twenty minutes, the attack continued. The bugs battered the RV, their claws gouging furrows in the metal, their proboscises stabbing again and again. The group huddled together, every muscle locked, every breath a prayer that the walls would hold.

Then, as suddenly as it began, the assault faded. The skittering receded, the shadows slipped away, and the only sound left was the ragged breathing of the survivors and the distant, inhuman clicks of the monsters as they moved on in search of easier prey.

George brought his hand up to his shoulder. His time in the cold water had stemmed the bleeding from where the asshole had shoved his thumb in. For that, he was at least grateful. Seeing food had sent the bugs into a frenzy, but if the smell of blood accompanied it, more would have arrived, and they would likely still be out there, scrambling to find a way in. And it was only a matter of time before one hit a window or the windshield and it gave way. He looked over to Dean and gestured to his shoulder with a nod. "How's your shoulder," he asked in a whisper.

Dean looked at the wound beneath his cut shirt. He smirked, looking back at the other. "Better than yours."

George let a silent gust of air escape in a short chuckle.

All five of them were still freezing. The interior of the RV was retaining a bit of the chill from the prior night but was beginning to warm with the sun. Gary had taken Simon's hands in his, blowing warm air in them and rubbing briskly until the skin shifted from the dull grey back to pink. They could hear the skittering of claws on the ground outside, and every so often, one of the things would land on the roof and skitter heavily from one end of the RV to the other, before flying away.

Another three hours passed, the sun edging its way across the sky, dragging its light and warmth with it. By the time it had moved out over the ocean, George and the others were nearly dry. Nearly. Outside, a handful of the creatures remained, occasionally probing at the side of the RV with their proboscis'.

"Why aren't they leaving?" Simon asked, listening as one of the creatures brushed against the side of the vehicle.

George looked at the boy, then his shoulder. "They smell the blood."

"But they went away when..." Simon couldn't bring himself to finish the sentence that would have ended with, *when they killed those men back at the cabin*.

"That's because they had food," George said. "There was a lot of blood, so the smell of mine got lost in the mix." His brow furrowed. "This is different. They know it's coming from in here."

"What are we going to do?" Bill asked, knowing there was really nothing they could.

"We just have to wait it out," George replied, his gaze moving to the windshield as a shape flashed past. "We should try and get some rest," he finished.

Gary scoffed, flinching as another insect landed atop the roof, probing it in a series of light thuds.

"You think it's safe?" Dean asked, looking over at George, who was seated in the driver's seat, legs stretched out to the side.

"I don't think we have much choice. We can't take the risk of being here when those pendejos come back to check." He pondered that thought for a moment. "I have a feeling it won't be long. They're probably waiting right now to come back and see what the bugs did."

"So, what do we do?" Gary whispered.

George and Dean both thought about it for a moment.

George brought his wrist up, checking his watch. It was just after five. "I think we're good," he said, wincing as he pulled his legs in. He brought himself to his feet, arching his back in a stretch.

"We should do this quickly," Dean said, stepping over to the door.

George nodded, looking out at three cars and a truck that were parked near the entrance office. "Let's give those a try first," he said.

Dean nodded, looking back at the others.

Gary had shaken Simon awake and Bill was just getting to his feet.

Dean looked back at them. "George and I will go try and find a car. You guys stay here. No sense all of us being out in the open. Just in case."

George glanced to where Simon was seated. He could see the worry wearing strong across the kid's face. He had the same, heavy worry buried within himself as well. Though they hadn't spoken about it, he hadn't stopped thinking about Coal from the moment they had stopped on the bridge. But standing there, looking down at the frightened boy, he could see that it may very well have been wearing far heavier on the youth than him.

George wrenched his eyes away, glancing at Dean as he reached out and opened the door to the RV. "Let's get this over with."

Dean stood there, waiting for the older man to finish scanning their surroundings. It had been at least two hours since the last of the bugs had lifted off in search of food or hosts elsewhere. But that also didn't mean they weren't in very close proximity. After a quiet moment, George pushed the door open and stepped out. "We'll be quick," Dean comforted as he stepped out, closing the door behind him.

The RV lot was large, with a long building at the back that looked as if it may have been a small motel at one point in time. Parked in front of it were a handful of vehicles. George was already halfway there and moving quickly as Dean pushed to catch up.

George approached the first vehicle, an older model sedan sitting on three inflated tires, one flat to the ground. He moved to the next, a smaller single bench seat pickup. The next down was an older, 80s model Land Rover. He eyed it, scanning the tires, windows and interior. He did a full walkaround, just like one would if considering the vehicle for a purchase. He even went as far as to kick one of the tires.

"I'll sell it to you for cheap," Dean said quietly from behind.

George glanced at him. "I think we found our ride."

He made his way to the driver's door and opened it. He looked around the interior for a moment, before sliding into the driver's seat. "The thing about older cars like this," he said, leaning down and looking at the steering column. "Not a lot of electronics." He reached over, flipping the glove compartment open and fished around. He grunted and then slid out, making his way to the back. He popped the back hatch and opened the small toolkit that was bolted to the side. With a slight grin, he reached in, coming back with a flathead screwdriver. "Bingo," he said, turning and making his way back to the front.

Inside, he popped the bottom of the steering column free and pulled the ignition wires out. Three snapping clicks later, the engine sputtered to life. He looked at Dean. "I'm gonna let her run for a minute. There's no telling how long she's been sitting here. By the time you get back to the trailer we should be ready to go."

Dean nodded, looking over the vehicle one last time with a smirk, and then turned, crossing the parking lot back to the RV.

Gary flinched as the door to the RV opened and light poured in.

"We have a car," Dean said. "George is letting the engine prime as we speak. We should be good to go."

"Did you look for Coal?" Simon asked, his eyes pleading.

Dean looked at him for a moment, his gaze shifting to both Gary and Bill. "No," he replied softly. "I'm sorry."

Simon held his gaze a moment longer, a single tear forming at the edge of his eye.

The sound of an engine approaching drew their attention.

"We should get going," Dean said, turning and stepping back out as George pulled the vehicle to a stop.

George sat in the driver's seat, watching the others file out of the RV. Dean opened the door and slid into the passenger's seat. A moment later, Gary got into the back, followed by Simon and then Bill. The last door closed and he put the old Rover into drive. He pushed down on the pedal and made it about ten feet before pulling it off and putting on the brake.

"What is it?" Bill asked.

George sat there, both hands on the steering wheel for a moment, and then dropped the vehicle into park, opening the door and stepping out. He looked out in the direction they had come from earlier that day. Then, he brought his fingers up to his mouth and let out a loud, piercing whistle. He chirped it twice and then stood listening. For the next few moments, he stood there, a deep sadness filling the empty space in his chest. He turned, sliding back into the driver's seat, anguish burning in him. Then he put the vehicle into drive and started away.

They had reached the edge of the driveway, when George slammed on the brakes, sending them all lurching forward.

"What!?" Gary burst, "What's happening?"

George shushed him loudly and the vehicle went quiet. He sat there, listening a moment longer and then leaned out the window, whistling again.

They all sat there, ears ringing from the quiet. Then a faint sound traveled past.

"I heard it!" Simon burst.

George dropped the vehicle into drive and started back down the road toward the bridge, almost chirping the tires as he did. A moment later he could hear the muffled sound of barking. He shoved the brake pedal to the floor, dropping the shifter into park, and jumped out. "Coal!" he shouted, throwing caution to the wind. "Come here, boy!"

He heard another bark and rushed to the edge of the road. A short distance down the embankment was another small culvert. He scrambled down and made his way over. Lying ten feet back, looking tired and scared, were two glittering eyes masked in matted fur. "It's okay, boy," he said, patting his leg. "Come on." George felt the rush of emotions, tears falling down his face as he looked into the two foot diameter pipe.

Coal made a whimpering sound and tried to scooch forward. George could see that his back legs weren't working, and he was trying to drag them. "Oh, no," he whimpered. He leaned in, crawling through the wet sludge. He grabbed Coal's front legs and inched back, pulling him with him. The dog whined as he did.

A very long two minutes later, George was making his way back up the embankment, Coal hanging in his arms.

"Coal!" he heard blast out inside the vehicle as Simon saw them approach.

Coal whimpered again, limp tail flapping against George's leg. It's okay, buddy. I'm right here. I got you."

Bill exited the vehicle and made his way over. As he did, he caught the dull matting of blood on Coal's haunches and saw the puncture wound. His eyes moved from the injury to George, who had another tear forming in his eye. The held each other's gazes, an entire conversation passing without word.

"Let's get him inside," George said, refusing to accept the second possibility.

Bill opened the back door and Gary leaned back, accepting Coal into his lap.

"I need you to keep him company," George said, looking to Simon, who was already holding Coal's head and was petting his softly. "Just give him comfort and tell him everything is going to be alright. Just. Tell him it's going to be okay."

Simon began speaking to the dog in a whisper, consoling him as best he could.

George's gaze moved to the limp tail, which ordinarily would have been thumping heavily. Then he made his way back to the driver's seat, scanning the sky once more before sliding in and closing the door. He stole one last glance at Coal resting with his head in the boy's lap, before putting the vehicle into drive and spinning the wheel. Moments later they were headed back north.

"You might want to put that to the floor," Dean said, his gaze moving to the sinking sun on the horizon. George nodded, stealing a glance himself before pressing his foot down.

Andy, the appointed leader of the New Visionary Militia, and self-appointed guardians of the Pacific Northwest, stepped out of the passenger's side of the large Four Runner as it rested to a stop. Three other doors opened behind him, two more vehicles coming to a stop behind as he closed the door and made his way ten feet before coming to a stop. The first thing he had noticed when his Lieutenant had pulled their vehicle to a stop, was the lack of bodies. The second was the lack of blood. As he stood there, anger swelling in his chest, his gaze shifted to the zip-ties that lay cut on the highway pavement.

Hawk, his lieutenant, came to a stop beside him. "Ah, shit," he grunted, readying himself for what was to come.

Ordinarily, Andy was a calm, level-headed fella. Hawk and the others had seen him get riled up a few times, and knew well, the molten fury that lay chambered beneath the laid-back demeanor.

The New Visionaries had formed in the first weeks after the initial attacks, a large group of men coming together to form what they believed would help secure a future for their families, and the families of any who may enter or pass through their territory. They had set up checkpoints, ensuring that they had a chance to inspect any vehicles that may enter into their territory carrying ill intent. In those first few weeks, they had turned away hundreds; looters, gang bangers, ill-mannered and disrespectful. They had even gone as far as to rescue and save a handful of women who were being held against their will by rapists and kidnappers. Those men had found themselves floating face down in the waters beneath the bridge. Their group had grown, and they now monitored every major road into Oregon and Washington. They were doing their best attempt to rebuild a society in the wake of the bugs' arrival. Andy's sister, Laura, had joined with them in monitoring the checkpoints just three weeks prior. And now, as Andy stared down at the cut ties in the road, his thoughts drifted to her. "That was them," he said, his tone uncomfortably calm.

Earlier that morning, they had heard a vehicle drive past the patrol station they had set up a few miles up the road to the north. They had just been preparing to return to properly dispose of the bodies of those responsible for Laura's death, and the death of six of their crew. Wives and children hadn't even had a chance to properly grieve, and now, due to a misjudgment, fueled by the desire for revenge, those very murderers had not only gotten away, but had well over a two hour head start.

Andy turned to Hawk, glancing at the men who had exited their vehicles and stood a short distance behind. "That was them," he repeated. He looked past Hawk to the others. "They're headed north," he called out. "They have about a two hour head start. But this is our territory. Our mountains. And nobody knows them better than we do. We're going to find them, and this time we're going to put a bullet in each one of them." He paused. "But save the old man. He dies slow."

The others watched intently.

"Well, let's go!" he shouted.

The others flinched, making their way back to their vehicles and piling in. Moments later, tires screeched across pavement and three engines roared north.

"I think it might be best to try and make our way back over to the 5," George said, glancing in the rearview mirror, sneaking a quick look at Coal who was sleeping with his head still in Simon's lap. A trickle of sadness touched his chest. "If... When they come looking for us, they already know the direction we're headed. We told them we were headed north. I doubt they're far behind."

"You really think they're going to chase after us?" Bill asked from the back.

"I would," George replied flatly.

"Yeah," Dean agreed. "Me too."

"Well, we still need to get through Seattle," Gary said. "I don't think we can make that trek on foot. Especially with Coal the way he is. We don't have a lot of options."

"Just keep it pegged," Dean said, looking at George, who nodded silently in response.

"Is he going to be okay?" Simon asked after a quiet moment.

"Who?" George said, knowing. "Coal?" He smiled, exhaling sharply. "Don't let his furry demeanor fool you," he replied. "He's a strong boy. And a fighter. It'll take a lot more than that to take him down." Though, for the last half a day, he'd already resigned himself silently to the fact that he had lost his best friend. "It's going to take a few days for the toxin to wear off and for him to be back up and on his feet. But you watch. He'll be back to normal in no time, running and jumping around." He smiled at the thought, relieved to have him back. "But we do have to get that wound cleaned. We can't afford to let it get infected. And I don't imagine he is going to like that much, so I might need your help. You think you could do that?"

Simon looked from Coal to Gary and then to George through the rearview mirror. He nodded. "Okay."

"Good. Then he's in the right hands."

Simon turned his attention back to Coal, gently rubbing the space between his ears.

"Look," Dean said, pulling his gaze from the downloaded map on his phone. "If we drop down and go west, we can cut up through Tacoma. I think we could curl out through Auburn and Berrydale. Take Highway 18 up and around to Highway 169. From there we can try taking the 405. If that's backed up, we can use surface streets. It might actually be smarter that way. If we're being followed, we just have to get above the city and right here," he pointed. "In Smokey Point, we can try to reconnect with the 5. Then it's a straight shot to Vancouver."

"And you think that will work?" George asked, glancing at the phone for a brief moment.

"It's better than trying to make it on foot, or getting stranded in the city," Dean replied. "Just one problem," Dean added. "My phone's at nine percent, and my charger was in my bag, which is now with those militia assholes."

"Anything in there?" George asked, gesturing toward the glove compartment with a nod.

Dean pressed the button, looking in the small compartment. "Negative," he replied.

"What about yours?" he asked, looking between Bill and Gary.

Bill shook his head. Mine's dead.

Gary offered an irritated look. "Mine died when we went swimming." He paused, looking across to Bill. "I don't think a charger's going to bring it back."

"I told you to go with Samsung," Bill replied, a strong *I told you so*, tone to his words.

"*I told you to go with Samsung*," Gary mocked.

"I did," Bill added for good measure.

"Well. You should probably use what battery you have left to get us to a sporting goods or surplus store. We should try to at least restock."

Dean nodded. "Got it." He opened his map and began searching. A few minutes later he had pinpointed a well-known sporting goods chain in a small town they would be passing through. He found a pen in the center console and wrote the directions, powering his phone off just in case they would need it later and didn't happen upon a charger. Then he slid it back in his pocket and let his gaze drift out the windshield to the ocean beyond.

Moonlight danced across the water as they drove up the coast, the air continuing to grow crisper the further they drove. George scanned the rearview and side mirrors every few minutes, expecting to see the distant glow of approaching headlights, but only darkness peered back. They followed the highway until their first cutoff and then followed that for nearly an hour, before reaching the sporting goods store.

They pulled into the parking lot and George killed the engine. He and Dean looked up at the large *Dale's Sporting Goods* sign hanging in big white letters above the entrance. "Alright," he said, glancing back at the others. "Let's go take a look." He turned in his seat, reaching back and petting Coal's face. "We'll be right back, buddy. You stay right here."

Coal lifted his head, whimpering slightly as he attempted to shift in the seat.

"It's okay, chico," he said. "We'll be right back."

The others stepped out. George looked into Coal's eyes a moment longer, before stepping out and joining the others.

"We should probably do this quick," Dean remarked, glancing at George.

George nodded. He doubted the others were very far behind. Even with having broken east, they had no idea how many of the militia guys there were, or how many vehicles they had. The one thing he was certain of was that they were actively being hunted. "Yeah," George replied. "I agree. Let's get what we can and get back on the road."

"That's if there's anything left," Bill said, nodding at the broken out front windows and scattered debris.

The first thing they noticed as they stepped into the large store was that it had been violently looted. Shelves and racks lay knocked over, glass counters shattered in and there were dropped items scattered from one end to the other. The passing four seasons had deposited all manner of woodland detritus throughout, and the moldy smell of damp earth filled the interior. Gary stepped over the broken remains of a cash register, and the shattered POS terminal it was attached to. The drawer had been pried open and all the contents were gone. A few feet away were two parts of a broken hammer.

They made their way further in. The clothing section had two racks still standing, with an assortment of outdoor apparel still hanging on rusting hangers. Mounds of dropped clothing lay scattered around.

"I'm gonna check the hunting section," George said, starting toward the back of the store. "Good idea," Dean said, remembering that neither of them had any firearms after they had been confiscated. None of them had anything other than their phones to use as weapons for that matter.

As they made their way further back, the damage seemed to lessen. It appeared as if the majority of the looting had been in the front of the store, with the back only having been scavenged. Shoes were still on the racks, boxes under the counter., racks still had fishing poles and tackle hanging from the little metal holders.

"I'm gonna try and find a jacket for Simon," Gary said to Bill.

"Okay," Bill replied. "You should probably grab something for yourself, if there's anything left." He paused. "And if you really want to be a dear, maybe find one in my size."

Gary smiled. "We'll see."

Bill smiled back, and then turned to follow after Dean and George.

George was making his way to the hunting counter when he breathed a gentle sigh of relief.

"I'll be damned," came Dean's voice from behind.

Sitting in the racks behind the counter were a small handful of hunting rifles, a few shotguns and some small caliber rifles used for target practice and sport.

"I would have thought this would have been the first to go," Dean said, stepping up beside George.

"Maybe it wasn't looters," Bill said, approaching from behind them. "Maybe the bugs got in, searching for people and tore the place apart."

"Maybe," George replied. "If people came looking and saw the front looking the way it does, they might have kept going, assuming it was all looted out."

"Well," Dean said, making his way around the counter. "Good for us."

"Damn good for us," George replied, following after.

George made his way over to the hunting rifles, pulling down a .30-06 bolt action rifle. He set that on the counter and removed a Colt Python .357 from beneath the counter. He scrounged up a holster belt and stocked twelve boxes of cartridges for each, which he tucked in a hard case ammo box.

Dean was a few feet away, pulling the slide back on a nine millimeter when Bill called out. "How's this look?" he asked, holding up a twelve gauge shotgun with a pistol grip.

"I think it compliments your eyes," Dean said with a grin.

Bill smiled back, taking the gentle tease in stride. "Maybe I'm just overcompensating."

This got a laugh out of both Dean and George.

"Dad!"

The three of them snapped their gaze in the direction of the voice, to see Simon walking quickly toward them. The boy's eyes were locked to the case that held a small collection of knives. "Can I have a knife?" There was pure excitement in the boy's voice.

Gary came stepping out of the shadows.

Bill looked at his son. "You're going to have to ask Papa Gary that. I don't have the authority to answer that question.

Simon turned to Gary. "Dad, can I have a knife?"

Gary looked at Bill and shook his head slightly. Then he turned his gaze back to Simon. "Okay," he said. "But under one condition. It has to be one of the small ones you can fold and carry in your pocket. I don't want you carrying some Crocodile Dundee knife okay?"

"A croca-what?" Simon asked, confused.

"I think you dated yourself a bit with that one, babe," Dean said, one brow lifting.

Gary grinned.

"Just pick one of the smaller ones," he said, glancing back at his son.

"Awesome!" Simon said, charging around the counter.

Gary looked at Bill, who was attaching a strap to the shotgun. "What is that?"

"This?" Bill said, holding up the weapon. "It's a shotgun."

"Are we hunting bears?" Gary asked sarcastically.

"We are heading to Alaska," Dean replied.

"There's a lot worse things than bears between here and there," George added, holstering the .357 and making his way to the small game rifles.

Dean holstered the nine-millimeter as Bill hefted the weight of a small revolver.

"That'll stop a bug in its tracks," George said, pulling his eyes from a small rimfire rifle.

Bill regarded him for a moment, settling his gaze back on the weapon. Then he reached out, handing it to Gary.

Gary took the weapon reluctantly, holding it in his hand and eyeing it like some foreign object.

"You need it," Bill said softly.

Gary resigned himself to that thought. From the beginning he had shied away from carrying any weapon other than a small fold out baton. He had a strong aversion to guns, always had. He didn't like them, voted against them and often preached about how the US should have been more like Australia or England. But after the prior day, and the days leading up to that, his opinion was beginning to skew. So, he took the pistol and put it into his jacket pocket.

George took a small .22 caliber rifle and made his way over to where the straps were. He picked a good leather one and affixed it, securing it tightly. In the beginning he had carried a .22 pistol. He'd gotten a few amused laughs about it from some of the survivalist types in the underground, but his quick response had wiped the smirk from their face. He'd look at their .30-06, or AR-15 and smile. *"You take down an elk recently?"* he'd ask, to which the response would be an obvious no. Then he's smile and pat the pistol, saying, *"I saw three dozen squirrels last night alone. At least I know I won't be starving..."* His philosophy was pragmatic. People in survival situations always go for the biggest, high caliber weapons. But the one thing they always fail to remember was, how often do you see large game? When was the last time you saw a deer while out camping? Or an elk, or bear? But squirrels, and rabbits, birds. Those were everywhere. It was hard to go anywhere and not see a dozen squirrels hanging from the side of a tree. And if you tried to take small game down with a .30-06, you'd be picking fur from a hole in the ground. But a .22? You'd never starve as long as you knew how to field dress and clean.

"I'm good to go," Dean said, pulling George from some distant memory.

George lifted his gaze, looking at the others. He hefted the brick of .22 ammo and smirked. "Let's hit it then."

The group made their way back out to the Land Rover parked in front and piled in. A moment later they were turning back onto the road, and George was punching the gas pedal to the floor.

-37-

"Plug me in?"

Dean reached over and plugged George's phone cable into the cigarette lighter adapter. He plugged the second into his. Instantly the glow from his phone grew brighter. He opened his map and double checked their route, cracking his window to let the cool night air in.

For the next three hours they made their way down and around the city of Seattle, and the smaller communities surrounding it. Three times they had to exit the freeway and circle around, avoiding large pile-ups and traffic jams. By the time they were reaching the outskirts of a small town called Mt. Vernon, the Rover had begun to chug, a gentle knocking sounding from behind the dash.

"Oh, come on girl," George said, reaching out and tapping the dashboard lovingly. "Don't give out on us now. Just a little further."

The engine continued to knock, the sound growing louder the further they went. George had tapered off the gas, dropping them to a steady fifty miles per hour. Then, three miles later there was a loud *bang*, and the dashboard lit up like a Christmas tree.

"Shit!" George hissed as the vehicle coasted to a stop.

The interior of the Land Rover began to fill with the smell of burning oil and smoke.

George leaned back, closing his eyes for a moment, both hands still at ten and two on the wheel.

"We should probably take a look," Bill said from behind.

George slowly shook his head. "Won't help. We threw a rod."

"And, we can't fix it?" Gary added.

George opened his eyes, shaking his head. "No." He turned in his seat, looking down at Coal. "Looks like you're getting carried, Buddy."

The others made their way out of the vehicle, moving to the front. Headlights illuminated the road leading to where it curved away a short distance ahead. A wall of trees stood sentry beyond.

"Here," Bill said, holding out his hand in Dean's direction. "Take my pack."

Dean nodded, reaching out and taking it. He slung it over his shoulder, adjusting it into place.

"Thank you," George said, watching as Dean reached into the vehicle and hoisted Coal out.

Dean nodded. "Of course. But we should probably try and move as quick as we can," He scanned the road behind them. "They find the truck, they'll know we're close." He turned and started off, adjusting Coal in his grasp. The others followed after.

It was a little over two hours later that they made their way into a small community. Bill, Dean and Gary had traded off carrying Coal, who was an easy eighty-five pounds. Three blocks in, George spotted a small animal hospital. They all decided the few minutes it would take to check it out wasn't going to kill them. Though, the militia group still hunting them would if they found them.

They made their way in, scavenging a good amount of cleaning supplies and antibiotics. George bagged a stash of Amoxicillin and some Carprofen to help Coal adjust back to walking once the neurotoxin wore off.

"We should probably get that wound cleaned," Bill said as George was zipping his pack. "We might as well. We're already here."

George pondered the thought. "Yeah. Okay."

They moved Coal into one of the rooms and cleaned the area around the wound. They shaved the area down, cleaned the wound and applied antibiotic ointment. Then they dressed it, and George shoved two antibiotic pills down his throat, holding his muzzle gently until he swallowed them. Coal didn't react during the cleaning. Thankfully the site was still numb from the paralytic toxin. The other upside, if you could call it that, was that the toxin was not only a powerfully strong paralytic, but coagulant as well. This, it had eventually been hypothesized, was likely due to the fact that when the bugs implanted their eggs, the wound wouldn't bleed them out, allowing for as many as possible to gestate.

"That's disgusting," Gary said, hearing this theory.

"It's just their nature," George replied. "Insects have been breeding like that for millions of years." He paused, patting Coal on the head. "Ever heard of the botfly?"

A shiver ran through Gary. "I don't want to talk about it, but yes. And they're the most disgusting thing I've ever had the displeasure of seeing..."

"You've seen one?" George asked.

"YouTube..."

"Ah."

The entire time they were speaking, Bill was eyeing the bandage. "You're sure there's no... There's nothing in there?"

George looked at the bandage. He drew in a breath and exhaled evenly. "No real way to know until..." He let the thought trail off. "But I think we would have seen something by now."

"I'm sure he's going to be fine," Gary assured, reaching out and placing a reassuring hand on Simon's shoulder. "I mean. It's already been like, what? Over twelve hours. Those things grow quickly." He winced at the thought.

George looked down at the dog whose tongue came out as he began to pant. "Yeah," he replied. "That's what I've been telling myself."

"It's getting early," Dean said, not wanting to interrupt, but time forcing it. "I saw an RV dealer just up the road a bit. Might be a good place to hunker down."

George patted Coal's side once more. "How about it?" he asked the dog. "Now that you're all clean and patched up. What do you say you go sleep off some of that toxin?"

The dog eyed him caringly, his tongue bobbing slightly as he panted.

"Tomorrow night, we'll be Canadians," Dean added.

The group made their way out and up the road a few blocks to the small RV dealership. Multiple vehicles were parked on the lot, and they made their way through, picking their own. George picked a smaller model, something not cramped, but cozy. Dean chose one beside his, and Bill, Gary and Simon started toward a larger one near the back.

"Can I stay with George tonight?" Simon asked as they were starting through the lot.

George heard this and turned.

Gary shot his son a puzzled glance.

"Because of Coal," Simon added. "He might get lonely. And he's hurt."

Gary smiled, a warm tickle working through him. His gaze shifted to George who was now smiling softly.

"Well," Gary answered, adjusting Coal who was held in his grasp. "I believe that would be up to George, and if he wants to have the company. He might want to get some rest on his own."

"Nah," George replied, smiling and looking at Simon. Then he glanced over to Coal. "I'd never hear the end of it. He'd just keep me awake all night whining."

"So, I can?" Simon asked.

Gary looked at George and smiled. Then he turned his attention back to his son. "Okay. But don't keep him up all night."

"I won't," Simon said excitedly, making his way over.

"Well," George said as he approached. "I suppose we better pick a bigger model. Wasn't planning on company when I chose this one."

Together, they made their way a few vehicles down, George settling on a slightly larger model. Gary followed behind, helping them get Coal inside and situated.

A short time later, George was seated at the small foldout table, a Zane Gray book in hand, headlamp illuminating the cream colored pages. Simon was sitting next to Coal who was snoring lightly, front paw twitching.

"He's going to be able to walk again?" Simon asked. "In a few days right?"

George pulled his gaze from his book, placing his hand over the headlamp as he looked at the boy. He looked at Coal who was still dreaming. "Yeah," he replied. "Like I said. He's a strong boy. He'll bounce back."

"Have you ever been bitten? By one of the monsters?"

George shook his head, dogearing the page he was on and folding the book closed. He pulled the headlamp from around his head and set it beside him, so that it illuminated the vehicle's interior. "No. Not myself," he replied. "I've come close. There was one time I thought I was going to, but I suppose I've been lucky."

"Do you know anyone who has?" Simon asked, now fully committed to the conversation.

"Not personally, no," he answered. "But I've had conversations with people who have." He paused, thinking about the best way to address the elephant standing between them. "I've heard it doesn't hurt, if that's what you're getting at. They have this, toxin in their saliva that almost instantly numbs the injection site." He thought about it for a brief moment. "Have you ever been bitten by a mosquito?"

Simon nodded. "Yeah. It itches."

George smiled. "That it does. But I bet you didn't feel it when it happened. Right? Just the itch afterwards."

Simon pondered the question carefully. "You're right."

George nodded, his brow lifting. "It's pretty much exactly that. Except that the bugs are about a thousand times bigger than a mosquito."

"Do you know where they're from?"

George thought back to that first day, when the creatures had arrived. He caught a mental picture of the objects flaming through the sky, the impacts, the chaos that followed as the creatures emerged. He shook his head. "No. Somewhere out there," he responded, looking up at the ceiling.

"Like from outer space?"

He nodded. "Like outer space, yeah. Like the old dollar theater horror movies back in the day."

"I used to like going to the theater," Simon replied. "I liked it. My dads would take me every week. I saw all the new movies. I like the superhero ones the most."

"Who's your favorite superhero?" George asked, his gaze narrowing.

"Green Lantern," Simon responded almost instantly.

"Green Lantern?" George asked. "I would have assumed Superman or Batman."

"No," Simon replied. "I like the Green Lantern. He can make anything with his ring, and he's part of this huge intergalactic group. And he can fly in space."

"So can superman," George replied. "But he also has super strength."

"Yeah," Simon replied. "But Green Lantern is funny."

"Ah," George replied.

"Who's your favorite?" Simon asked.

George put a moment of thought into it. "Oh. I suppose I'd have to go with..." He pondered it a moment longer. "I think probably Wolverine."

"Oh," Simon replied. "He's cool."

George smiled, holding back a chuckle. He lifted his wrist, checking his watch. "It's getting late. Going to be light soon. We should probably get some sleep."

"Okay," Simon said, scooting down and curling up against Coal.

Coal shifted, nestling his head into Simon's armpit. A breath later they were both asleep.

George folded the book back open, finishing the chapter before he himself turned in for the day.

A still silence filled the small recreational vehicle. George was lying there, eyes half open, when he heard the approaching thrum of bug wings. He listened as they drew closer, a small swarm of half a dozen he guessed by the sound. They drew closer, slowing as they passed over the vehicle.

A few dozen feet away, one of the insects landed atop the RV that Dean was sleeping in. He awoke with a start, his hand darting out for the rifle leaned against the small foldout bed.

He lay there, listening to the heavy skittering as the bug made its way in small circles on the roof. He held his breath, listening. Then, remembering the bandaged wound on his shoulder where the militia asshole had drug the knife blade through his flesh, he glanced down, noticing the thin hue of red that had permeated the white gauze. That tiny amount had likely been what had drawn the bug to his vehicle. He reached down, grasping the thin blanket he had pulled from a cupboard and draped it over the wound, hoping to quell the odor.

The insect above skittered in another tight circle, before thumping its proboscis against the roof twice. Then, it lifted off and Dean listened as the thrum of wings faded away.

George lay there, listening, when he heard a soft whimper. He turned his face to see Coal twitching lightly, front paws kicking out. In an instant he was awake, on his feet and moving quickly to where the dog was lying. He knew that when the bugs injected their eggs into their hosts, they would normally secrete a viscous fluid that would harden around the injection site, forming an almost cocoon-like appearance in order to keep the impregnation site safe. Coal didn't have any of that hardened crust around the site, so he was still hoping it had only been a puncture wound, nothing more. Even one larva could be enough to kill the host, as it grew by feeding indiscriminately within before chewing and clawing its way out. He brought his hand down, resting it atop the warm fur just above the bandage. He held it there, looking down at his best friend as front legs kicked in a dreamy run. A moment later, Coal's eyes fluttered open and he looked up at him.

George smiled, reaching up and rubbing the dog's face softly. "It's okay, buddy." He said, petting him another few strokes. "Go back to sleep." He pulled his hand away and made his way back to the fold-out. A few minutes later he was back asleep.

A familiar sound pulled George from his sleep. As he lay there, breathing in the smells of the new recreational vehicle, he listened. Then the sound repeated, slightly softer. He drew in a deep breath and stretched his neck, pushing himself up to a seated position on the fold out. Lying across from him, still curled at the boy's feet, was Coal. He was peering back at him through the dim interior. Coal whined again.

"You gotta pee, boy?" George asked, mentally clocking the last time he had seen the dog use the bathroom. "Yeah. You gotta go."

George checked his watch. The sun was just dipping beneath the horizon outside. His watch read six twenty-three. He pushed himself up and stepped over, petting Coal on the head for a moment while he mentally prepared himself for the pain he knew was about to follow. He reached down, sliding his arms under him and hoisting him up. Pain flared through his shoulder at the motion and he grunted, gritting his teeth together as he stood. He turned, stepping to the door and finagling his hand around the knob. In a slightly awkward motion, he gave it a shove. His shoulder screamed out again.

He stepped down the two stairs to the concrete and made his way over to a small grassy patch. As he did, he scanned the area around them, his ears pricking up as he took in the quiet lack of sound. Birds chirped in the distant trees, and a small flock flew overhead, making their way to their nests for the night. A lone crow cawed somewhere further in the small city. He knelt, setting Coal down. The pain flared. As he set the dog down, its back legs folded out. "Shit," George sighed. "Sorry, buddy," he said, quickly forming a solution. He reached down and unclasped his belt. Then he slid it under Coal's haunches, careful to avoid resting it across his little doggy bits as he'd referred to them once at the vet, when Coal had the unfortunate displeasure of a rather nasty urinary tract infection. He lifted gently, hoisting the dog's back legs up with his good arm and offering him the support he needed to feel like he was standing.

Coal stood there, sniffing the air for a moment.

"Come on, buddy," George said, looking down at his companion.

Coal brought his nose to the ground and sniffed, making a motion to walk forward. George moved with him, giving him the support he needed to find that perfect spot. Then Coal lifted his head, sniffing the air once more and released a long, steady stream of urine.

"You've been holding that one," George said in mild amusement as the liquid kept coming.

When Coal was done, George helped him spin in a small half-circle in order to give his fresh release a quick sniff. Then he bent down, hoisted him up and started back toward the RVs.

As George was nearing the one he and Simon had slept in, the door to another opened and Gary stepped out, rubbing the sleep from his eyes.

George took note of the mess of hair atop the man's head, and sleep wrinkles still worn across his face.

"Good morning," Gary said, smiling as he arched his back in a gentle stretch. His face shifted. "Here," he said, starting forward. "Let me help."

"It's okay," George said, wincing lightly as he adjusted his hold on Coal. "I got it." He paused. "Looks like you had a good night."

Gary's face tightened. "Oh, you shut up," he said with a grin.

Bill emerged from behind him, stopping in the doorway. "Morning, George."

"Buenas dias," George replied.

George started to make his way back to his RV, when Bill called out quietly.

"George."

George turned.

"Thank you," Bill said with a deep sincerity. "For last night." He smiled at Gary. "We needed that."

George smirked.

"It's been difficult to be *intimate*," Bill added. "So. Knowing that Simon was safe, allowed us to be able to relax a bit. Thank you."

George smirked again, this time adding a gentle nod. "Any time," he said, turning and making his way toward the trailer. Three steps later he stopped in his tracks, turning his head to a sound that had just barely drifted past his ear. He stood there, listening. Then the sound reappeared, louder. He snapped his gaze to the other two. "Get inside. Now!"

Bill and Gary exchanged a fearful glance, and as they were making their way back in, they heard the sound that had caught George's ear, an approaching vehicle.

George made his way into the RV and closed the door. He leaned down, setting Coal on the small fold out bed. As he did, Simon stirred awake. George looked at him and put a finger to his lips. Then he hoisted his rifle up and thumbed off the safety, moving to the front of the RV and peering out of a crack in the curtains that were drawn across the windshield.

The sound of engines grew into the sound of three or four, and a few minutes later, those vehicles came rolling into sight. George watched as a small procession of cars and trucks drove down the highway, his skin tensing as the one in the lead slowed, faces peering in his direction. "Shit," he whispered as they slowed to a stop.

"Is it the people from before?" Simon asked.

George pulled his gaze from the crack. "I don't know. I think so." He brought his finger back to his lips, emphasizing the motion. Then he turned his gaze back out the window.

The vehicles behind the one in front slowed to a stop. One of the men leaned out, shouting something to the front. The man in the passenger's seat of the lead vehicle was leaned across, eyeing the RVs. He said something to the driver and they leaned their head out, shouting something to the vehicles behind. Then they lifted their hand in the air, waving the others forward. A moment later the truck pulled away, the others pulling their feet off the brakes and following.

George stood there, watching as the vehicles continued north. He waited until he could no longer hear the engines before pulling his gaze away. "Stay right here," he said, making his way to the door and stepping out.

Bill and Gary were stepping out at the same time as George and they met halfway, Dean just a moment later.

"That was them, wasn't it?" Gary asked as they approached.

"Yeah," George replied. "If I had to take a guess, I'd say it was."

"So, what do we do?" Bill asked, realizing all the implications that went with that.

"It's obvious that we can't keep going north," Dean said, skipping the good mornings. "Not on this road. And we still need to find a working vehicle."

Gary pulled his phone out, thumbing it open to the map. "We can take surface streets through the town," he said, spreading the map with two fingers. "From here," he said, turning it so that the others could see. "We can take Road 9 all the way up into Canada." He turned the phone back, scrolling the map. "Here's where it's going to be a problem." He turned the phone back for them to see. "Once we get past Vancouver, there's only one road that takes us up and around to Anchorage. And it looks like nothing but mountains and wilderness."

Dean sighed, glancing at George. "We'll be wide open."

"That's *if* they continue north into Canada," George replied. "I'm hoping they stop at the border and make their way back, thinking maybe we turned and headed west toward Montana. That would buy us some time."

"We just need to get across the border and I think we'll be good," Dean added. "It's just getting there that's the part that's got me nervous."

"Agreed," George replied.

"Then I say we get a truck and get the hell out of here."

George nodded, looking to the others. "You guys pack up," he said, looking between Gary and Bill. "Dean and I will find us a vehicle. "Twenty minutes, max."

Bill nodded. "Yeah. Okay."

"Let's go find our ride," George said, turning and making his way back toward the highway.

"I don't like this," Dean said a few minutes later as they were crossing the parking lot of a small convenience store. "You know as well as I do that they aren't going to give up. They aren't just gonna stop and turn around because they hit the border." He took the next two steps in silence. "Border's don't exist anymore."

"I know," George replied. "But what was I going to say? That they are going to keep hunting us until they eventually find, corner and kill all of us?" He looked at Dean. "They have a kid. They're already scared, and we need them to stay focused, not jumping at shadows. We've already got enough to worry about with the bugs. But at least those, we know we can avoid by not going out in the daytime. These other assholes." He shook his head. "They chased us into sunrise once already. And I think that guy in the lead is even crazier than the others were."

"That's what scares me," Dean replied.

"Let's just find us something with four wheel drive, gas up and we'll worry about the rest once we get back on the road. I doubt they're going to turn around anytime soon, but I'd like to be long gone from here, just in case."

"Heard that," Dean said, gesturing to a full sized pickup truck a short distance away. "That could work."

George eyed the large Tundra, nodding. "That it could."

Bill stuffed the clothing he had pulled out and folded the night prior into his pack. Behind him, Gary was shoving a bag of labeled pills into a pouch. He had emptied al the containers, eliminating the wasted space and consolidating all of the medication they had found into a freezer bag, dozens of smaller Ziploc bags within.

"I hate this," Gary said, lifting his gaze. "I hate it."

"I know," Bill replied, turning to see the first of the tears falling from his husband's eyes.

Gary sniffled, the beginnings of a sob choking back.

"Oh, Sweetheart," Bill said, setting a bundle of socks down and making his way over to where Gary was seated. He wrapped his arms around him and pulled his head to his stomach.

Gary burst, sobbing heavily into his gut.

"Shhhh," Bill comforted, rubbing his hand through his hair. "It's okay."

"We should have stayed in L.A.," Gary sobbed. "We never should have left."

Bill stood there, rubbing his fingers across his husband's scalp. "We didn't have a choice."

Gary pulled back, eyes red and puffed as he looked up at him. "Yes we did. We could have stayed. We didn't have to leave. At least it was safe there. There was food, security." He paused. "Your sister."

Bill felt a sting of pain at the comment.

"We have a son," Gary said, his brow furrowing. "We're supposed to keep him safe, to help him learn to grow and adapt to this *new* world. And look at us. All we've done is pull him from the safest place he could have grown up and dragged him out into a world filled with psycho redneck assholes and God knows what else." He stared up at him. "This was a bad decision."

Bill stared down at him for another moment, desperately wanting to comfort him, but unable to still the building irritation. It wasn't his fault. It had been a cooperative agreement, but like always, when things went south, it was completely his fault. Gary was never the one to make the mistake. "This was a decision we *both* made," Bill corrected, carefully navigating the following words. "But we're already here, so it doesn't matter. George and Dean are out there, right now, finding us a working vehicle. We *will* get through this." He stared down, watching another two tears fall from his husband's eyes. "And we need to keep it together, *for* our son." He moved his hands to Gary's shoulders, squeezing tightly. "We've been through worse," he said, peering deep into his husband's upturned eyes. "Remember Arlington?"

Gary held his gaze, a flood of memories rushing past.

It had been eleven years prior, the year before they had adopted Simon, that the two of them had flown to Dallas for Gary's aunt's funeral. They had been there for a few days and decided to take a little trip out, to check out the city and surrounding areas. It had been a Friday night when they had found themselves in Arlington, after spending the day at the nearby amusement park. They'd decided to go out for the night, finding a local bar to have a few drinks to unwind. That night had ended with multiple police units involved, and Gary being held at knifepoint by a drunken bar patron that had made the connection between Bill and himself, and had quite loudly voiced his opinion on *faggots* as he had so eloquently chosen to refer to them as. Gary had spouted off at the man, something about being a neanderthal who was probably just angry because he and his cousin were still hiding in the closet. This had brought the man's friends into play, one who he could have had no idea *was* actually the man's cousin. This had gotten Bill involved, and fifteen minutes later the police were talking the man's blade away from Gary's throat. Bill had walked away with two fractured ribs, a cracked tooth and a broken pinky. Gary had nearly lost his life.

"This is just something else we're going to get through and laugh about later," Bill reassured.

Gary sniffled, choking another sob back.

"Come here," Bill said, leaning down and putting both hands on Gary's cheeks. He stared into his eyes. "I love you, Gary. And I will *never* let anything happen to you, or Simon. You understand me. I meant it when I said until death do we part."

Another tiny sob escaped Gary's lips.

Bill leaned in, kissing him softly on the lips. When he pulled back, he lowered his hands and smiled. "Now, get your shit together. We need to pack and get the hell out of here before those redneck assholes come back."

This brought a smile to Gary's lips. A breath later they heard the sound of a vehicle approaching.

George pulled across the parking lot, slowing the truck to a stop and leaving the engine running as he climbed out. "We've got our truck," he called out, letting the others know it was them.

A moment later, the door to an RV opened and Bill emerged, pack already across his back.

George started toward the RV Simon and Coal were in. "Load everything up, I'm going to get Simon and Coal.

"I'll give you a hand," Dean said.

"I got it," George replied in a snap. "Just go grab your stuff."

"Okay," Dean remarked, hands lifting defensively. "Stubborn ass…"

George turned and started toward the RV.

Simon was sitting with his hand running through Coal's warm fur, when the door opened and George stepped in.

"Grab your stuff," the older man said sharply. "We've got to get out of here."

He made his way over, slinging his new pack into place and grabbing his rifle. He double checked that the safety was on and held it out. "Be *very* careful," he said, as Simon's gaze widened. "I just need you to hold it until I can get Coal in the car."

Simon nodded hesitantly.

George reached down, scooping Coal up and made his way outside. He saw the look on Gary's face as Simon stepped out, cradling the rifle in his hands. "Safety's on," George said. "It ain't chambered."

Gary shot him a disapproving look and made his way over, gently taking the rifle from Simon, who offered it up willingly.

George slid Coal into the backseat, grunting from the motion. A moment later, the opposite door opened and Bill climbed in.

"Nice truck," Bill said, eyeing the interior.

George smiled. "Yeah. That's what we thought." He looked back toward the front. "Four wheel drive and capable of handling the snow where we're going."

Bill nodded.

Less than five minutes later they were all inside, and George was pulling the truck out onto the highway.

"Turn left here."

George slowed, taking the turn. A he pulled onto the road, he saw a crumpled road sign lying beneath the front end of a police cruiser. Lying a few feet away were three long decayed corpses.

"This turns into Road Nine," Gary said. "It's pretty much a straight shot to Canada."

"How far?" George asked.

Gary typed in the directions. "One hour."

George nodded, okay with that number.

"Did you get gas?" Bill asked, looking through the space between the front seats and trying to get a glimpse of the instrument panel.

"Didn't need to," Dean replied. "It was already full up when we got it."

"Well," he replied. "Lucky us."

"Lucky us indeed," Dean replied. "How many miles to Anchorage?" he added.

Gary reopened his phone. A moment later, he looked up. "Twenty-one hundred."

"I doubt this thing gets that good of gas mileage," Dean said. "What about Vancouver? We have to go through it to get to Alaska."

"Eighty Miles," Gary said a moment later.

"Okay," Dean said. "We'll stop in Vancouver. Fill back up and load up a few cans. That way, if we won't have to worry about finding ourselves out of gas in the middle of nowhere."

"Good thinking," George replied.

"Well, you know. Every now and then I have my moments."

George smiled, an overturned bicycle with a skeletal frame lying beneath it pulling his gaze from the road as they passed.

"I really hope this cold theory's true," Gary said, eyeing the dead youth as they passed.

"I don't see why it wouldn't be," Dean replied from the front as he reached out and popped the glove compartment open. "Hmph," he snorted. "I'll be damned."

George glanced over as Dean pulled a small revolver from the glove.

"What did you find?"

Dean hefted the weapon in his hand for a moment. "Looks like a little .302."

George smirked. "My ex-wife used to carry one just like that in her purse."

Dean eyed the gun for a moment longer and then placed it back in the compartment and closed it.

Outside, a large blue house stood vacant, front door open wide. Moonlight caught across the word HELP painted in white across the sloping roof. In the yard were three corpses, clothing tattered from the prior seasons.

Dean watched the house disappear into the night as they drove past. Overhead, the last of the day's light was fading into obscurity, stars slipping from their slumber and sparkling against the midnight blue above.

Bill looked out at the charred remains of a home. The brick fireplace stood tall, blackened remains piled around it. A burned out, rusting vehicle sat on rusted rims in the driveway, a discarded children's car a short distance away, the kind that had a small motor and could be driven by remote. He flinched as a hand came to rest on his leg, yanking his gaze from the window to meet with Gary's.

Gary squeezed gently and then leaned down and kissed Simon atop his head.

Bill reached over, putting his arm around them both, pulling them into a gentle hug. He let his gaze drift back out the window, watching as an abandoned middle school drifted past.

It was a little under an hour later when George pulled the truck to a stop.

He sat there, both hands resting on the wheel at ten and two, staring ahead silently.

It was Dean who broke the stillness. "We could try and go around."

George stared out at the piled up line of vehicles leading away. "We should have thought about this," he growled. "Goddamnit." He leaned forward, placing his forehead on the wheel between his hands. "Goddamnit."

The group had made their way north, nearly all the way to the border. Now, they sat there on the outskirts of a small border community, a parking lot running for miles in front of them.

"We have four wheel drive," Dean added.

"Oh," George snapped, holding a hand out toward the windshield. "We're just going to drive over the cars and through houses." He was tired, angry and irritated that in the rush of getting away from the militia group hunting them, that he had allowed this single oversight to slip past. He was always a planner, always the one who had clear and concise direction. "Sorry," he said, drawing in a deep breath and exhaling in a gust.

Dean let a thin smile touch his lips. "We're good."

In the backseat, Gary pulled his gaze from the line of abandoned vehicles and glanced at Bill, finally resting his gaze on Simon. He reached out, patting him on the leg. "You ready to get some more exercise?"

Simon looked up at him unamused.

"Come on," Gary said, forcing a smile to his face. "We'll call it practice for when we're surviving in the frozen north." He tapped Simon's leg and reached out, opening the door.

George sat there, the flames of disappointment smoldering as Bill stepped out of the truck, followed by Simon. For a moment he just sat still, staring ahead, hands still on the wheel like by some miracle, Moses was going to come along and part the sea of stalled vehicles blocking their path forward.

"Come on, old man," Dean said, reaching out and tapping George on the leg lightly with the back of his hand. "Let's get our steps in."

He sat there a moment longer, pushing his disappointment down as Dean climbed out into the night. Then he brought his hands up, fingers rubbing his eyes. "Ah, shit," he grumbled before stepping out. "I liked this truck."

The group hoisted their packs and guns into place and started down the line of parked cars. There were hundreds. Where they started, four solid lines sat formed, but the closer they got to the border, the less organized those lines became, as people in the beginning had tried edging around and cutting each other off. The line of traffic seemed to be the perfect representation of how things had been in the beginning; utter and complete chaos, followed by a transition period of the world grasping to catch its bearings. That had been followed by those left creating clean and simple lines in order to survive.

The moon overhead was bright, casting its silver glow across the river of painted steel. The group made their way through, weaving in and out, sometimes up and over the stalled procession. It was nearly forty minutes before they saw the rising metal gates that had been the US Customs and Border Protection. As they approached, they saw what had caused the chaos they had just trekked through.

The fold down gates at the crossing were drawn shut, two Humvees parked at angles across the entry point. Guns, mounted in turrets sat atop both. There were pools of spent shell casings around them, glittering bronze in the moonlight. Dozens of corpses lay near the crossing, tattered clothing riddled with stained holes. Two dozen dead bugs lay atop and crumpled between the nearby vehicles. George guessed that people had been trying to make their way north in the beginning, and at some point, the sun had likely risen up with hundreds of those same people still congregated around the then military controlled checkpoint. He also guessed, having spent the better part of his life in the military, that the soldiers manning those turrets either wanted to be anywhere but where they were, or were the types of soldiers who had enlisted for exactly the type of setting the bugs had created. In that, George also had to assume that the sun had come up, the bugs had come out, and the men on the guns had begun to fire indiscriminately. Anyone who had been in the front, panicked or trying to force their way through had been caught in the crossfire. The rest had likely scattered like cockroaches under fluorescents.

"Jesus," Dean whispered as they approached the defunct checkpoint.

Gary was taking up the rear, Simon and Bill just in front of him. Moonlight played across the scene, darkness casting eerie shadows across the carnage. His foot crunched against broken glass. The air around them was silent, save for their footsteps lifting up.

"Imagine," Dean said, his feet sending a dozen spent shell casings clinking across the dark pavement. "You're just trying to escape. You survive days, not getting eaten or impregnated, only to get gunned down by the military. What a shit-show."

"They were probably just as scared," George replied. "Think about it from their point. You're some eighteen year old kid who enlisted for whatever reason you did, and then *this* happens. I guarantee that whoever was manning those guns, was thinking about their family the entire time they were working those .50s." He shook his head. "They were just doing what they were ordered to."

Dean looked at the Humvees as he made his way past, a flicker of disgust working through him. A short distance away were three corpses tangled up in a spool of razor wire, stained clothing slashed and tattered. He'd never liked the military prior, and even less now as he stared down another of the results of its actions.

The same piled up traffic continued on the Canada side, with vehicles spread out through the surrounding fields. Doors sat open, personal belongings strewn between in a pastiche of brightly colored suitcases and luggage, clothing and bullet riddled corpses rotting away in the tall grass.

They continued past, snaking their way through the rows of stalled vehicles for another half an hour, before traffic faded away. Beyond was the open road leading west toward the coastline.

George had found another four wheel drive truck and had managed to hotwire it. He was getting quicker with every one. It was only a few minutes later before they were back on the road and making their way across toward Vancouver, a little over an hour away.

"We should be to Vancouver in about an hour," Dean said, looking up from his phone. "So long as we don't run into any traffic."

George nodded, watching as the yellow lines disappeared beneath the truck.

"I'm thinking we should probably stop there for the night, before we head north." Dean paused, watching a row of houses drift past. "That way we give those militia assholes time to either go further, or head back, being as they haven't found us. If we could at least take that worry off the table, I'd be happy."

"Yeah," George replied. "I agree." He turned his focus back to the road. He had made the decision to drive through the night without using the vehicle's headlights. It forced them to go slower, but the stealth it offered more than made up for the time lost. Time they had an endless amount of. It was safety that seemed to be growing less and less abundant the further north they went.

It was a little over forty-five minutes later they were entering the outskirts of Vancouver.

"Um," Gary said from the back, his phone light illuminating his face. "Yeah. I think we should find somewhere around here to stay." He pressed the button on the side of his phone, killing the light. "We have to cross another bridge to go north, and I'm just not sure I have that in me. Not after…"

The cab fell silent as each of them drifted back into the shared memory.

"I'm okay with that," Dean said. "George?"

George sat with the question for a moment. "Yeah. I'm good with that." His gaze drifted to the small residential neighborhood they were passing through. "This looks like as good a place as any," he said, slowing the truck and turning onto the next side street they passed.

The first few houses on the street had broken front windows, what looked to be nothing more than passing vandalism. The homes further back sat quiet and untouched. He continued down a few more houses and then slowed, pulling into the driveway of a small one-story home painted light blue. He coasted the truck to a stop and reached out, turning the engine off. "We're going to need to get gas in the morning," he said, his thoughts returning to the stockpile of gasoline they had left in the Tundra.

Bill opened the back passenger door and stepped out, stretching before reaching into the bed and hoisting his pack out.

The others piled out, George and Dean scanning the surrounding neighborhood as they did. Overhead, a gentle blanket of grey was edging in, blocking out the sea of stars.

"I'll check it out," Dean said, starting toward the house.

George scanned up and down the street, his gaze drifting back to the main road they had pulled off.

The interior of the house was dark as Dean stepped onto the small porch. The curtains were drawn, and as he glanced at the neighboring homes, he saw they were the same. He approached the front door and lifted his hand, knocking lightly. "Hello?" he called out. "Anybody home?" He looked at the nearby homes, scanning the windows for any movement. Then he reached out and tried the handle. Locked. He looked over to where George was standing, Bill, Gary and Simon a few feet away. "I'm gonna try around back," he said, starting back down the steps and making his way around the back of the house.

The small backyard had a dark green garden hose that was strung across and was attached to a single sprinkler near the middle. A small doghouse stood a short distance away, a silver tie-out chain attached.

He made his way to the backdoor and tried it. It was locked as well. He stood there for a moment and then stepped back. He lifted his leg and planted his foot firmly, right beside the door handle. It broke free with a loud crack and swung inward, part of the door jamb snapping free and falling to the linoleum floor just inside.

He stood there, listening for a moment and then brought his flashlight up, clicking it on as he made his way in.

The back door led directly to the kitchen. There was a small dining room off to the side, and the living room beyond that. A handful of prints hung on the wall, old thrift store nature portraits hanging in wooden frames. As he made his way into the living room, he saw a large family portrait hanging above a large sideboard decorated with a lace runner. There were almost ten people in the photograph, and judging by the small porcelain dolls sitting atop the runner, he assumed that the home had likely belonged to the older couple smiling from the edge of the group.

He made his way to the front door and unlocked it, opening it up and stepping back. "It's clear," he said.

The others started forward, making their way in and setting their bags down beside the front door.

"Anything in the pantry?" Bill asked as he set his rifle against the doorframe.

"Does it have a pantry?" Gary asked.

Dean shrugged with a smirk. "I didn't take the time to check." He held his hand out. "But the kitchen's that way."

"This'll work," George said, making his way through the living room toward the small hallway leading back.

The house was a small three bedroom, with two off to the side, and the master at the end of the hall. A bathroom sat between them, with a half bath connected to the master. George chose one of the smaller rooms. It had a pullout couch and looked as if it had been a sewing room or office at some point in its past. The other was a plain guest room, bed made up properly. He assumed Dean would be taking that one, and left the larger room for Bill and Gary. He stood there, looking at the pull out and then turned, making his way back into the living room. He sat his bag down beside the plush couch. The house had that old musty smell from windows having been sealed for the prior five seasons. The odor of antique cloth furniture filled the air, a feeling of remembrance accompanying it, like old, lamented memories layered atop dust.

"Taking the couch?" Dean asked.

"Yeah," George replied. "That way I can keep an ear out." That wasn't the real reason he'd decided to take the living room. It was because as he had been standing there in the room with the pull-out, he'd realized that Simon was probably a bit old to be sharing the bed with his parents.

"Good call," Dean said, turning and making his way toward the sound of Gary's excited voice in the kitchen.

"I don't want to talk about it," Bill said, shaking his head as his gaze lowered to the table.

Moments prior, Dean had remarked on the quality of the wine they were currently sipping versus the wine they had experienced in the basement of the house they'd stayed in those few days prior. This had not only touched a sore spot from the events that had followed, leading up to them having to abandon the small stash of bottles Bill had brought along, but the events themselves.

Bill continued. "I know that everything that happened afterward far outweighs losing a few bottles of expensive wine, but ugh..." He lifted his hands, shaking them in frustration in front of him. "That was six of the best bottles of wine ever produced in the last sixty years, and a port over a hundred..." He shook his head again. "I bet those assholes passed it around like it was two buck chuck..."

"This one isn't too bad," Dean said, lifting his glass and taking a sip from the wine found earlier in the pantry.

Bill stared at him flatly.

"Well, look at what I found," George said from behind, stepping into the dining room with a smile. He held a small, white box with two colorful insect-looking creatures hugging. "I used to play this when I was younger with my folks."

Bill looked up, eying the box. "Cootie?" A puzzled look drifted past his face.

George smiled, setting the box down and pulling the top down. "Figured it was fitting for the times. You roll dice to build your bug. Whoever finishes first, wins."

"Seriously?" Gary asked, looking back at them from the stove, where he was cooking a large pot of pasta with sausage and clams. "Bugs...?"

"I want to play," Simon said, reaching out and hoisting a part from the box.

"Alright," George said, digging in for the instruction book. "We should probably give this a read though. It's been quite a few years since I've played, and I'll be honest. I'm a little hazy on the rules."

"I'm good at games," Simon said, smiling. "I'm gonna win."

George raised an eyebrow. "That's if the dice are on your side. That can change very quickly, young man. Trust me."

"Did I hear a little acrimony in those words?" Gary asked, grinning playfully.

George looked over at him. "Let's just say I've learned more than a few valuable lessons about dice from Vegas craps tables in my life."

Gary chuckled, turning back to the simmering pot and giving it a quick taste with his spoon. "Everyone hungry?" he asked, setting the stirring spoon down.

"It's smells amazing, Babe," Bill said, moving the glass in front of him to the side to clear space for the plates Gary was pulling from the cabinet.

"Well," Gary said as he pulled five of them down, pausing to grab one bowl. "Be grateful the power's still on and their freezer was stocked up. Who knows when we'll get to have clams again..."

"We're headed to Alaska," George replied, smiling as he took a sip from his glass. "Clams are the last thing I think we'll have to worry about not having."

"I was speaking metaphorically," Gary replied, setting a plate down before him, before making his way in a circle around the table. When he was done, he set the bowl down in front of where Coal was lying atop a blanket Dean had folded out for him. "I didn't forget about you, big guy," Gary said, reaching down and ruffling the fur atop Coal's head.

Coal looked up at him, his upper body shifting.

Gary made his way back, returning with the pot of pasta and setting it in the center of the table. A moment later he brought the pot of sauce that had been simmering for the last twenty minutes.

A few minutes later all of them were seated around the dining room table. Simon and Dean had finished eating and the others were multitasking, working their forks and a set of dice. Simon, as he had predicted, had won the first game, completing his little cootie first. Dean had won the second and they were well into their third. Coal had finished his serving of pasta and sauce, complete with four clams that Gary had shucked from their shells and a half a sausage, cut into small bite-sized portions.

"I think the hardest part," Dean said, taking a sip from his wine glass, "is knowing that there will come a day when there is no more coffee... I think that's the day I may just have to throw in the towel."

George scoffed. "We'll just have to make our way down to Costa Rica or Guatemala."

"Just getting this far has been a nightmare," Gary said. "And you want to try and make it to Costa Rica?"

"We'd be going by boat," George theorized. "The bugs don't like water. I don't see them flying out over the ocean looking for food. Hell. For as far as we know, places like Hawaii and Costa Rica could be completely untouched."

"There would definitely be less of them," Dean added. "Less land means less food, which means less bugs. Theoretically."

George was about to reply, when the lights went out, plunging them into darkness for a moment as their eyes adjusted to the dim lighting pressing through the drawn curtains.

"Well, shit," Dean muttered.

"We all knew this was coming," George added, setting the dice in his hand down. "It was only a matter of when."

"It could be a breaker," Gary said hopefully.

George shook his head. "No. That was the grid."

"How can you be sure? We could have popped a breaker."

George looked at him. "With a lightbulb?" He hovered on that for a moment. "No. I'm actually surprised the grid stayed up for as long as it did, with no one maintaining it."

"Well," Bill said. "At least it alleviates what my biggest fear has been."

"And what fear might that be?" Dean asked.

"Fire," Bill added. "Remember the Camp Fire? The Dixie Fire? Both of those were caused by unmaintained power lines. Now imagine one of those raging, but with no firefighters to put it out... The entire state of California could potentially go up in flames."

"Well," George said. "Good thing we're not in California anymore."

Gary sighed, setting his fork down on his plate. "Maybe this is nature telling us it's time to get some sleep."

George nodded.

Dean lifted his glass, draining the last of it. "Well. I was gonna lose this game anyways." He shot Simon a sideways glance. "Cause someone over here. I won't say names, is a little cheat."

Simon looked at him in awe. "Am not!"

"On that note," George said, rising from his chair. "You all have a good night." He turned and started back toward the other room.

Dean smiled, reaching out and ruffling the boy's hair. "I'm just messing with you. Good game." With that, he pushed his chair out and stood. "See you in the morning." He followed after George.

Gary looked at Simon and smiled, his gaze moving to Bill and back to the boy. "You should probably get to bed too, mister. I think we're a bit past your bedtime."

Simon looked at him incredulously.

"Eh!" Gary interrupted, before the boy could offer the usual, there's no school rebuttal. "I don't want to argue. It's been a long day, and you're already starting to get cranky. And your father and I would like to have a nice, calm day tomorrow."

Simon stared at him for a moment, his gaze drifting to Bill.

"Don't look at me," Bill replied, his eyebrows lifting. "Daddy Gary says it's bedtime. It's bedtime."

"Stupid," Simon grunted, taking his cootie and pushing it forward before standing and making his way out of the room.

Simon looked at Bill and sighed.

"It's only going to get worse," Bill said, looking across the table at him. "Wait till he hits his teens."

"Ugh," Gary replied. "Were we this bad?"

Bill smiled, the grin turning into a chuckle. "Do I need to remind you of my teenage years?"

"Please," Gary replied with a coy smile. "Don't."

They looked across the table, peering through the darkness at each other.

"We're going to be okay, right?" Gary asked, his tone shifting.

Bill leaned forward, reaching across the table to take his hands up in his. "No matter what happens, I won't let anything happen to us. I promise."

Gary gave his hands a tight squeeze. "I'm just scared."

"And it's okay to vocalize that," Bill replied. "Remember what the therapist said. Keeping things bottled up—"

"Only leads to the bottle popping," Gary interrupted. "I know."

"Then don't feel bad about sharing your emotions." Bill looked deeply into his eyes. "I'm not your father." A beat passed. "He was an asshole, and he's gone now."

Gary's gaze dropped to the table in quiet remembrance for a moment, a sourness filling his chest.

"Sweetheart," Bill said, pulling his gaze to him. He squeezed his hands. "I've got you."

Gary let a smile work across his lips, though faintly. "I know."

"I love you. With all my heart."

Gary nodded. "I know."

Bill looked at him, smiling. "Jerk."

This brought the smile further across Gary's lips. "I love you too, I guess."

"Come here," Bill said, rising up and making his way around the table.

Bill wrapped his arms around Gary's shoulders, pulling his face into his stomach. For the next few minutes, they stayed there, comforting each other in that simple gesture. It was a short time later that they made their way to the master bedroom in the back and let sleep drag them away.

Outside, the sun lifted up above the horizon, streams of shapes rising up like embers from a crackling fire. The shapes shifted and swirled, coalescing into small, murmured clouds as they turned, making their way in every direction.

The sun was still visible above the horizon when the group made their way out of the house and loaded their belongings into the back of the pickup truck. They had added a small stockpile of goods taken from the pantry inside, split between a handful of heavy duty shopping bags. A quiet calm hovered between them, and other than a polite greeting, no words were shared.

They loaded the vehicle and climbed inside. Dean checked his map one last time, offering directions to George, who pulled the truck back out onto the main highway and hooked left, leading them down the road that would take them through the heart of Vancouver and across the bridge into the vast wilderness to the north.

As they snaked their way through the city, they noticed that a good portion of the traffic had been pushed aside, as if someone had plowed a path with a bulldozer, opening a single lane through.

"I don't like this," Dean said, eyeing the crumpled front end of a small Mercedes sedan as they passed.

"Hopefully it was from the beginning," George replied.

"What?" Gary asked from the back.

"Someone cleared a path," Dean replied. "Pushed all the cars out of the way."

"Well, that's a good thing, right?" Gary asked. "We don't have to do it."

"Just makes me worry about what we're going to find further north," Dean said. "More people, more problems. And who's to say it wasn't those militia freaks. I'd really hate to get to Alaska and find those assholes up there waiting for us."

"You really think they're still following us?" Bill asked. "I mean. We haven't seen anyone in two days. And we don't even know if those cars we saw back at the RV park were part of their group. We could just be working ourselves up over nothing."

"That was them," George replied flatly. "They aren't going to give up."

"But how can you know that?" Gary asked, siding with his husband.

"The men in those vehicles were hunting." He lingered on that thought, replaying the memory in his mind's eye. "They were hunting for us."

"But how can you know that?" Gary repeated.

"Because," George replied. "This isn't the first time I've been hunted."

A silent glance was shared in the back seat.

"I just know," George added, knowing the couple in the back was still struggling to believe him. "Trust me."

"And you think they've come this far?"

George stayed quiet for a moment. Then he sighed. "We killed members of their group. We killed that man's sister, and brother-in-law. Yeah," he replied. "They've come this far. Our only saving grace is that we didn't tell them the location we were heading. But it's only a matter of time until they figure it out. Alaska's the only location that makes tactical sense. Further north is the Arctic, and that's damn near uninhabitable. I just know that once we get to Fairbanks, we need to have a different story. And I really hope they've forgotten our faces by the time they arrive, because I think it's only a matter of time before they do."

"But we didn't kill those people," Simon said, his voice low. "The bugs did."

"We know that," George replied, glancing at him through the rearview. "But they don't see it that way."

The truck's cab again fell silent. In the back, Gary reached out, grasping Bill's hand and squeezed.

It was a short time later that the group was crossing the short bridge that led through Stanley Park into West Vancouver. From there, they hooked left and started their way up the 99.

They followed the small coastline north, and a little under an hour later, a forest of towering trees engulfed them.

A dull slate hung draped over the sky, a chill moisture breathing through the open driver's side window.

In the back seat, Simon shivered lightly, wrapping his arms around his chest. "It's cold," he said, suggestively commenting that George should roll his window up.

"You better get used to it," Gary smiled, rubbing his hands together briskly. "In a few months you're going to think this is warm."

"Ugh," the boy grunted, shuddering at the thought.

Night had overtaken the woods, and darkness shrouded the trees in an impenetrable cloud of black. Headlights cut their path down the highway, dotted yellow lines ticking past like second hands on a clock. George had suggested they continue on without their headlights, but the moment they had passed into the woods, that idea had gone out the window. The cloudy skies combined with the trees blocking out nearly all remaining light had forced them to use their lights. Without, they would have driven off the road on the first bend.

They passed a small handful of small communities, each dark in their own quiet abandon. A short time later they slowed, edging their way around a small work van that sat stalled out in the middle of the lane, front end crumpled and stained. The carcass of a large black bear lay rotting a short distance away, skin peeled back to expose the sun-bleached bone on the side of its massive head.

Bill watched as they inched their way past, stealing a glance into the empty work van. Both airbags had deployed, but the vehicle sat empty. He took a silent offering of comfort in that.

"It's really dark," Simon said as the truck began to pick up speed again. "I don't think I've ever seen this dark."

"It's because there's less light pollution the further north you go," George said, his gaze tracing the edges of the road for any flicker of green, a tell-tale sign that a deer or something larger could come darting across.

"What's light pollution?" Simon asked.

"Light pollution is how they refer to ambient lighting cast from the millions and millions of lights at night. Car headlights, streetlights, businesses," Gary replied. "You remember when we went on that cruise to the Bahamas, and the captain turned out all the lights on the ship, so that everyone could look up and see the stars?"

Simon did. He had loved that trip. "Yeah."

"You remember saying that you had never seen so many stars in your life, and that you didn't know there could be so many?" He smiled. "Well. That's because there is almost no light pollution that far out in the ocean. All the lights from the cities reflect off the atmosphere, and makes it hard to see the stars. Now that the power grid is down, all those lights are out."

"Eventually," George added. "We're going to see the stars just like our ancestors did." He liked the thought. "My ancestors were Mayan. Do you know who they were?"

"No," Simon replied.

"Well," George continued. "The Mayans were one of the original peoples of what we now call Central America. At one time, they were the biggest civilization in the world. And one of the many things they were very good at was reading the stars. They were masters of astrology. They had some of the most advanced calendars in the world, all revolving around stars, and the constellations. They still reference those same calendars today. And that was all because there was no light pollution. They could see every star out there." He leaned forward, stealing a quick glance up. "I think some of the old ways are going to eventually come back to us. Certain things are never truly lost."

"Somewhere, right now," Dean said, looking out the window at the black enveloping the edge of the road. "There's some middle-aged, Topanga Canyon white lady sitting on a yoga mat, looking up and waiting for Mercury to enter retrograde."

This brought a laugh out of George, the sound cracking the quiet conversation. "Oh," he said after a moment. "That was good."

Gary and Bill exchanged a quick, puzzled look.

A breath later, a flicker of light trickled through the trees ahead.

Dean' finger shot out.

"I see it," George replied, gently edging his foot off the pedal.

The light flickered again, headlights working through the pines as another vehicle made its way down the road in their direction. Moments later, the trees peeled away, and headlights shined directly at them.

"What do we do?" Bill asked, his hand grasping the armrest on the door.

"Keep driving," George said.

As the other vehicle approached, George tried to look inside, but the headlights obscured the view. He caught a quick glance of what looked to be four men in the car.

It passed, and George locked his gaze to the rearview mirror. Dean was doing the same with the side.

Then, a hundred yards back, brake lights lit up, illuminating the surrounding trees. The highway became bathed in red.

"Shit," George hissed, his foot pressing down on the pedal.

The taillights behind shifted as the vehicle spun around, headlights now shining brightly in their mirrors. A second later they grew brighter as the pursuing vehicle snapped on their brights.

"It's them," Gary said, as a ripple of fear worked through him.

"Yeah," George said, pushing down on the gas pedal. Both hands moved to the steering wheel, his gaze flickering between the road ahead and the blazing headlights in the rearview. He reached out, pulling his seatbelt across his chest and clicked it into place. Dean followed suit.

The truck was pushing sixty as the last of the inlet on their left disappeared behind. The road ahead curved back into the dense woods. Behind them, the vehicle had gained, now holding steady a good twenty yards back.

They came around another long curve and George felt his breath stop in his throat. A hundred yards up the road, two vehicles had pulled across, parked nose to nose with a small gap between them. Headlights illuminated the part of the road they were parked in, and he could see a small handful of men standing around them, rifles leveled. "Seatbelts," he said, the word coming out in a growl.

"George," Gary started to argue, one hand reaching out to grasp the hold on the door.

"Hold on," George grunted in response, pressing the gas pedal to the floor. "Lean down and be ready for the airbag," he said to Dean, who edged down in his seat as the first of the bullets took the side mirror to the truck off.

Gary screamed, leaning down and pulling Simon in beneath him. Bill leaned over them, bringing his arm up to shield his head, though little good that would do if one of the rifle rounds found its mark.

George leaned over, barely catching a view over the dashboard. "Ah, shit," he grunted as the truck barreled toward the space between the cars.

Moments later, they impacted. Steel crunched against steel, and both of the truck's airbags deployed, the fabric slamming George in the shoulder and side of the face. He fought the wheel, his vision swimming. The vehicles outside smashed to the side, and he heard a mixture of gunshots, angered shouts and screams as one of the vehicles flipped sideways, rolling atop one of the men who had been too slow to get out of the vehicle's trajectory.

Gary, Bill and Simon were thrown forward, their seat belts holding them violently in place. Gary felt something *pop* in his lower back and let out a small yelp.

Moments later, George was punching the airbag out of the way and crushing his foot back down on the gas pedal.

Another volley of rifle rounds punched into the back of the truck, one round spiderwebbing the back window.

"Stay down!" George shouted, ducking as another two impacted into the tailgate.

Behind them, the men who had formed the barricade rushed to get into their vehicles. The third car had stopped, and men were piling in. One of the vehicles, a smaller sedan, was the one that had been flipped on its side, but the second, a larger truck, was still on its wheels and running, though nearly a quarter of the front end had been ripped away by the impact. The men leapt in, four climbing into the back of the truck's bed. Hands slapped the top and both vehicles peeled away with a screech of rubber.

George pulled his gaze away from the mirror, a flicker of colored light catching his eye. The check engine light had come on and a litany of other indicators were illuminated across the cluster. "No shit," he grunted, turning his head to glance into the back seat. "Anybody hurt?"

"No," Bill replied, checking Simon once more.

Gary grunted as he sat up. "I think I pulled something in my back." He winced.

"We can ice it later," George replied. "Right now, we need to get the hell away from those assholes."

"What if there's more?" Bill asked, worried that they might run into another barricade, and that the next could be even more fortified.

"That was it," George replied, glancing into the rearview as headlights turned a corner behind, falling into place.

"How do you know?" Bill asked.

"They're militia, not local police," George replied. "One car radioed ahead; the rest set up the roadblock. But it's likely they've already radioed to the others we saw back at that RV park. There's still another vehicle missing. He stole another look at the instrument cluster, watching as the temperature gauge slowly began to edge its way up toward the H.

Behind them, the two vehicles began to close the gap. The one in the lead was a quarter mile back and gaining. The road snaked more and more the further they drove, a large river coming into view off to their right.

George flicked his gaze to the rearview as the distant sound of a horn caught his ear. Headlights flashed and the second of the vehicles fell back. It was probably the one they had plowed into, George assumed. They had hit it hard, and after seeing the other flip sideways, he was surprised it had started at all. It had to have been badly damaged. He was surprised theirs was still running.

The second vehicle continued, gaining on them quickly. As they turned a curve, he stole a glance, seeing that it was the vehicle that had passed them, coming in the opposite direction prior, and was also the one that had been in the lead of the procession he had seen while hiding in the RV park. "Come on, you assholes," George growled to himself, his foot pressing down a little further on the gas pedal.

They were already cruising at a steady sixty-five, thirty over the posted speed limit, and ten over what he would have considered safe. He didn't know the road, and one hairpin turn could quickly result in the end of their escape. But he couldn't let up. The car behind was gaining, and he knew it was only a matter of time before weapon's fire resumed. "Get down," he said, glancing in the mirror to see the other vehicle lurch forward, making its move. "Get as low as you can."

Behind him, Gary and Bill pressed down, creating another shield over their son.

"Dad," Simon whimpered.

"Shhh," Gary consoled. "It's going to be okay. We've got you. We're right here."

"Get that pistol ready," George said, watching as the other vehicle sped toward them.

A moment later, their truck lurched forward as the car rammed them from behind. Tires screeched as the driver jerked the wheel to the left and gunned it. The chasing car edged up a few feet and then lurched to the right in an attempt to spin them sideways in a pit maneuver.

George pulled his foot off the gas and smashed down on the brake pedal in one fluid motion, sending them jerking forward again. As he did, he jerked the steering wheel to the left, sending the front of the truck smashing into the other car. Like a jiu jitsu fighter flipping a reverse, the front fender of the truck crunched against the back quarter panel of the chasing vehicle and sent it skidding to the side. The driver of the other vehicle jerked the wheel, overcorrecting and sending it spinning sideways. Rubber caught the pavement and it spun back around. As it did, the tires caught and momentum yanked the car sideways, sending it tumbling. It rose up into the air, coming down hard on its side. The speed they had been going sent it tumbling over and over. One of the back doors opened and two men were ejected out, flying at nearly fifty miles per hour into the air, landing with wet thuds on the pavement. The car continued to roll, crushing one of the men beneath with a sickening splat, before impacting into the side of their truck.

George felt the truck lurch to the side and gripped the wheel. He struggled not to overcorrect. Then he heard the loud *pop*, and the steering wheel jerked hard to the right, sending them careening off the side of the road and straight toward the small river.

The truck careened down a small embankment and slammed to a stop. A small yelp escaped from the back seat. Smoke began to rise as metal clicked loudly. For the next few moments, they sat there, the sound of the engine clicking backed by the sound of water flowing past.

George's head was still pounding from where the airbag had deployed, slapping him in the side of the face. He sat there, hands still grasped to the steering wheel, when he heard movement. He swallowed, blinking twice as the pain across his chest pulsed. Then, he reached down and unclasped the seatbelt.

"You good?" he heard Dean ask from beside him.

George nodded. "Yeah. I think so."

He craned his neck to look behind him. Gary was sitting up, both hands on Simon's shoulders and was looking him over. Bill was staring at the headrest in front of him. Coal looked up from where he had been lying on the floor. Then, another sound caught their ears, and George snapped his gaze on Dean. "Shit," George grunted, reaching out and opening the driver's side door.

He stepped out into the flowing water, oblivious to the cold. He made his way to the bed of the truck and hoisted his rifle from where it was strapped to his pack. As he did, Dean stepped up, doing the same.

"Get ready," he said, working the bolt on his gun.

"Stay here," Dean said, looking to where Gary was watching them intently.

Gary didn't respond. He was still in a daze from the impact. Simon sat silently beside him, shivering slightly.

"Let's go," Dean said, making his way back up the ravine.

George followed behind, pulling his rifle against his chest as he navigated the muddy incline. As they reached the top, his gaze drifted from the bodies lying sprawled across the blacktop, to the smoking car that was lying upside down between the two lanes. Shattered glass was scattered from one edge of the road to the other, and other than the faint *clicking* coming from the settling engine, only the sound of an approaching engine, and the whimpered cries of a man hanging upside down in his seatbelt could be heard.

"Down," Dean said, taking point. George was still dazed from the crash, and he could see the slight distance behind his eyes. He likely had a concussion from where the airbag had smacked him in the head.

But they'd have to tend to that later. With the sound of the second vehicle approaching, they had more pressing matters. He lowered to the ground, dropping to a prone position, rifle held in his grasp.

George did the same, lying a few feet away. They waited there as the approaching car fell into view.

The small SUV slowed a short distance back, its headlights illuminating the scene. From where George and Dean lay, they could just catch flickers of the hurried conversation being held behind the closed windows of the vehicle. A moment later the engine turned off and four men stepped out.

"Ren," One of the men said, gesturing to the river with a nod. "Check the river. Dave, you check on them. Lalo, you're with me."

George instantly recognized the voice. It was the pendejo who had tied them up and left them for the bugs. His grasp tightened on the forestock of the rifle, and he shifted his position, lining up his crosshairs with the man's chest.

The other men fanned out, the one they had called Ren, making his way almost directly toward where George and Dean were laying. The others started toward the overturned vehicle.

When the man approaching was twenty feet away, Dean pulled back on the trigger, sending a bullet slamming into his chest. The gunshot shattered the night air and the man fell backward, a grunted belch escaping as he collapsed to a heap on the pavement.

Beside him, George fired, his shot going low and hitting the leader in the side, just below his gut.

The man howled as he dropped to the ground. The other two pointed their weapons in Dean and George's direction and started firing indiscriminately, not knowing where the shots had come from. One bullet impacted into the dirt a foot away from Dean's face, and he returned fire. Half of the other man's face disappeared into a puff of red mist. Blood fountained up in arterial sprays, and he hovered there for a moment before collapsing in a heap. The other turned to run, but a bullet from George's rifle plunged into his back, shattering his spine and ricocheting through his lung. He pitched forward, face slapping against the cold blacktop.

Dean rose to his feet, rifle scanning the area. The leader, whose name eluded him at that moment, lay writhing on the ground. The man in the car cried out, begging for help and crying that his leg was crushed.

The two made their way forward, each listening for any sounds of more approaching vehicles. The road was silent.

George pulled his pistol and knelt down, taking aim and sending a .357 round through the side of the man in the car's head. The whimpering stopped.

As he turned, he saw Dean standing over the other.

"Fuck you!" the man on the ground belted, coughing up a spatter of blood that rolled down the side of his cheek.

"It's over," George said, making his way over to where he lay. "I should leave you here," he said, looking down at the spreading crimson beneath the bottom of the man's shirt. "Like you did to us."

"You killed my fucking sister!" he blurted, more blood forming at his lips. He groaned, wincing deeply in pain as he curled to his side. "God. Fuck."

George looked down at him. "Your people shot first," he said blankly.

"Fuck you," Andy whispered, his gaze drifting to the pavement a few feet away. "I won't stop."

"I know," George said, looking down solemnly at the dying man.

A single gunshot rang out, and the contents of the man's skull splashed out onto the pavement.

Dean watched the blood pool around bits of splattered brain matter and flecks of skull. "Is that it?" he asked, his gaze locked to the scene. "Did we end it?"

George stared down at the dead man, nodding slowly. "Yeah. That's it."

"What about the others?"

George looked between the dead men, shifting his gaze back to Dean. Slowly his head shook back and forth. "I don't think we have to worry about them. If they do come this far..." He paused, looking down at the dead man on the ground. "I think we've made our point."

Dean pulled his gaze away, settling it on the other vehicle. He sighed heavily and turned, making his way over to the small SUV.

George stood there, staring down at the man who had tied them up and left them to die. He felt no pang of emotion. He had killed a lot of men during his time in the military, and each time, he had felt something. Sadness, remorse, victory, satisfaction. But as he stood there, staring down at the other, he felt nothing other than a dull relief. And even that was no more than a vapor.

"You aren't going to believe this."

George wrenched his gaze away, looking to where Dean was standing. "Simon's going to be happy as a pig in shit."

George shot him a puzzled glance, giving a single, questioning nod.

Dean reached in, pulling a small backpack out and smiled. He held the bag up in one hand, and in the other, the small video game console the boy hadn't let out of his grasp prior to the bridge.

George felt a smile tug at his lips. A single breath escaped, a gentle sigh of relief escaping. "Gary," he called out, looking at the pack in Dean's hand. "Bring Simon up here. We've got a surprise for him."

They heard talking down the embankment, and a few minutes later, Gary emerged from below, Simon just behind him. A moment later, Bill ascended the top, Coal held in his arms.

"Don't look," Gary said, holding the side of Simon's face to keep him from looking at the dead men in the road.

"Hey, Simon," Dean called out. "I found something I think belongs to you."

Simon's face wrinkled in puzzled confusion.

"Go on," Gary said, glancing at Dean, himself just as puzzled.

Dean stood there, hand behind his back as Simon approached. When he was about five feet away, he smiled. "Tell me if this looks familiar to you," he said, pulling the console from behind his back and holding it out.

Simon's eyes lit up like a Christmas tree. "My switch!!" he shouted, closing the space between them in a flash. He snatched the console out of Dean's grasp and eyed it in stunned amazement.

"I got something else, too," Dean said, reaching in and pulling out his backpack.

"My backpack!" he burst, his attention immediately turning back to the console, which he powered on. Just to check.

Dean looked over to Gary who was sobbing softly, a steady stream of tears running down his cheeks.

Bill approached and put his arm around him, smiling.

Gary turned, burying his face in his chest.

"Is it over?" Bill asked, his gaze moving from Dean to the four men lying dead.

Dean nodded, glancing at George and then back to him. "Yeah. It's over."

George made his way from corpse to corpse, collecting the weapons they had dropped and placing them in a small duffel bag that had been ejected alongside the two dead men further down the road. It was still early in the night, and his head was pounding. He could feel the gentle pull of vertigo each time he leaned down to pick one up. When he was done, he made his way back to where the others were congregated near the small SUV. His gaze drifted between each of them. Coal was seated on the ground, and as he approached, he rose up, his back legs shaking beneath him. He made two steps forward before they gave out and he fell to a seated position. He whimpered, his tail making a slow, jerking motion to one side. His tongue hung from his mouth and he panted lightly.

"Hey, boy," George said as he approached, reaching down and petting him between the ears.

Coal struggled again to his feet. This brought a warmth to George's chest and he knelt down, taking Coal's face in his hands and pressing his forehead against his. He stayed there, holding his companion for a moment. Then he looked up, gaze working again between them. "What do you say we finish this trip?"

Dean scoffed, shaking his head. "That sounds amazing."

"Yes," Gary replied. "Please."

Simon was already sitting in the back seat, his face illuminated by the glow coming from his console's screen.

"That sound good to you, buddy?" George asked, reaching down and petting Coal between the ears.

Coal looked up, panting. In a series of jerky movements, he managed to turn himself around and staggered three steps before Dean bent down and hoisted him up. He set him in the back seat and Simon reached out, helping him scoot into the space between his feet. The boy pet his neck for a moment and then fell back into his game.

Dean did another check of the overturned vehicle, coming back with another pistol and a small satchel of ammunition. A few minutes later, Bill returned with their gear from the truck and they continued their way north.

Night filtered by, making way for day and, night again. Though the hours spent in the dark grew shorter and shorter, dropping from fourteen or so hours, down to just under six, with even those having a dusky warmth still on the horizon. The further north they went, the longer the days became, until they were relegated to traveling for just a few hours at a time, seeking shelter in roadside houses and shops, or in the confined space of their vehicle, clothing pressed against the windows to block out any prying eyes. It was nearly another week before they found themselves crossing into the Northwest Territories. As the group made their way further north, the chill in the air grew stronger. Even in the summer warmth, they found themselves flipping the heat in the vehicle on more than once. By the end of the eighth night, they found themselves taking refuge in the tiny town of Whitehorse.

George stepped out of the vehicle, zipping his jacket up as he did. It was just after four thirty, and they had driven for the last six hours straight through. They had managed to siphon three gas cans full of fuel at their first stop after Anchorage, and that had gotten them to where they were. By the amount on the gauge and remaining reserve in the last can, he assumed they would need to refuel and fill up before leaving the tiny community they were in.

"It's chilly," Bill said as he stepped out, looking around the vacant street.

They had passed a small airport on the way in and a handful of industrial buildings and shops. They had opted to drive further in before stopping for another long day. The air had gotten slightly cooler, but it was still in the low fifties, nothing compared to what winter threatened to bring.

As if thinking exactly that, Gary spoke up, calling out across the interior of the vehicle. "If you think this is cold, I can't wait to see what you'll have to say when November hits."

"Can't wait," Bill replied with an unamused smirk.

Gary blew him a kiss and then reached in, hoisting Simon's bag out from the bag cargo area and handing it to him.

"I was hoping to have enough time to resupply before we had to lock down," George said, glancing at his watch and then to the setting sun. He brought his hands up, cupping them and blowing a warm breath into the curled space before rubbing them briskly together.

"We can head out in the morning," Dean said. "It's only another two days to Fairbanks, and we're still pretty good in the way of food and water."

Coal jumped down from the floor in the back, sniffing the air and making his way to a small patch of grass to relieve himself. He'd been walking increasingly better over the past week, and at that moment was moving as if nothing had ever happened.

He still had the small bald spot where they had shaved the hair to treat the wound. George had chuckled two days prior, saying he hoped that patch of fur grew back before winter, or Coal would find himself wearing a new pair of doggy long johns. This had elicited a round of laughter, and a brief explanation to Simon about what long johns were. Once he had been brought up to speed he'd had a chuckle himself.

As they were making their way to the front of the small roadside inn, George stopped, cocking his ear. He shared a quick glance with Dean and snapped for the others to get inside. Down the road, just a few blocks away, a vehicle had turned onto the highway and was headed in their direction.

Dean rushed to the door, grasping the knob and attempting to turn it. It didn't budge. He tried the next with the same results. "Shit!" he barked, moving to the third.

Behind him, George had brought his rifle to his shoulder, holding it ready to raise and fire. Bill and Gary had moved just behind him, Gary holding Simon at his back and Bill holding his rifle in hand.

"Might wanna speed things up," George called out, watching as the vehicle fell into view.

"I'm trying!" Dean barked back. "They're locked."

George drew in a breath, raising the rifle barrel and scanning behind the pickup truck that was now just a block away. "Be ready," he said, not taking his eyes off the vehicle.

Dean tried the last door, cursing in frustration and entertaining the thought of trying to kick it down. But it wasn't the movies, and the last thing he wanted to do was hyperextend his knee, or tear a ligament trying an action hero move. So, instead, he turned, pulling his pistol and moving to a concealed location behind a covered garbage can.

The vehicle coming down the highway slowed as the driver noticed George and the others standing there, weapons in hand. George took note of the three passengers, one male, a female and what he would come to realize as they passed, was a girl about Simon's age. As it approached, the man said something to the woman and she leaned her seat back, placing her head behind the side panel between the windows in order to block any potential gunshots. The girl in the back lowered down, peering just over the edge of the back passenger window. The man eyed them cautiously. Then, he did something George in no way could have anticipated. He lifted one hand and waved, his gaze flickering from George to Gary and then Simon who was peering out from behind.

George swallowed, exhaling an even breath of relief. He pulled his hand from the forestock of his rifle and lifted it, giving a single wave in return.

And just like that, the truck was gone, disappearing down the highway in the same direction they would be going when the sun set once more.

"Holy crap!" Gary exclaimed in a gust of breath. "Oh, that was intense."

Dean stepped out from behind the garbage can, pistol still in hand as he stole another glance in the direction the vehicle had vanished in. "What are you thinking?" he asked George as he approached.

George looked once more down the highway. "I think they're local," he replied, finally lowering the rifle to a relaxed position.

"How could you tell?" Bill asked, still feeling his heart pounding in his chest.

"No supplies," George replied as if it answered everything with those two short words.

Bill gave him a puzzled glance.

George sighed. Not irritated, but relieved. He nodded to the top of the SUV, where three gas cans sat tied, a small pile of tied up supplies visible in the cargo section at the back. "It's obvious they weren't part of that militia group, or they would have had more vehicles. And I doubt they would have brought women and children along hunting us. And I didn't see any supplies. So, it's safe to assume they live locally, or just passing through to somewhere close." He glanced up the highway once more. "I caught the vibe that they were just as surprised to see us as we were them."

"Yeah," Bill said. "The little girl was about Simon's age."

"They seemed friendly," Gary added. "Friendly enough at least. They waved."

George picked up the flicker of hopefulness in the other's remark. He hoped he was right, but judging from the defensive position the occupants had taken, he highly doubted they would be returning to put themselves in harm's way. They had seen full well that he and their group were well armed and on guard. Unless they returned with a larger group, they'd have one hell of a fight on their hands. And he was pretty sure they had also taken notice that he and the others didn't exactly have a stockpile of anything worth plundering. "Yeah," he remarked. "Seemed that way." He pulled his gaze from the highway and turned, looking at Dean. "Let's go check the office. See if we can't find us some keys."

Bill looked up from his book to where Gary sat, his face pressed to the thin crack running between the drawn curtains. Outside, the sun was well into the sky, the day's light casting a ribbon of gold across the room. "Come to bed," Bill said, dogearing the page he was on and folding the book closed. He set it on the end table and tapped the side of the bed beside him. Simon was already fast asleep in the next bed over.

Gary watched a moment longer before pulling his gaze away and pressing the curtains together, sealing out the thin ray of warmth. He turned his gaze to where his husband lay. "Nothing," he said, a look of disbelief worn on his face. A thin smile threatened to pull at his lips. "It's daylight, and not a single one."

Bill looked at him, reaching over and pulling the covers beside him back.

Gary made his way over and sat, removing his shirt and laying back. "I've almost forgot how it feels," he said, turning his face to look at Bill. "I used to live in the sun."

"I know," Bill replied, smiling softly. "You were my little iguana."

Gary reached out, pushing him playfully.

"Okay," Bill corrected. "Sea otter. They're cuter."

"Are you saying I'm furry?"

Bill looked at him for a moment before letting his gaze trace his husband's body down to his waist. He offered a mock grimace. "You could use a shave," he said, wrinkling his nose. "It's starting to look like the Amazon down there."

"Ugh!" Gary scoffed, shoving him harder.

Bill smiled, grabbing him and pulling him into a hug. Their lips pressed together.

Gary smiled, wrinkling his nose as he pulled back. He lifted his hand, rubbing his upper lip. "You want to talk about furry. You're the one that's starting to look like Magnum PI with that caterpillar you got there."

Bill leaned back, bringing his hand up and pressing his fingers across his moustache like a debonaire gentleman. "I think it looks sophisticated."

"At least it's finally past the John Waters phase."

This time Bill gave Gary a gentle shove. "Jerk."

Gary smiled, edging closer and putting his head on Bill's chest. "I could get used to this," he said, lifting his face to place his hand underneath.

"Motels?" Bill asked.

Gary lifted his face, slapping Bill on the chest lightly, before resting his face back down. "The quiet."

Bill nodded, his head pressing down into the pillow. "Yeah. The last few days have been nice."

They both lay there, pondering that thought.

"The first few days after we left," Gary said. "I think I might have gotten a few hours, max, a night. sleep." He sighed. "That goddamned buzzing," he growled.

"Are you surprised?" Bill asked.

"About what?"

"That we made it?" Bill replied.

Gary scoffed lightly. "Don't start celebrating just yet. We haven't even reached Alaska yet."

"Six hours," Bill replied. "We'll be to Fairbanks by tomorrow night."

"You mean tomorrow day?"

Bill smiled. "That's the one I'm going to have to get used to again." A beat passed. "My day night cycle is so fucked."

"Language," Gary said, tapping him lightly on the chest.

Bill smiled, looking over to where Simon lay, his chest moving up and down, the gentlest snore coming from his lips. "Just six more hours."

This time the smile did work across Gary's lips, and he closed his eyes, listening to the sound of his lover's heart thumping rhythmically in his ear.

Twilight hung in the air, a cool breeze billowing through the open windows as the Northwestern landscape drifted past. Simon's hair wafted to the side and he reached up, pushing it out of his face. Beside him, Bill sat with his gaze locked to the sprawling vastness. They had been driving for the last five and a half hours, having crossed from Canada to Alaska a short time earlier in the night. The grey sky overhead hung thick and heavy, smothering the rolling expanse below, a pastiche of tributaries and tiny streams crisscrossing the verdant brown and green tundra. They had passed the tiny town of the North Pole a short time prior, this hosting a whole slew of questions from Simon. He was old enough to know the truth about Santa Claus, but being a ten year old boy, and seeing the North Pole for real. That begged him to entertain the thought that if the town was real, maybe there was a certain magic behind it after all, and that meant that the other might be true as well. In the end, George had punctuated the conversation by telling him he was in his own right to believe whatever it was he wanted to. George believed that dragons were real, at some point, and unicorns, so why couldn't Santa. This had led to another entire conversation revolving around all the known cryptids they could remember; Bigfoot, the Loch Ness Monster, Mothman and the Chupacabra. George had said his grandma had sworn she had not only seen the Chupacabra, but a duende as well. She swore by it. This had led to him spending the next twenty minutes explaining the folklore behind the tiny goblin-like creatures known for stealing children away in the night and playing ill-intended tricks on those unlucky enough to cross their paths.

They had driven the following hour, relegated back to quiet observation of the landscape, the sun already pressing its glow up on the distant horizon, though, with the daylight cycle being so long, it felt like it never truly disappeared that far beneath. Twenty minutes later they saw a sign reading, *Anchorage, 5 miles.*

As they reached the edge of the city, the sun was peeking above the skyline, its warm golden glow pouring across the cold tundra. George slowed, dropping the vehicle from the steady seventy he'd been driving down to a cool fifty-five. Then he pulled his foot off the pedal, tapping Dean on the leg.

Dean pulled his gaze from the window and looked ahead to where a large blockade had been built across the road. They were still about a half a mile out, but they could see where multiple shipping containers had been stacked atop one another, creating what looked to be a large, rectangular pyramid, with a single gated entrance at its base. The road they were driving on ran straight through the middle of it.

"What are we doing?" Dean asked, not taking his eyes off the approaching checkpoint.

George had slowed the truck to just under twenty-five miles per hour. He studied the checkpoint, counting at least a dozen men at different points across the staggered tops. As they drew closer, he could see where foxholes had been built out of stacked sandbags, and men stood at the ready behind two on each side. "No choice," he said. "Turning around ain't an option. Just keep cool and I'll do the talking."

In the back, Gary and Bill shifted nervously.

George slowed the truck, placing one hand out the window and offering a wave as they approached.

Four men approached, stopping in the road and holding their hands up. George saw that they were dressed in military fatigues, and each one was geared out, sidearm on the belt and AR-15 held at the ready across their chest.

One of the men stepped forward, holding his hand out in a stopping gesture.

George placed the truck into park as the man edged his way around, keeping a good ten feet of space between himself and their SUV. The other men watched cautiously from a distance, eying the scattering of bullet holes that riddled the vehicle's exterior, markings left from their exchange back on the highway.

"Where are you coming from?" the man standing off to the side asked.

George eyed him, stealing a quick glance at his rank and insignia. "Believe it or not, Los Angeles," he replied, adding a polite, "Corporal," to the end.

The man eyed him for a moment, his gaze working through the truck to the others. Then it drifted back to him. "You run into trouble along the way?" he asked, his gaze now working across the bullet holes as well."

George nodded. "Yeah," he replied. "Some."

The man regarded him distrustfully, a squint flashing through his gaze. "Anything we should be worried about?"

George studied the man, wanting to glance at the others, but forcing his gaze to stay engaged. He shook his head, smirking lightly. "We took care of it."

The other glanced past him, to Dean who watched carefully from the passenger's side.

"You military?" the man asked.

"Retired," George replied.

"Which branch?"

George sniffed, the cool air chilling the inside of his nostrils. "Army." He pondered offering more than that but opted instead to keep quiet.

The man nodded.

"What brings you to Fairbanks?" the man asked, glancing into the back, his gaze settling on Simon for a moment.

"We have this theory," George replied. "We caught a bug in one of our traps back in LA. The cold killed it. So, we figured that with them being cold blooded, they might be less inclined to venture this far north."

The man eyed him, smirking again.

One of the men in front of the truck shifted, bringing his hand up to an earpiece and saying something they couldn't hear.

"It's a good theory," the man replied, easing slightly. He peered out into the tundra beyond. "We've got a few that have made their way up, but nothing like what I've heard it's like down south." He pondered that thought, looking out in what looked to almost be admiration at the rolling hills. Then he shifted his gaze back. "How bad is it down there?"

George drew in a deep breath, exhaling slowly. "Bad."

"Yeah," the other replied. "We've been getting less and less communications."

"Probably a lot less now," George said. "Now that the grid's gone down. Not a lot of folks with backup generators."

"I'd imagine," the soldier replied. "They make too much noise."

George nodded.

A long moment passed in silence.

"Well. I'm going to need to see some IDs," he said, glancing again between them. "Some routines still hold."

George nodded, reaching into his pocket and pulling his wallet out. He fished out his ID and handed it over.

The man took it, glancing past him to Dean and then back to Gary and Bill. "Yours as well," he said, not yet glancing at George's.

The others fished their IDs out, handing them to George, who handed them to the soldier.

"You stay here," the man said. "I'll be back with these in a few." And with that, he turned and started to where the other men stood watching.

"What the hell is going on?" Gary asked.

"Just standard protocol," George replied. "Don't put too much thought into it. A lot of databases are still up, running on backup power. They're probably just going to run our names and see what pops up. He glanced in the rearview and then to Dean. "Nothing we should be worrying about?"

A litany of shaken heads replied in silence.

"Well. Then we shouldn't have anything to worry about."

George sat, watching as the soldier read off the information detailed in their IDs to someone on the other end of the headset. One by one the cards were shifted to the back of the small stack. Once the last had been completed, he turned and made his way back to the truck.

The soldier reached out, handing the IDs back to George, who handed them to Dean. "I'd like to glean a little more information about this *altercation* you mentioned."

George held his gaze for a moment. Then, with a sigh, he recounted the entirety of their interaction with the militia men, from their initial stop, to the incident on the bridge, to the chase on the highway. The entire time the soldier listened intently.

When George was finished recounting their tale, the soldier looked through the window at Simon. "Is this true?"

Simon nodded, not taking his gaze from the man. "Yeah."

George breathed softly, realizing that not only was the man they were speaking to a soldier, but quite likely law enforcement as well, either prior or following. Children aren't able to pick up on the subtle intonations of adult conversations, and where another adult could read between the lines, going right along with a lie being spun, children needed stronger cues. That would generally come from a stolen look at a parent or guardian, or a guilty look on their face if they were trying to remember a scripted response. Smart tactic, George thought, catching the man's gaze once more.

"Okay," the soldier said, eyeing them each once more. "Well. We have rules that you are going to need to follow."

George felt the tense uncertainty suddenly fall away.

"Most are the same as before. Same laws apply. But everyone here is required to add to the community. There's no welfare here, no government cheese or food stamps. If you live here, you pitch in, simple as that. Understood?"

Another resounding round of nods returned.

"Okay. Then why don't we start with your professions. What did each of you do before this?"

Each of them offered their skills. George omitted a fair amount of his, relegating his entire service record to simply *active duty* with four tours in Iraq. When complete, the soldier stepped back, gesturing to the other men with a nod. They stepped aside and the large front gate slid sideways.

"It sounds like you've had one hell of a trip," the soldier said, the first inclination of a smile crossing his lips. "Welcome to Fairbanks."

George put the vehicle into drive and started forward. No one spoke.

As they crossed the threshold, the other soldiers offered polite nods. One gave a single wave. George offered one in reply. Then the city unfolded before them.

"I thought we were going to offer the other story?" Bill asked quietly.

George peered cautiously at him in the rearview. "These are actual military," George replied. "I figured they've heard similar stories from others. Didn't want to get caught up."

Bill nodded, understanding.

"Oh, my God," Gary said, eyes widening as he leaned forward, hands clasped to the backs of the front seats.

The sun was now hanging in the sky, and the city of Fairbanks was a gentle buzz of activity. Vehicles made their way down the highway and a bustle of community was thrumming in the air. A helmeted stranger on a motorcycle crossed the main highway in front of them, making his way into a small residential area. A woman ahead was jogging, light jacket covering her multicolored clothing beneath. A military humvee trundled past, six armed soldiers seated in the back, weapons in hand. As they drove further, George saw that the heads of some of the bugs were hanging like ornamental trophies on pikes just off to the side of the road. They made their way further in, driving slowly into the center of the city. All around them, commerce seemed to be alive, the thrum of daily routine unphased by the world to the south.

George pulled their vehicle into a small parking lot, putting it into park. All five of them sat there, silently watching the community carry on around them, only a handful of residents taking notice of their presence.

In the back seat, Gary reached out, clasping Bill's hand in his. He leaned over, pressing the side of his face into the mess of hair atop his son's head and smiled. "We made it," he whispered, a single tear working its way from the corner of his eye.

-EPILOGUE-

The sun had just crested the horizon, casting its golden pallor over the battered skeleton of downtown Los Angeles. The city's towers, once proud, now loomed like headstones in a graveyard of shattered glass and twisted steel. Somewhere deep beneath the concrete, thousands of survivors were just settling down for their night.

Above, a black river of alien insects rose from the ruins, their wings beating in a deafening, discordant chorus as they rose up into the coral colored sky. They swarmed upward, twisting in tightly grouped murmurs between the buildings, their chitinous bodies glinting in the morning light. The air seemed to vibrate with thousands of beating wings. Like a shifting cloud, its shape ebbing as it blocked out the sun, thousands of the creatures flowed together, before dropping back to the earth in search of their next meal.

In the earth, a low rumble began, dust and debris falling from the towering structures. It slowly morphed into something bigger, the buildings beginning to shake as if the earth had begun to quake. The ground shook, rattling the bones of the city. Birds erupted from their hiding places, shrieking as they took to the skies.

Beneath the city, the survivors felt the tremor, hundreds of frightened survivors looking to each other in terror. Above, the asphalt buckled and split. A mound of earth, concrete, and rebar heaving upward, sending entire apartment blocks toppling like toys. The ground ruptured, vomiting forth a torrent of debris and dust.

From the gaping wound in the earth, something impossibly vast began to emerge. First, a leg; armored and jointed, as long as a city bus, punched through the rubble. Then another, and another, each one ending in a hooked talon that gouged deep furrows in the street. The mound collapsed outward, a massive creature ripping its way from beneath, its carapace dark and catching the morning light. It's massive head rose up, its immense shape taking form as it stepped slowly from the gaping hole.

Impossibly large mandibles clicked together, spraying viscous fluid that splashed out, steaming where it landed. Like an armored beetle, the size of a small house, it rose, shaking the piled dirt from atop it in a violent shudder. Its gaze shifted, turning to the twisted landscape surrounding it as a dozen black eyes surveyed the city with a cold intelligence. It opened its mandibles once more, a deep, bone vibrating tremor building. The sound that followed erupted with a force that hook the remaining windows in the surrounding structures, vibrating down into the tunnels below. Survivors in the underground stared up in terror, wide gazes locked to the tunnel ceiling as dust began raining down.